C000151928

DEAL WITH THE DEVIL

DARK DESIRES BOOK 1

M.L. MOUNTFORD

For my amazing husband and two wonderful daughters.

LUCIFER

HE WAS LATE. Time was not precious to me—I was immortal after all—but he wanted something from me, and he was doing himself no favours. I'd arrived at the bar earlier than we'd arranged, but by making me wait all he was achieving was pissing me off.

I was happy with the surroundings, which was in his favour. If he'd kept me waiting and had taken me to a shit-hole, blood would have been spilt—probably his.

London by night was glorious. The lights, the people and, most importantly, the sins. The city oozed with desire which led people to sin, and that was where I shone.

I was seated at the best table in the place, perks of being me. I always got what I wanted. I'd flashed a brilliant smile at the waitress when I arrived, and she did everything she could to keep me happy—nothing was too much trouble. The world was mine.

I took in the bustling lights of the city from the massive floor-to-ceiling window in front of me. I could see for miles from the top of the Shard. He'd chosen the location, and I was more than happy. It suited my needs.

It was a high-end club, and therefore the people inside were beautiful—well at least on the outside. Men and women danced, drank, and flirted. There was a lot of desire in the city tonight; I could sense it, and it made me feel powerful.

The music was loud, the bass pounded through my chest, and my eyes were assaulted by the severity of the neon lights that flashed though the room. Places like this, though, were like a second home to me, and to be honest, it was no hardship.

I could sense him before I saw him. He made his way through the throng of people on the dance floor. They swayed to the music, bodies grinding together in harmony with the beat.

Daniel Turner was on his way to a meeting he would never forget.

Mr. Turner was visually not what I expected. People sought me out for so many different reasons. The majority of people who needed me for the reasons Mr. Turner did, usually weren't like him.

They tended to be shy, timid, and very much lacking in self-confidence. Not Mr. Turner. There was more to this man than I first imagined. *This will be interesting.*

On his way through the crowds, he was gaining a fair amount of female attention, and as he made his way to me, he flirted with a number of them.

He worked in finance, but his muscular six-foot-one frame did not quite fit that job. His build did not scream finance, yet he wore a clearly expensive designer suit, so he obviously wanted people to know he had money. Mousey brown hair was worn slicked back away from his face in a distinguished style, and dull, blue eyes scanned the bodies of the women who danced before him.

As I took him all in, I would have made a bet that he was a wolf, but I knew better and that he was indeed just human.

"You're late." I stressed the words, making sure the displeasure in my voice was evident.

"Sorry, London traffic. My apologies—" He stopped, clearly waiting for me to introduce myself.

"Luke Albright, though you can address me as Mr. Albright." I was aware that was not the name he expected, but he did not push it further.

I motioned for him to sit down and without skipping a beat raised my hand to summon the waitress. She was with us immediately.

"Would you like a drink, Mr. Turner?" I already knew that he wanted one—who wouldn't given the circumstances?

"Double tequila, neat," he addressed the waitress in a demanding tone, never once raising his eyes to look at her.

This guy was a prick, and I would enjoy my time with him should he choose to accept my terms. I raised my own glass to the waitress, indicating I wanted another. I flashed her my best smile, and she nodded while hurrying off.

"So, can you get this done?" He asked, straight down to business.

"First of all, Mr. Turner, I have some questions for you before we discuss the terms of our potential agreement. Is that acceptable?" He nodded.

"What is the nature of your relationship to the woman in question? Who is she to you?" I knew all of the answers already, but I wanted him to tell me. I wanted to feel it.

"She is my everything. I need her, and she was ripped away from me. I need her back. I *have* to have her back." When he answered, I could see the desire and want for this woman. But there was something else... anger. It bubbled just below the surface.

"She is yours? In what way?" Again, I knew the answer.

"In every way. Everything about her is mine, and I want

her back!" The anger grew; it was visible under the façade, but it was taking more for him to control it.

"If she is yours, Mr. Turner, then why is she not with you?" The potential agreement was beneficial to both of us, but he needed me more—and, in all honesty, I enjoyed having my fun and toying with people.

"Because she's a fucking snowflake who couldn't handle me. I… may have lost my shit on a couple of occasions and scared her. There was no need for her to vanish off the face of the fucking Earth." I knew it was more than just him losing his temper, so I continued to prod him.

"A couple of trips to the hospital and a restraining ordered would suggest to me that she is less of a snowflake and you are more of a bully, Mr. Turner." I didn't care either way what the outcome of our meeting was, but I liked the game too much to make things easy for him.

"Go fuck yourself," he said with a scowl, pushing up from his seat.

"Sit," I ordered. He did so immediately. It was a command that his body obeyed. My hands were clasped together, fingers laced, and my eyes had gone as black as the night sky. My demeanour had changed in an instant. He knew he'd fucked up.

"My apologies, Mr. Albright. Sometimes my temper gets the better of me," he admitted, looking at me sheepishly.

The waitress returned with our drinks and placed them on the table in front of us. He didn't acknowledge her as he downed his drink in one gulp. I thanked her, and she smiled at me. There was pure lust in her eyes; that was often the way with human women… and a fair few men.

Everybody wants a bad boy, I thought to myself.

When this meeting with Mr. Turner was done, I'd find her, take her to the toilets and get her to suck my dick. She had, after all, been an excellent waitress and deserved a tip.

Her eyes scanned the length of my body, from my face, down over my chest, and rested on my crotch; I thrust my hips a little, and I noticed her visibly flush. I could hear her heart beating faster in her chest, and she was undeniably aroused when she scuttled back over to the bar.

A smile graced my lips. I would never tire of the effect I had upon people. They were the perks of the job, and I *always* made time to indulge in them.

"Tell me, Mr. Turner, why would you not seek out the services of a private investigator? Surely they would be able to track her down for you?"

"No, no, I don't want them involved," he said immediately in a hushed tone.

"But why? I'm sure it is something they would be able to do. I don't think it would take them very long to find her."

"Are you saying this because you can't do it? Are you not able to find her?" His façade was slipping, and the anger was becoming more visible.

"Not at all, Mr. Turner. I can, of course, do this for you. I just want to know why you've turned to me? There are other, easier methods at your disposal. Given the circumstances, I would have thought you would utilise them. I tend to be a... last resort."

"Private investigators would leave a trail." His voice was low, almost a whisper.

"Go on," I prompted, gesturing with a wave of my hand for him to continue.

"I don't want to just find her. I want to find her, and I want to fucking kill her. A private investigator would be compelled to tell the police, and then I'd get put away. I want her dead, so I can be free to live my life." His voice was a low, angry growl.

"That woman is my entire world, and if I can't have her, no one can. She'll die at my fucking hands, and she'll be glad it was me who ended both our pain. *Now* can you help, Mr. Albright?" He had conviction; I'd give him that.

"That depends, Mr. Turner. Are you willing to pay? I can give you what you seek, but everything has a price. *Everything.*" I could see the anger in him, raging, coursing through his veins. I knew he would say yes.

"What… what happens to me?" This was a common question. Most people wanted to know what would happen to them afterwards. In all truth, this was as much a mystery to me as it was to him. We wouldn't know till it happened—I could guarantee it would not be good. I wasn't going to tell him that though.

"You get what you want from me; I fulfil our agreement. Then you live your life. When the times comes, you become mine. After that, I do not know. It depends on you, Mr. Turner." I could tell that he hadn't been expecting that response. He sat for a while in silence, contemplating the decision before him.

"Alright. Agreed. When can I have her?" He was impatient and reckless. Both of which were good for me. He'd make mistakes and get into trouble. He would likely be mine sooner than he thought.

"Did you provide my people with the information we requested?" He shook his head as he pulled out some documents from the inside pocket of his suit jacket.

"No, but everything I have is in there. She's been gone two years, so a lot of it is probably outdated, but it's all I have." He looked dejected when he passed me the information.

I examined the picture of Mr. Turner and the woman. He was a few years younger, and they looked like a normal, happy, young couple. It must have been prior to his darkness taking over. She was pretty, and they looked good together. I leafed through the other documents. None of them would be much use compared to my contacts. My team were quicker, better, and everywhere. All-knowing.

"I'll have someone look into it straight away. This is your last chance, Mr. Turner, your final opportunity to walk away. Once you shake my hand the deal is done, and there will be no turning back." I held my hand out.

He observed it for several seconds. Finally, he leaned forward with purpose, taking my hand and shaking it.

The deal was made; it was done.

"Thank you, Mr. Albright," he said, smiling at me.

"Daniel, please… call me Lucifer," I said with a grin.

Now, where's that waitress.

2

TESS

I'D BEEN TAKING photos of the venue in preparation, prior to the arrival of the guests and bridal party. Simon was at the hotel, taking photos of everyone getting ready.

"Simon, the guests are starting to arrive. How long will the bridal party be?" I'd called him for an update so I could get everything ready.

"The groom and his party left about fifteen minutes ago, so they should be with you soon. I'm leaving now, and the bridal party will be heading out in about ten minutes. How did the set-up shots go?" He was such a perfectionist.

"The venue is beautiful, so it hardly took any work. I'll see you when you get here."

I loved weddings. Everything about them: the outfits, the decor, the food, the wine, the dancing, and the love shared between two people.

I, however, was nowhere near getting married—hell, I didn't even have a boyfriend. That was a bit hard when you were as closed off as I was.

This was my job. Simon, another photographer, had asked if I could help him out with the shots for the day. He was doing the formal ones, and I was in charge of the candid photos. As a freelance photographer, I did a lot of different jobs.

Weddings, though… I was a sucker for them.

I'd always loved capturing different images ever since I used my first camera. My mum got it for me, and I never looked back. I was lucky that one of my passions was my job. I knew it wasn't that way for most.

The location was spectacular. The happy couple had chosen to have both their ceremony and reception at a boathouse in Central Park. I'd walked or run around the park at least once a week since moving to New York but had never really paid much attention to the boathouse nestled on the lake.

It was stunning.

The ceremony room had huge, fully glazed doors that wrapped around the entire room. Deep, dark wooden floors were broken by a cream carpet which served as the aisle. Along the edge of the carpet were huge lanterns with pillar candles flickering inside. Either side of the aisle, there were ornate cream coloured chairs with light-green bows on the backs. At the end was an archway decorated with green foliage and a variety of stunning flowers.

I began taking photos as the guests arrived; I guessed there were around 200 people there, so I knew I had lots to do. I noticed the groom, best man, and ushers had arrived and snapped some photos.

Everyone made their way inside the beautiful venue, and the groom ventured up to the floral archway and stepped to the right of it. His best man followed.

Both men were very handsome, around mid-thirties. Tall with broad frames. They wore black tuxes. No one looked bad in a perfectly fitted suit.

At least that's what I thought until I saw one of the ushers who approached the archway. I noticed both the groom and best man rolled their eyes slightly as he approached them. The usher was small in every sense of the word, and his suit made him look like a child. He was probably around the same age as the others but had a shaved head and a round face. The best man seemed annoyed and quickly dismissed him.

As the usher made his way back down the aisle, he saw me and wiggled his eyebrows. I thought he was trying his best, *"How you doing?"* but I ignored him. Even if he had been my type, I still wouldn't have done anything; I was working, I was a professional, and he was definitely not my type.

Simon found me and filled me in on how we would be shooting the ceremony. He'd be at the front taking the majority of the shots, and I'd float around in the background grabbing any photos I thought worked.

With everyone in place the wedding procession started. The music was a classical piece, and I recognised it as Pachelbel's Canon in D Major. I didn't know a lot of classical music, but this one was common at weddings. Rock was much more my thing, and I loved seeing live bands in any setting.

The doors opened, and the bridesmaids entered. There were two smaller ones who entered first, and I guessed there were about four and six; they threw petals from little baskets. Next were the adult bridesmaids; they made their way down the aisle on the arms of the ushers. I took shots of them all.

The last pair entered, and it was the usher I'd seen earlier. He was escorting an elegant-looking woman, in her early thirties. She was much taller than him, even without her heels on. She smiled, but I could see she was putting on a brave face. I knew it because I'd worn the same face so many times.

He, however, was completely oblivious to her discomfort. As I continued shooting, I saw him sway slightly, and the bridesmaid wobbled on his arm. He'd clearly already had a few drinks.

With the pair reaching the end of the aisle it was the bride's turn to make her entrance. Heads swivelled to the doors as they opened, and she entered.

I was watching the groom. I thought that you could always tell how much a couple loved each other by looking at the groom's face when his bride entered. I remember a couple of weddings where the groom looked indifferent, and I felt sorry for the women having to be with pricks that didn't appreciate them.

This groom, however, was not one of those. His eyes lit up when he saw her, and they glistened slightly with tears. The biggest grin spread across his face.

I don't think anyone had ever looked at me like that.

I'd captured the groom's reaction for them to cherish always. Those were the shots I loved taking.

With that, I turned my camera on the bride and her father. She wore a stunning mermaid-style dress, ivory and lace with beautiful beading. She carried a huge bouquet of ivory flowers and foliage. A floor-length veil followed behind her. I snapped shots of family and friends in awe of the beautiful bride. Some beamed, some cried, and no one could take their eyes off her.

The ceremony had gone perfectly, and I had helped Simon with the formal family shots. We both took photos during the speeches and cake cutting, and the afternoon was drawing into night.

It was common to stay at weddings until at least the first dance, but this couple had wanted us to stay until the very end. They wanted everything captured.

I never saw the point in that. Most couples had an open bar, so the final shots of the night were mainly of drunk idiots in various stages of stupor.

I carried on though; I was getting paid no matter what the late-night shots looked like.

The first dance started with the happy couple moving in harmony. Sheer bliss was visible on both their faces. *This one will last*, I thought to myself. As they moved together, they gestured for others to join them, and people did. It was that moment I noticed the usher from earlier as he staggered onto the dance floor, no partner to dance with in sight.

He stood on the spot swaying by himself. The happy couple looked anything *but* happy to see him, so I decided not to get any shots. The best man guided him from the dance floor to behind me.

"Christ, Barry, you're wasted," the best man snarled.

"Fuck off, Stuart, what has it got to do with you?" the usher snapped back.

The best man, Stuart, was not impressed and apparently didn't have time for Barry's bullshit. "Pull yourself together. You're an embarrassment." He turned to walk away, but Barry grabbed his arm.

"Who the fuck do you think you are to talk to me like that? I'm the bride's brother," he spat.

"Exactly. You should know better than to ruin your sister's big day." Stuart snatched his arm from Barry's grasp and walked away.

I became aware Barry was very close behind me as I continued taking shots of the guests mingling and dancing.

"Well hello there, beautiful," he breathed into my ear. The smell of alcohol filled my nose. He was much closer than I thought he'd been.

"Excuse me," I said, trying to move to another location.

He grabbed my arm and turned me to face him. "Are you British?" he asked, still swaying.

"Yes, could you please excuse me?" I was trying my best to get away, but his grip was tight, and he wasn't letting go.

"Don't rush off," he slurred. "Don't you want to party?"

"I'm sorry, but I'm working." It wasn't a lie, and I thought that was better than saying he repulsed me.

He still hadn't let go of my arm. "Say something for me, anything, I don't care what. I love your accent."

This had happened a few times since I had moved to New York. Apparently, a lot of American men were hot for my accent. Not that it did me much good—I wasn't ready to go there just yet after everything that had happened.

"I'm sorry, I really have to work." I was insistent and managed to free my arm from his grip.

He was persistent, though, and moved to block my path. "Come on, there's no need to be like that about it," he breathed his words into my face, and the smell of alcohol on him made me retch a little.

He began to walk forward, and I had to back up to prevent his sweaty body from making contact with mine. I'd tried to be polite.

"Look, I'm not interested. Leave me alone and get out of my way."

Everyone was still dancing, so no one had noticed what was going on.

"Come on, *baby*; I can show you a good time. I've got a friend we can call. We'll both take turns on you. You won't regret it." He was deadly serious.

Well fuck, I thought to myself, *that I was not expecting*. I was through being nice.

"Wow, well what an offer that is. Firstly, if you are that bad in bed you need to ask a friend to come and help, I'll have to pass. Secondly, I'm no one's to "take turns on." Now leave me the fuck alone before I break your nose, you small-dicked prick."

I noticed the best man had again spotted Barry was

causing problems and was on his way over to us from across the dance floor.

Before he could reach us, however, Barry grabbed my wrist and pulled me towards him.

"You are a feisty little bitch, aren't you? I'll fucking show you," he hissed.

I was done. I was tired of men thinking they could put their hands on me and that I wouldn't do shit about it.

When I'd moved to the city, I was broken and scared and hated the feeling. I wanted to learn to protect myself, so I'd enrolled in self-defence classes. I'd been going the entire time I'd lived in New York and was pretty proficient.

I twisted my wrist and pulled free from his grasp; it wasn't too hard given his intoxicated state. I then grabbed his own wrist and twisted it back upon itself to an awkward angle, and he let out a throaty shout.

The music was too loud for anyone other than the best man to hear—he was now nearly on top of us.

I leaned in to Barry and said, "Touch me again, and I'll rip your arm off." In order to reiterate my point, I applied a little more pressure to the wrist lock, and he collapsed to his knees.

Stuart arrived. "What the hell is going on?"

"Your friend tried to grope me. Can I leave him with you?" It wasn't really a question.

"Miss, I'm so sorry. God damn it, Barry, you dick. I'm putting you in a cab home now before you can do any more damage."

"Fuck you, Stuart. She's a fucking tease, she was asking for it," he said through gritted teeth.

I smiled while I applied a little more pressure to his wrist.

"Argh," he moaned.

"I have it, Miss, I'll take it from here. Again, I'm so sorry for the trouble."

I let go of Barry's wrist, and he cradled it like a newborn. Stuart pulled him to his feet, grabbing his uninjured wrist and pulling him away from me.

Barry turned to me. "Fucking stuck-up bitch," he shouted.

I looked him dead in the eye and blew a kiss in his direction.

3

LUCIFER

MOVEMENT to my left-hand side woke me. I stirred, opening my eyes to see what it was. I recognised that I was still in my London home. I had places all over the world—it was easier for business that way.

My main home, though, was the innermost circle of Hell. That was all mine; no one could enter unless invited. It was my most private sanctum.

On my left was the waitress from the club the night before. She was sprawled out on her stomach with her arm draped over the edge of the bed. She was naked, her lower half covered by a bedsheet.

Before I could admire her, there was a noise to my right. I turned and noticed a brunette fast asleep. She was on her side, facing away from me. The curve of her figure enticed me to touch her naked ass.

It had been a good night.

After Daniel had left, I'd found the waitress easily and invited her back to my place. She'd asked if it was okay to bring a friend along. Well, who was I to say no to that?

I thought back to three of us moving as one as I kissed

them, they kissed each other, hands roaming everywhere. I'd taken both of them over and over throughout the course of the night. Stamina was key. I didn't want to disappoint anyone. By the look of the two of them beside me, I'd say I was successful.

I hadn't asked their names, it didn't really matter. It was doubtful I'd see them again—very rarely did that happen.

Lust was one of my favourite sins, and I'd indulged in it anytime I was given the opportunity. There was *so* much of it displayed by these two women last night. It was safe to say I had an extensive sexual history; when you were as old as me, it was hard not to. I took most sexual opportunities that presented themselves to me. Who wouldn't?

As I lay there, remembering the events from the previous night, I became aware I was being watched. I felt eyes burning into me. I raised my head to scan the room, and there she was.

At the end of my bed stood Bee, arms folded across her chest while she shook her head in disapproval.

"Lucifer, you're too old for all of this shit. There are matters that require your attention," she said wearily.

I climbed from the bed and made my way to the full-length windows of my bedroom. I was naked and hadn't bothered putting any clothes on just because Bee was there. She'd seen it all before. Sure enough, she didn't flinch.

I placed a hand on the window and looked out; I was hungry—I'd have to grab some food before I did any work.

"How was the meeting?" she probed, all business today. I waved my hand dismissing the question.

Bee—or Beelzebub, to address her by her full name—had known me the longest of all my demons. She was a fellow fallen, arriving in Hell shortly after I had been tasked to rule it. She had helped with my rebellion, so she'd been cast out like so many of my disenchanted brethren.

She was my second in command, my chief-lieutenant, and a force to be reckoned with. Bee had proven herself to me on countless occasions over the years.

She was around five-foot-six and had a small, compact, athletic build. She was very capable of looking after herself and putting a stop to anyone who challenged her. Queen Bee, I called her. She hated it.

Today her long, flowing black hair was fixed to the top of her head in a severe bun, scraped back from her face and exposing her milky white skin. Not much scope for a tan in Hell really, despite the heat.

Her piercing blue eyes fixed on me. "Really?" She nodded her head in the direction of my bed and the still passed-out women.

There was never anything amorous between Bee and me; she loved me, and I knew that she would always be by my side, but those romantic feelings were never there. She was extremely loyal, and I trusted her implicitly.

"You know I can never say no to a pretty face… or two." I smirked at her, and she shook her head.

"Do you never tire of it?" She studied me, waiting for my response.

In all honesty, I didn't. Why would I? Despite my initial misgivings, which had landed me in Hell, the human world had brought me innumerable pleasures and I partook in as many as I could.

"My dear, there is very little I tire of. Except *his* bullshit," I said, nodding my head up to the heavens. He hadn't bothered me for a while, though. The tussle between Heaven and Hell had been steady for some time. For now, things were easy.

"So the meeting? Are you going to fill me in?" she probed once more. She was business first and everything else second.

"He agreed to the terms. He was a prick though; he kept

me waiting." I turned to see her reaction and walked over to the huge closet.

"How dare he," she said, but I could tell in her tone she was mocking me.

I searched the closet and pulled on some loose-fitting trousers. I made my way to the large sofas where Bee had made herself at home. I'd closed the door to the bedroom. I doubted either girl would be awake yet after the previous night's activities, but I decided to stay on the safe side.

"Honestly, Bee, he's a piece of work. You'd like him," I said, raising my eyebrows at her.

"Dick," was the only comeback she had.

"He wants a woman, and he wants her so he can kill her. No matter what happens, we'll be getting his soul. It's just the level of Hell that he'll end up in. That is still to be determined."

"You think he'll mess up?" she asked. She was sharp; I could always rely on her for that.

"I do, and I think his soul will be ours to torture much sooner than he thinks. He's hot-headed, and that will be his downfall. His temper will get the better of him, and eventually he'll pay for it with his life."

She studied me for a while. "So a girl? Do we have anything on her?" Bee already had a plan, I could see it in her eyes.

I made my way over to the living area and picked up my suit jacket. Various items of clothes littered the floor. Our activities had started in here last night and moved to the bedroom after we had all disrobed.

I plucked the information Daniel had handed me last night out of the side pocket of my jacket and strode back over to her. "This is all he had. Apparently, she's been gone two years. So it's a little outdated." I handed the bundle to her, and she began scanning it.

"This won't be much use, but least there is a photo." She held the photo in her hand as she studied the couple. "They look happy," she commented.

"Things change," I remarked, remembering the look of possessiveness in Daniel's eyes as he spoke of the woman.

Then we started our search. The information we had would be distributed to all of our eyes and ears. The reach of Hell was vast, and we would have her tracked down in no time.

"I'll take this down to be actioned; it shouldn't be too long. What should we do once she's found?"

"I want to know as soon as you have anything. I'll be handling this one personally. I might even take a hands-on approach," I said with a smirk that she was all too familiar with.

"Really, Lucifer, this one too?"

"Hey, he kept me waiting, so now he can wait a while. If things happen and I have a little fun along the way, then what's the harm? The girl still dies either way, but at least this way she can say she fucked the Prince of Darkness." I laughed, but Bee simply rolled her eyes.

I thought about taking what Daniel wanted most. He had, after all, said she was his. Well, after I finished with her, she wouldn't even remember his name. No, my mind was made up. I would have some fun with her before she died—making him sweat would be an added bonus.

I stood up from the sofa and Bee was aware she was being dismissed.

I made my way across the floor to the bedroom door, opening it and stepping through. I saw her watching me as I looked out into the living room.

"Now if you'll excuse me, I have a *couple* of matters to attend to." A wide smile played across my mouth as I closed the door, glancing at Bee who was shaking her head.

I removed my trousers again and climbed onto the end of the bed, trailing a hand up each woman's body until I got to their backsides and squeezed. Both women stirred and turned to look at me.

"Ladies, you've slept long enough. I want to know which of you can come the most." And with that, I began to find out.

4

TESS

"Can I have another please, Harry?" I asked the bartender, raising my glass to him.

"Be right with you, Tess," he said with a smile.

It was busy in the bar tonight, so I sat and took in my surroundings while I waited. I felt at home here; it was comforting.

My first apartment had been a short walk from O'Malley's Bar, and I'd stumbled on it one night when I was out exploring. At that point, I'd been stuck in my apartment unpacking and adjusting to my new life. I'd felt the urge to get out and familiarise myself with the area surrounding my new place.

As soon as I'd walked into the bar, I was met with warm smiles and a good feeling. That first night in the bar was when I first met Emma. She was a waitress there, and we quickly became friends.

It had been so long since I'd had a female friend, we just clicked. I'd been alone for so long. I had my ex, but I was still alone. He did that; he'd isolated me.

But now I had Emma.

She was a typical American "girl next door" but with an edge. Her blonde hair was cut into a short wavy bob, and she had a thick fringe. "It's bangs, not fringe." Emma would always correct me. *"You're in America now, you need to speak American,"* she'd say. She was small at five-foot-two, but that never stopped her. Since she was slim with a big chest, I always said she looked like she'd topple over. She'd used her "assets" to her advantage, though, on many occasions. Emma was forward and not afraid to go after what she wanted. The complete opposite of me.

"Where's your head at tonight?" She appeared behind me, making me jump. I turned to her and shook my head.

"I'm just a bit tired, long day." It wasn't a lie, but there was more to it, and I didn't feel like sharing tonight.

As she bounced to the bar to gather a tray full of drinks, she looked at me. "That's bullshit and we both know it. Spill."

"Fine, today is the anniversary of me deciding to leave London. It just weighs on me a bit that's all." She knew about my past—well, not all of it, but most of it. I couldn't find the strength to tell her everything. I was still so ashamed and embarrassed. I had done nothing wrong, but the whole thing still brought up those feelings. I hadn't been strong enough then, but I was now.

"So why are you moping? Surely that is one of the best things you ever did? Leaving that asshole and getting to meet me." She winked at me with one of her grey-blue eyes. "We're going to a club when I get off work, so we can celebrate properly."

"I don't really feel up to it, to be honest, Em." I had mixed emotions about the day. Happiness and sadness, but not in equal measure.

"It's happening, deal with it." With that, she took the tray of drinks and disappeared.

I watched her deliver them to a large group at the front of the bar. She was flirting with one of the guys. *Shameless.*

Harry had filled my glass up for me. I turned to thank him, and that's when I saw Jerry. He was the owner of the bar, and it was rare for him to be here this late on a Saturday night. "Hey, Jerry, what are you doing here so late?"

"Well, if you're here, sweetheart, someone needs to make sure Emma does some work and doesn't chat to you all night." He shook his head, but I knew he was joking.

I feigned a look of shock, and then smiled at him. Ever since I'd first found the bar and Emma, I had pretty much come here every night. Everyone made me feel welcome— hell, I had the same seat every night, and Jerry never seemed to mind me propping up the bar. He was a lovely man; I thought of him like how I would have wanted a grandfather to be. I never knew my grandparents, but I wished I'd had Jerry.

Emma returned to the bar, standing next to me. "Tess, tell Jerry that we have this and that he can go home. It's late, and I'm sure his wife wants him back." She worried about Jerry being out alone late in the city, and so did I.

Before I could agree with her, he raised a hand cutting me off.

"I'm going now. Make sure you and Harry lock up properly and put the cash in the safe," he said to Emma.

"Jerry, I've worked here for four years; I know the drill," she reminded him.

He pulled on his jacket and turned to us both. "Night, girls, take care."

"Night, Jerry," we said in unison.

With that, Emma turned to me, holding up a piece of paper. I could see that on it was scribbled a telephone number. She grinned, and I immediately knew it belonged to the guy from the group at the front of the bar.

"Let's see how many others I get tonight," she said, giggling. She was serious, though. Emma was a free spirit and pretty much slept with whoever she wanted. If she saw someone she was interested in, she went for it. She never held back, unashamed about her wants and desires.

I envied her.

I was the complete opposite; I overthought everything when it came to men. It was as if they were a completely other species. I knew that my fear of the opposite sex had something to do with what I had endured in my past. However, even before that I had an issue with confidence.

"By the way, I met the perfect guy for you. He's from my gym, and he is *so* your type," she said, eyeing me.

This was a regular occurrence for her, thinking she had to set me up and make me happy with a man. I'd told her so many times that I didn't need a man to be happy and that if it happened, it happened but that I wasn't settling again.

Truth be told, I didn't think I was ready. I was still adjusting to my new life and getting comfortable in my own skin. So, at the moment, men were off the table.

Don't get me wrong, I'd had relationships before, but I never had the freedom Emma experienced. I'd only had sex with someone I was in a relationship with, and most of those had been long-term. I'd been with my ex for nearly four years, and that was a massive shit storm of epic proportions. Hence me moving to another country to escape.

When I moved to New York, I'd vowed to start afresh; I had counselling to help me deal with my issues and thought I'd try a different approach when it came to men. So many women had multiple one-night stands and actively went after whatever the hell they desired. I wanted that: the level of freedom that leaving your insecurities and inhibitions behind would allow.

Just after coming to the city and starting my new life, I

went to a club. I'd had a few drinks and danced to any song that came on. There, I met a guy; he was cute, I think. I'd had a lot to drink. He started dancing with me, grinding against me, so I thought *fuck it, let's do this*. A fresh start and new me.

We danced and drank till it was closing time and he asked if I wanted to go back to his place. I decided that I would—why couldn't I be one of those people? Free and liberated. So I went back with him.

As soon as we were through the door we were kissing, hands groping at each other, clothes being ripped off and thrown across the room. He guided me to his bedroom and onto the bed. We removed the last of each other's clothes and got down to it. The build-up was fantastic, but once it started, it was two minutes of him thrusting until he fell to a heap on top of me, rolled off, and went to sleep. I felt cheap and extremely unsatisfied.

I had really wanted it to be good—no, amazing. As I lay there, I couldn't help thinking of my ex and what he would say if he could see me. Tears pooled in my eyes as I heard the man next to me snoring. I gathered my clothes and left the apartment.

I knew at that point, one-night stands weren't for me. That sort of thing couldn't fix me; I was too broken even for that. I would never be like Emma, and that was okay. Everyone was different.

The city had changed me—though it was for the better. My confidence was slowly returning; I didn't second guess everything I did. I had friends and was no longer alone. I'd begun to talk and work through what had happened to me, and I was able to protect myself better.

Moving to New York had been a good thing. At the time it had been a necessity to leave London, but looking back, moving here made me better. It helped me put my broken pieces back together. There was that part of me, though, that

I still wasn't ready to open up. It would have to remain closed off.

The bar was now closing, and I stayed to help Emma and Harry lock up. I knew I was going out with her; I didn't really have much choice in the matter—she usually got what she wanted.

As we locked the door of the bar, we waved good night to Harry and jumped in a cab.

"Where are we going?" I asked her.

"Anywhere we can dance and drink. We're celebrating the day you started your new and improved life, and more importantly that you met me," she said with a smirk.

I knew I was going to regret this in the morning.

5

LUCIFER

I WAS STILL IN LONDON, waiting for news about the woman. I'd arranged to meet with two of my most trusted leaders to discuss the goings-on in Hell, and to see if any issues had arisen.

I arrived at the restaurant early, not expecting them to be there. Again, I was afforded the VIP treatment: the best seats and exceptional service. I'd ordered a bottle of the finest Pinot Noir; I knew my guests would appreciate it.

Bee joined me first. I thought the two of them might arrive together considering they were both coming from Hell, but that was not the case. She saw me and made her way to the table.

Today her hair was worn in an equally serious-looking high ponytail. She wore black skin-tight trousers and a bright green high-necked sleeveless shirt, ever the fashion icon. She looked powerful and gained a fair amount of attention on her way to the table.

"Am I the first here?" she asked.

"Yes, I'm sure he's on his way, though. Wine?" I asked, gesturing to the bottle.

"Excellent choice. I'll indulge, if I'm off the clock?" she questioned, already knowing the answer. I wasn't fond of drinking alone when talking business, and she knew that.

I didn't answer, and simply poured her a glass of wine. She took it, cupping it in her hand. I did the same. I inhaled and took a deep sip; I got herbs and mixed berries, as well as summer flowers. It was a good wine. Over the years, I'd come to appreciate the finer things: wine, food, and women.

Bee set her glass back on the table. The look on her face let me know she also appreciated it. She sat scanning the restaurant, surveying her surroundings with purpose. She was always on the lookout for danger and threats. Hell and its inhabitants had, after all, been a target for a long time. Forever.

My thoughts were interrupted when I saw him arrive at the front of the restaurant. He addressed the maître d', who at this point looked petrified. I had a certain effect on people, and he had the complete opposite. It was easy to understand why.

Leviathan was six-foot-seven and extremely muscular. He looked half-giant due to his massive size. He wore a navy suit, with a light blue shirt. He'd dressed up for the occasion, though, as that wasn't his normal attire. Armour was much more his comfort zone. A shaved head with grey eyes completed the look.

He had arrived in Hell shortly after Bee had. Another of my allies in the holy war. Leviathan—or Levi as we now referred to him—had been instrumental in the battle, but unfortunately it hadn't led to a victory.

For their devotion to me in the fight, both Bee and Levi had been stripped of their titles as angels and had been cast down to join me in Hell. I'd felt immeasurable guilt that their fate was sealed with mine, but I had come to terms with it over the millennia. They had both told me it was their choice to fight alongside me and that their actions were on them alone.

We had become close over our many years together, and there was no one I trusted more than these two. Both Bee and Levi's loyalty to me had never faltered, and I knew I could always count on them for anything, should I need it.

"Wine, Levi?" I asked as he came to the table to join us, nodding his head as he did so. The maître d' had quickly scuttled back to the front of the restaurant. The gaze of several of the other guests remained on our table, all as low key as they could possibly be. Sly glances here and there—it was often that way when the three of us were together.

"Thanks. Are we eating or what?" he asked, straight to the point. There was never any messing around with Levi.

"Yes I've already ordered for us. It shouldn't be long." I knew neither of them would mind that I had ordered on their behalf; they appreciated my taste.

Since Bee had fallen first, she became my second in command and Levi my third. Both had proven themselves on multiple occasions over the years; they had deserved their titles.

Bee was responsible for the Sin of Pride. It was, therefore, her responsibility to oversee all things relating to Pride within Hell. She had informed us that things had been going well and that they may need to expand due to the influx of new sinners. Levi agreed with the potential plan for extensions.

Levi took his obligations seriously and managed his circle of Wrath with a strong hand. He had to; it was one of the trickier circles. No one was more up to the job than this beast of a demon. Over the next few minutes, he informed us that he had been experiencing some issues with some of his more problematic inhabitants.

"Do you need any help? I can come and exert some force

if need be. Try and calm things for you?" I knew he wouldn't ask if things weren't getting bad.

"That might be useful, show the bastards who's boss," he said, nodding appreciatively.

"Anyway, enough chat about work, what else is going on with you two?" I asked, knowing the answer already. Both needed pushing to let loose, and if things had been busy in their Hell for them, it was unlikely they'd have left for some time.

"Very little," Levi grunted as Bee agreed.

"Not all of us have the luxury of leaving on a whim as you do, Lucifer," she said whilst raising an eyebrow at me.

"Ouch," I feigned, hand over heart and acting wounded by her words.

Our food arrived, as well as a couple more bottles of the wine. We continued chatting through the food and drinks, and both Bee and Levi relaxed into themselves. It had been a while since we'd all gone out together, and I think the three of us needed it.

We laughed and joked, aware we were gaining a lot of attention from the other diners. None of us cared, though, and we continued on through our lunch.

"Have we an update on Mr. Turner's woman?" I asked Bee, knowing she would be up to date on all of the affairs down in Hell.

I hadn't been home in a while; business had kept me up in the human world longer than I'd expected. It was a common misconception that the Devil was stuck in Hell, sealed inside for all eternity. I could, in fact, come and go as I pleased. I did have to go back though; I couldn't live in the human world indefinitely. Hell was a part of me, and therefore I had to return to it.

It was Levi that replied, "She's in America. We don't have

an exact location for her yet though. We should have it in a couple of days." He trusted the way things worked.

"Shouldn't take too long," Bee confirmed.

"Excellent. I'm eager to meet this woman and see what all of the fuss is about." It wasn't a lie; I *was* keen to find this woman and ruin the touching reunion between her and Mr. Turner. Him knowing that I'd been with her would ruin him. I was looking forward to that.

"I expect an update as soon as we have a location." They knew I was going to be hands-on with this, literally. They both nodded in acknowledgement.

We had continued to gain attention in the restaurant, mainly because of our appearance. We were quite the trio to look at, but it wasn't just that. All three of us were old—not in our looks but in the auras we expressed to the world. We exuded confidence and self-assuredness. People were often drawn to us, probably for that reason. I liked to think it was because of our natural charm and charisma, but it was more likely the power that radiated from us.

I was less bothered about what drew people to us and more that they were drawn to us in the first place. With that thought in my mind, I decided Bee and Levi deserved some downtime. Far from the worries of Hell. They were owed a little bit of fun.

Eyes continued to wander to our table and tongues wagged. *Let's see just how much of a good time the three of us can have.* I'd eyed partners for all three of us and summoned the maître d' back over to the table.

"Do you have a private dining room we could use?" I asked him as he nervously stood by Levi.

"We do, sir," he replied quietly.

"Excellent, prepare it for us please," I instructed him. "Have it ready for six guests."

At this point, Bee and Levi were intrigued. "What are you up to, Lucifer?" Bee asked.

"You two work too hard, you've earned a treat. Go with the maître d', I'll join you shortly." Neither of them argued and they left the table.

With that done, I went over to the people I'd picked out. Two were a couple. The man I thought very much Bee's type, and the woman had Levi written all over her—or at least she would soon. They hesitated at first, as was so often the case, but after a little gentle persuasion they agreed to join us. I waved the maitre d' over and instructed him to show the pair to the private dining area.

I made my way to a group of women, eyeing the small brunette the entire time I crossed the room. Her gaze never left me. I interrupted their conversation, holding my hand out to her.

"You look bored, care to join me?" I said, ignoring everyone else and only focusing on her. The rest of her party fell silent, waiting for her to respond. She said nothing; she simply stood and took my hand. As we made our way across the room, I could hear the surprised voices of her friends whom she had just abandoned.

"I'm Luke. Pleased to make your acquaintance," I said smoothly.

"Sasha," was all she could reply.

I pushed my way through the door to the private dining room, guiding Sasha in behind me. Once we were in I saw Bee straddling the man from the couple. They were sat on a large chair, and she was riding him, eliciting feral moans from him every time she ground her hips against his.

Across the room, Levi had the woman from the couple bent over the table, taking her from behind. His strong hands were firmly on her hips as he drove into her and she held onto the tablecloth to prevent herself from moving. She pushed back into his thrusts, pleasure clearly riding her hard.

I pulled Sasha over to a sofa situated in front of a fireplace. I laid her down on it, and she made no attempts to get up. "Are you ready, Sasha?" I questioned. She could only muster a nod, completely caught up in everything surrounding her.

With that, I joined the others, partaking in the pleasures of the flesh.

We deserved to let loose; after all, Hell was an exhausting mistress.

6

TESS

I SAT AT MY COMPUTER, working my way through the photos from the wedding. I needed to get them edited and ready so I could send them over to Simon. Once he had them, I could get paid.

As I looked through the shots, I found the photo of the groom as the bride made her entrance. It was beautiful, and I knew they would love it. I continued working through them; I was really pleased with the job I'd done. So many beautiful photos of their family and friends, laughing and smiling, not knowing I was there capturing every moment.

It was clear looking back over the photos and the faces of the family and friends, that this couple were loved. There was elation in everyone. As nice as the formal shots were, it was the candid shots I always enjoyed most—there was no posed stiffness.

I carried on through the photos, but stopped when I came across one of Barry, the over-eager usher who had pushed his luck with me. *Prick*, I thought to myself.

That seemed like a good point to stop to make a coffee

and keep myself going with a much-needed caffeine shot. I made my way from the desk to the kitchen in my condo.

This was the second place I'd had in the city. The first was rented, a choice I'd made to see if I was going to stay in New York. I knew I couldn't go back to London, or even England, but I decided to rent initially as I wasn't sure if New York was for me. I'd contemplated other cities: Boston, LA, Houston, to name but a few. I'd also considered Canada or Australia. Once I found my feet, though, I couldn't imagine being anywhere other than New York.

The condo I was in now was mine; I'd bought it about a year ago and couldn't have been happier.

When I'd told Emma I was planning on buying a place in the city, she went into overdrive. I was glad to have her friendship, and knowledge. Buying a place in America was different from that back in England; thankfully, though, she helped me through the whole process.

Emma was born in New York, so she knew it like the back of her hand. I'd told her I wanted to stay close to my old apartment, and she'd agreed the Upper East Side was very desirable. She viewed so many different places with me.

I remember walking through the door to the condo off 79th Street. It was fairly close to my old place and the bar, and I immediately got a good feeling about it. When I'd first gone to view it, it was mainly a shell and needed a lot of work, but the layout and vibe I got was positive. Emma had agreed with a beaming smile.

I wasn't afraid to get my hands dirty and do the renovations myself, within reason. I knew there were certain things I couldn't do, but that was where Emma again came to the rescue. She had a lot of male contractor friends who were very keen to be in her good grace and gave me a discount on the work I needed. I just had to make sure none of them were there together at the same time.

When I'd left London, I sold my mum's place, so I had a decent amount of money to put towards buying the place. We also managed to get a really good deal due to the state of the place and the amount of work it actually needed. Hard work never deterred me, and all I could see was the potential.

I loved everything about it. As you entered there was a small hall that led you to a kitchen on your right, a decent-sized kitchen at that, which was good as I loved to cook. Further on, there was a large living area with a huge window at the end of the room where you could see the tops of the trees that lined the street below. To the left of the hall was a bathroom, a large walk-in closet, and my bedroom, again with a huge window along the end of the room.

Once the sale had gone through, Emma helped me with getting the place ready for the contractors she'd lined up. She'd promised drinks and who knows what else. I owed her big time. She'd assured me it wasn't any trouble.

We ripped up the old carpeted floor to reveal beautiful hardwood underneath that I decided I wanted to keep. Walls were prepped, and as much as we could do ourselves, we did. The whole place had been re-done. New bathroom, kitchen, re-plastered walls, and the flooring had been sanded and re-stained.

Once the contractors had completed their work, Emma was back to help me decorate. I could do that myself and didn't see the point of paying any more money than I needed.

When all the work was done, I couldn't have been happier; it was mine. My own little slice of city life. The first place I'd finally been able to put my stamp on.

My mum's place was still all her style. I hadn't touched it since she died, and the place I shared with Daniel was all him. This one, though, this was me.

The kitchen had bright white cabinets with dark wooden

worktops, white tiles and stainless-steel appliances. There was a small window which let in little light making it seem dark, but that's why I'd chosen white cabinets, to make everything bigger and brighter.

I brewed my coffee and made my way to the desk in front of the huge window in my living space. The room was big enough for my desk, two sofas, and a table and chairs. I'd chosen light colours again in here to brighten the space and to complement the hardwood floor.

I was happy here. It was my safe place, and I couldn't imagine being anywhere else.

I stopped my reminiscing and focused again on the present as I tucked my legs under me and went back to the wedding photos. I'd be finished soon, so I dropped Simon a quick email to tell him they'd be with him by the end of the day.

I carried on editing until it became late, and then finally sent the images through to Simon. The whole thing had gotten me thinking about whether I'd ever get married. There was a time when I had genuinely believed that it would have been to Daniel. When we met, he'd been so sweet and gentle. Nothing was too much trouble, and I honestly believed he loved me. We moved in together after around ten months, and things were amazing. Until they weren't.

Things changed when he got his new job, about a year into our relationship. He became angry with everything, mainly me. It started off with small things, being secretive with his phone and money, and him criticising the smallest of things, from my outfits to the food I'd cooked.

Then things got worse. I'd become alienated from my friends—he did that. He stopped me from going out with them and ruined the trust and friendship with anyone close to me. He isolated me so I was alone and had nowhere to go, no one to turn to other than him. He became my everything.

My mother had died a few years before we'd met, and I'd never known my father, so all I had were my friends. He scared them away; he drove a wedge between us, to the point where they were no longer there when I needed them the most.

So it was me and him. He wore me down so much that I believed the vile and horrible things he said about me. I believed I was worthless, that I was worse than the shit on his shoe. Yet I stayed. I stayed after he hit me the first time, and the second and third. I stayed after he'd beat me so badly that I had to go to the hospital. I stayed after he did it again. And again.

We'd been together around four years when I finally built up enough courage to leave. I'd waited till he was working away on business and packed everything I had from our place. Then I left, going to a hotel.

It didn't take long for him to find me the first time. I phoned the police, who came immediately and removed him. I moved to another hotel, but again he found me. I went to the police and took out a restraining order; it failed to do anything other than piss him off even more. He followed me; I was always aware he was watching—I'd become familiar with the sensation.

I had to leave London. Not just the city, I had to leave England. I had to disappear if I wanted to live. I knew I had no other choice.

I shivered at the thought of what would've happened if I'd stayed, or if I'd married him. But I'd been strong, although I knew I'd never fully recover. I was free now, safe.

My life had changed so much since making that decision and moving halfway across the world. I honestly couldn't imagine being anywhere else. I'd come to love my new life and everything about the city. I'd been in New York for two years, and I'd begun to feel like my old self.

Fun and free of the troubles that had plagued me in London.

Love still eluded me, though. To be honest, I wasn't really trying to find it; I'd only just found *myself* again. I wasn't prepared to settle. I wanted epic love. I knew my worth now and was determined that I wouldn't compromise. I didn't want fairytale love; I knew that didn't exist. I wanted real, raw passion, and love that made me weak in the knees. I wanted a partner who could accept me for who I was, baggage and all. I think I wanted something that didn't exist.

So, I'd be alone, but I was happy, and at least I was alive.

7

LUCIFER

I'D RECEIVED word from Bee that the woman was in New York, so naturally that's where I was now.

I'd used a portal to get to my place there. It was a convenient way of moving from A to B without drawing much attention. I had the wings obviously, but people tended to stare when I used them. Portals were much more efficient. They were simple to use, and I could open them indefinitely. A few other demons had access to them, but it would drain their power. Thankfully, that was not the case for me.

Portals were easy to use; any unlocked door would do. All I had to do was think where I wanted to go with my hand on the door, open, walk through, and I was there. Quick and easy.

As I'd arrived, I made my way to the living space. Like London, this place had amazing views of the city and was in one of the best areas. I was the Devil, after all; I had a reputation to uphold. It was plush and affluent; it was important for me to be comfortable in my surroundings. Comfort and ease were the reasons why I picked all of the places myself.

New York, like London, was a city of sin. I could feel it

oozing from everywhere. Many people here had already succumbed to it, and there was no indication of it slowing down. People desired more and more, which led to an increase of sin. I relished in all of it. It gave me power.

It had been a week since my meeting with Mr. Turner, and we now had everything we needed.

Everything.

There was a large dossier on the table, and it had her name on the front. Tess Adams.

I headed to the kitchen for a drink. I was going to learn everything about her before I introduced myself. I wanted her before I handed her over to Daniel. I'd do that by getting to know her, making her feel at ease, and then taking her. She was to be mine before she would become his again.

Whiskey in hand, I made my way back to the living area and sat in front of the large coffee table. I pulled out the stack of papers that had been collected; the dossier was substantial. Surveillance photos, birth certificate, medical records—my demons had done well.

It was rare that they could not accomplish a task I assigned them. Things were completed with ease and speed. Demons, after all, were substantial in numbers.

Tess had been born on the outskirts of London in the early nineties, and she was twenty-seven years old. Her birth certificate showed that her mother was called Sarah Adams and that she'd worked as a nurse; the father section was left blank.

There was nothing known about her father in the entirety of the information.

Interesting.

Her mother was an only child, so no other family. Her grandparents were dead; they had died before she was born. Her mother was also dead. She'd died of complications from a routine surgery when Tess was in her late teens, just as she'd begun her degree.

She had absolutely no family.

She was alone.

A perfect target for someone like Daniel Turner.

I continued on through the file. The family section was probably the smallest; after all, there were only the details about her mother.

Details of her time in London, her schools, university, jobs she'd had. Very thorough.

The next section was associates. All of her previous boyfriends were detailed—to be fair there weren't that many. I was surprised. She was attractive; I would have expected her number to be higher. It looked like she'd mainly had long-term relationships. There were details of a one-night stand after she came to the city, but nothing recent.

Her relationship with Mr. Turner was by far the largest section.

They'd met on a night out in a club and got serious quickly. Ten months later she had moved into his place in the city, renting out her mother's place where she had been staying.

Shortly after that, the friends disappeared. Fewer posts on social media while he had isolated her. He moved quickly and efficiently. She became his, and his alone. No one was left for her to turn to.

Around a year into the relationship, the violence started —small things at first, by the looks of it: bruises and cuts.

He began to break her down. I recognised his methods; I had used similar ones, albeit for very different reasons. For my enemies, not someone I cared for. There were few I cared for: a handful, maybe just Bee and Levi.

She became withdrawn, retreating further and further,

becoming more reliant on Daniel. His method had worked for him.

As I read through the folder, I knew she felt like she couldn't leave—where else would she go? Who would want her?

I leafed over to the medical records, which showed that she was on birth control despite not being sexually active for some time. Well, that was unexpected. I was going to have her regardless, but it was good to know. Not that I could get her pregnant, it took more than sex for that to happen. I also knew I couldn't catch anything—or pass anything on—no creature carried diseases of any sort due to our healing capabilities and immortality.

In general her medical records were extensive and showed he had laid hands on her many times, and she had suffered. Broken ribs, a punctured lung, a broken nose, bruises, and so much more. She was a punching bag, and yet she'd stayed.

She endured him for years.

There was little police information. Incidents had been reported, but he was slimy and had cash, so not much of it stuck. She had also refused to make statements, which meant no witnesses.

Then it appeared enough was enough; something must have pushed her over the edge, and she left.

It did not appear that this went down well with Mr. Turner. I imagined him returning to find that she had gone, all trace of her removed from his life. I pictured the rage he felt: *How dare she leave me? She is mine.*

After that, she moved from hotel to hotel, not settling anywhere for long, in case he found her.

He did; every time.

He stalked her, pushed her to her absolute limits.

The police information detailed she had obtained a

restraining order against him. The police had tried, but she never stood a chance. He was obsessed.

She had made a decision; I could see that from the next set of documents. She was leaving.

She was clever and there was little information about her decision to move. I could see she had flown to America, bought her ticket using cash. She had sold her mother's place in London to fund the adventure. She would need money for her new life. Once she arrived in America, the trail went cold; he would have struggled to find her.

I, however, did not struggle. It had taken one week to find her and learn everything about her. My people would find everything eventually.

I wanted to learn about her new life, immerse myself in it. Get to know her and seduce her. I knew that would anger Daniel the most. Me, taking what he believed was his and defiling it. I would do it, and I would enjoy it, and I would make sure he knew every detail.

Since arriving in the States, she had maintained a low profile. She'd been very clever and careful. There was no social media for her. There were a couple of pages for her job, but no personal names, and the contact info was all company-related. No photos of her. In fact, searching online for her would bring up her old life in London. There was nothing for her New York life.

She had bought a place in the city, on the Upper East Side. I glanced through the photos—it was nice. Comfy looking.

She had a few friends, mainly those linked to the bar she frequented regularly, which would be a good place to introduce myself. Her closest friend was a waitress from the bar, Emma Wade. Now, from the information on her, she was my kind of woman. Not a full file on her but there was enough.

Feisty. After I'd finished seducing Tess, I'd have to pay Emma a visit, get to know her better.

Tess's job appeared to be the most important thing in her life, so that could be a way in. I thought the bar would be more conducive to my plans—get her a few drinks, loosen her up a little. It wouldn't take much.

Since she'd been in America she hadn't had any romantic relationships. I could change that for her. After all, I was sending her to her death; the least I could do was give her a good night, one she'd never forget. Everyone deserved a bit of pleasure before all of the pain.

I carried on reading through the file, learning more and more about her. I was surprised to see that Tess had attended self-defence classes; she clearly wasn't planning on staying a punching bag any longer.

I eventually came across a photo; she was smiling and laughing in the bar where she practically lived.

She was pretty. I'd enjoy fucking her.

With that, I headed to the bathroom. I was going to shower and prepare myself for a night out in New York.

Well, Ms. Adams, I thought to myself, *it's about time we were properly introduced.*

8

TESS

SINCE LEAVING Daniel and moving my life across the world, I'd decided I was never going to be unable to look after myself again.

He'd beat me black and blue, and I was determined no one would ever lay their hands on me anymore.

When I got settled into the city, I'd joined a gym, enrolled in self-defence classes, and tried to take up running.

I say tried, as it took a few attempts to master. Running was not for everyone, but once I got the hang of it, I found it empowering, and it was great cardio.

I'd downloaded the Couch-to-5K app and started it about three times before I had to have a talk with myself and stop dicking about. After I completed the course and ran my first 5K without stopping, I was hooked. Since then, I'd run at least twice a week in Central Park. I was the fittest I'd ever been, and I felt good for it. An added bonus was that my arse looked *amazing*.

Today, though, it was my self-defence class.

I was currently changing into my gym gear, ready to release some of my pent-up aggression.

It had been a particularly testing day which had involved taking shit from a group of bitchy, whiny models. I loved my job, but some gigs were better than others.

Today I'd been working on some shots for an independent fashion magazine. The models were so pretentious and self-absorbed. I'd had to bite my tongue repeatedly so I didn't let my disdain for them known.

They'd been angry with me that I couldn't get their perfect shot—it was obviously my fault and had nothing to do with them at all. As a freelance photographer, I was often bitched at by models because everything was a travesty.

I'd tried to joke with them, but that hadn't gone over well. Granted my joke may have made reference to them needing either a good meal or a good fuck. I thought it might have sorted their shitty moods out—I was dead wrong. I'd clearly touched a nerve, which meant I was spot on. My money was on the fuck, and in all honesty, I was exactly the same.

Who didn't need that?

It had been forever since I'd had sex. I was very appreciative of my vibrator.

Tonight, though, I'd be working up a different type of sweat—not involving my battery-powered friend.

I made my way to the same class I'd been attending since I'd moved to the city.

I didn't think Daniel would find me, especially since I was being careful. I hoped that after all this time he'd moved on with his life. I immediately felt a pang of guilt. If he *had* moved on from me, that meant some other poor girl was now being isolated, controlled, and beaten. I shivered at the thought. Selfishly, though, I was free, and I was relieved.

I was adamant that I wanted to be able to take care of myself in case anything happened. I couldn't be that lost little girl anymore. The class had been the first step in changing that.

I'd learned so much from it and was confident that I could handle any situation that arose. I still attended weekly though, since I didn't want to get complacent. Plus it was a good outlet for my aggression.

Josh was an added bonus.

He was my instructor, and not only was he a great teacher and a nice guy, but he was *so* hot. One of the hottest men I'd ever seen.

Josh was tall, around six foot two with a muscular build. He was mixed-race with short hair, and he was beautiful.

Too much time had passed for me to do anything about it; at this point he was just eye candy and a really good instructor.

Still, I didn't mind volunteering to help with any demonstrations. Being close to him and feeling his strong hands on me in any circumstances was hot, and to be fair, it was the most intimate I'd be getting with anyone. God, it was so depressing.

I'd used a couple of small moves on nights out when I'd been grabbed or leered at. The most I'd had to use my skills was when Barry had grabbed me at the wedding. What was it with men thinking it was okay to grab women? I knew drinking played a part, but that still didn't give them the fucking right.

Because of the events of the day, and my built-up sexual energy, I was ready to blow off some steam. As expected, Josh asked for a volunteer, and I immediately agreed. I was more than happy to have him pressed up against me today.

Josh wanted to show us how to break free from someone grabbing us from behind and trying to choke us. I'd practised the move in class several times, so I was familiar with it.

"Right, ladies, please say hello to my glamorous assistant for this demonstration," Josh introduced me, and I took a bow as the other ladies laughed, watching us intently.

"If you feel someone come up behind you and try to hook their arm around your neck, you should immediately attempt to tuck your chin to your chest to prevent them from being able to choke you." As he gave the instructions, we acted it out with me tucking my chin as close to my chest as I could.

I could feel every inch of him pressed against me; it was the only male contact I'd had in far too long.

Concentrate Tess, you horny bitch.

"Your attacker is likely to lock his hands together to give himself more leverage. At this point, you should take a step to the side and at the same time, grab the assailant's wrist." We continued acting out the steps he was describing.

I grabbed his wrist; his skin was soft and smooth. He was hot to the touch. I was just hot, full stop.

"Once in this position take your arm and strike the attacker's groin," he told the class. I followed his instructions, careful not to actually catch his groin.

Jesus, it's hot in here.

"When you've struck the groin then you'll find most men will double over. At that point you should raise your elbow to their face, which should incapacitate them." We acted out the final move while everyone else looked on.

"Nice, Tess, thanks. Now pair up and let's try that out." He dismissed me, and the class partnered up. He made his way around the room, correcting any mistakes and explaining certain aspects of the moves.

He really was a good teacher, and I was glad I'd found him.

The lesson carried on for a while longer as we focused on more moves and aspects of defence.

"Thanks for helping out there, Tess. You could be teaching yourself now you're such a pro," he said with a warm smile.

"Doing them in slow motion with you is one thing, doing them in real life is completely different," I replied.

"Let's hope you'll never have to test them out," he said, suddenly seeming serious.

"See you next class, Josh," I replied as I walked from the room.

I was still worked up. I think my aggression had gone and it was now replaced by sexual frustration. I thought I'd try and burn some more energy off before I called it a night, so decided to go for a swim.

I always had my swimming gear with me in case I wanted to do a few lengths.

I was new to running and enjoyed it, but swimming was my go-to. I loved it, always had. My mum jokingly said I should have been a mermaid as I seemed so at home in the water.

When I was little, she used to take me once a week, and it just felt so relaxing to me. I was a confident swimmer and felt like I could go forever.

It was late evening and at this time, the pool was pretty much empty, just an older man swimming breaststroke in one of the lanes.

I dove into the opposite side, so I wouldn't splash him. The water was cool, and it felt good against my hot skin. Hot not just from the class but from my thoughts about Josh. I did half a length under the water, then tumble turned at the other end of the pool, and went into front crawl.

I swam and swam, lost in my own thoughts. I think I swam for about fifty lengths, but I honestly wasn't sure. I stopped, realising by now I was the only one left.

I wasn't sure when the man had left. I'd been so focused on my breathing and movements that everything else had fallen away.

I found the water soothing; it had a calming effect on me.

As I caught my breath, I noticed that it was 9 PM. I'd said I'd meet Emma at the bar. She apparently had something important to tell me. I assumed she'd hooked up with someone new and wanted to debrief. It was probably the guy that had given her his number a few nights ago. She'd taken quite a shine to him.

Bracing my arms on the side, I pushed myself up and out of the pool and made my way back to the changing rooms.

I'd grabbed my shampoo and other stuff from my locker. As I made my way to the showers and into one of the cubicles, I noticed I was alone.

I turned the shower on, stripped, then stepped under the warm water. I lathered my hair to get rid of the chlorine smell, and tipped my head back, rinsing away the shampoo.

My mind wandered again to Josh's strong hands, grabbing me from behind, and I realised I was still horny.

I have time.

I moved my hands from my hair, down my chest, and over my breasts. Farther still, down my stomach till they reached their destination. I began to rub, thinking of Josh whilst I did. I quickened my pace as I rubbed and gently pulled at my clit.

The intensity inside me increased, and I could feel it building.

Then I heard two female voices enter the showers, chatting about the spin class they'd just finished. I couldn't stop, I didn't *want* to stop.

The water continued to cascade over my head, down over my body, while my hand increased the movements. I imagined it was him; he was behind me, his body pushed against me, his strong hands wrapped around me while he applied the perfect amount of pressure to push my limits.

I bit my lip at the thought of his fingers on me, inside of me and it was too much.

The feeling engulfed me, and it took everything in me not to moan loudly. Instead, I stifled it, biting my lip harder as the waves of my orgasm continued to take me.

I breathed heavily, revelling in the pleasure.

Fuck, I needed that.

Feeling a bit more relaxed, I finished getting showered.

As I stepped back to my locker, I noticed it was around 9:30 PM. If I hustled I could be at the bar at around 10 PM.

Emma was expecting me, so I knew she'd have a drink waiting for me; she always did.

9

LUCIFER

I'D FULLY APPRAISED myself of the information provided in the dossier. I knew her—well, on paper, anyway. What she was actually like would be fun to find out.

We now knew all of Tess's routines. We knew her whereabouts, and everything was in place. Of course, I never did that myself; other people did the menial labour on my behalf. Why have a dog and bark yourself?

I wanted to know where she would be at all times and what she was doing. That allowed me the best opportunity to pick my moment, tonight.

The information in the dossier showed that most nights around 10 PM she'd go to O'Malley's and sit at the end of the bar, farthest from the door.

I'd arrived at about 9 PM and settled into a booth so I could see both the entrance and her usual seat. This would be a good vantage point and allow me to observe from afar before I made my move.

I'd been given a description by both Daniel and my people. I also had a photograph, though I didn't need it. I knew I'd be able to tell who she was from what Daniel had told me; this was what I did.

"Whiskey, please," I said to the waitress who came to take my drink order.

Whiskey was one of the many pleasures of the human world. Smooth, smoky, and earthy. A good whiskey slid down your throat and provided a warming burn that I never grew tired of.

Of course, it never had the effect of getting me drunk—that was impossible—but I enjoyed it regardless.

I surveyed my surroundings and took in the atmosphere of the bar. Irish music blared noisily from multiple speakers littered throughout. The booth I sat in was all dark wood with red leather upholstery. All of the wood in the bar was a dark, mahogany colour. It looked rich and gave the place character. The floor was tiled, and the walls painted a pale colour, likely to bring a bit of light to the otherwise dark decor.

On the wall to the right of the bar was a huge neon O'Malley's sign—in green, obviously. It cast a glow over that end of the bar—the opposite end to Tess's seat.

Continuing to take in my surroundings, I noticed the other creatures who mingled amongst the humans in the bar.

This was often the way in big cities like New York and London. The darker beings would be confident enough to mix freely. Of course, looking at them, humans wouldn't be able to tell the difference and would be clueless about their origins.

"Come on, sweetie, we'll show you the best time. I guarantee you won't regret it. It'll be out of this world," an attractive female vampire said to a handsome man at the bar. She wasn't alone though; her vampire boyfriend was also trying to tempt the man into going with them.

It was clear to me the man had little say in the matter.

The three of them *would* be going home together. In all fairness, the two vampires would show him an amazing time—he'd experience pleasure like he never had before.

I did, however, wonder whether he would wake up in the morning.

Unlikely.

At the front of the bar, in a booth similar to mine overlooking the window, sat three witches. I knew they hadn't seen me. If they had, they would have approached me, pledging their allegiance to the Prince of Darkness.

Witches were like that, groupies.

I surveyed the rest of the patrons in the bar—they appeared to be human.

Keeping a low profile was often problematic with creatures; they would often gravitate to me. To the humans, I was just another guy, albeit a very handsome and confident one, but a guy nonetheless.

To everyone else, though, I was known.

Feared or revered depending on which side you were on.

I got attention from both those who knew me as Lucifer and those who didn't. I'd used my looks and charm to my advantage for many millennia.

On occasions like this, though, it didn't help. Trying to maintain a low profile was hard when you were constantly being hit on. Four women and a guy had approached me already tonight.

The waitress was the keenest of all.

Standing around five foot two, she had a slim frame with short, wavy, blonde hair. Her uniform was tight, and although it was only black pants and a white shirt, she wore it well.

"My name is Emma, and I'll be looking after you this evening. If you need *anything* please just let me know."

She's attractive, I thought to myself, and in other circumstances I'd have probably fucked her, but tonight I had pressing matters. I was all business.

At 9:55 PM the door to O'Malley's opened and she entered. Without fail, she went to the farthest end of the bar and perched on a stool, grabbing the bartender's attention with a wave of her hand.

Five minutes later she was handed a tumbler with amber liquid. *Whiskey*, I thought to myself, *she has taste*.

I surveyed the back of her for a while, studying her. She was tall, around five-foot-eight with a curvy hourglass figure. She wore tight jeans that accentuated her in all the right places. A white t-shirt and boots completed the look.

Long auburn hair she wore in loose curls fell all the way to the small of her back. She was talking to the bartender, with whom she seemed friendly. She hadn't turned yet, so I was unable to see her face. Regardless, I knew it was Tess.

"Thanks, Harry, you're a lifesaver. I hundred percent needed this tonight. Keep them coming." Her accent was undeniably British.

"No problem, Tess. Rough day?" the male bartender asked her.

"Photoshoot with a group of stuck-up models who needed feeding. Apparently, it was my fault I couldn't get the shot that they wanted. Nothing to do with them being a bunch of whiny bitches."

She carried on laughing and joking with the guys and girls behind the bar. She was clearly a regular, and they enjoyed her company.

I'd finished my whiskey, so I signalled to Emma for another. She acknowledged my request with a huge beaming smile, and I saw her go to the bar, opposite where Tess was sat. They talked a while, and I saw the waitress not very subtly motion in my direction.

I was sure Emma had meant to do this slyly, but obviously

I pick up on everything. With that, Tess turned and locked eyes with me.

Her eyes were bright green, the brightest I'd ever seen, and her skin was ivory smattered with freckles. Her hair was pushed behind her ears away from her face. Her lips were full, and I noticed she bit the bottom when she saw me looking at her. She quickly turned around in embarrassment.

It was clear to me Emma had told her she was trying to fuck me. Tess had been curious, naturally. The pair of them laughed.

I studied her from behind, trying to get a read on her. I picked up nothing from her. I continued trying to pick up on anything she was giving off, but I drew a blank.

It was very rare that people came across as a closed book; most people radiated sin and desire, or at least some sort of emotion or need. Tess, though, was like a void. I'd have to go over and chat with her to probe deeper and draw her out.

This was the intended course of action anyway, but now I wanted to know more about her. She was nothingness to my senses. I was intrigued. What made her different?

I saw Emma turn away from Tess, and she returned with my drink. She placed it on the table. "Is there… *anything* else I can do for you, sir?"

"No thank you. I'm fine." Her pride was clearly wounded, and she returned to the bar.

Once this was done, I'd return and help heal her ego. After all, sex was another of my favourite pleasures.

Emma had returned to the bar, opposite Tess, who again turned to look at me. She wore a silver necklace that she moved between her fingers. I think it was a subconscious movement, but it drew my attention to her chest. I noticed that the tight white t-shirt she was wearing strained to contain her ample breasts, and I imagined what I would do to them when I freed them.

There was no doubt about it, Tess was a beautiful woman.

But I was Lucifer; I'd had my share of beautiful women over the years. Many, *many* beautiful women had shared my bed over the past millennia. I had come to appreciate all women in their own way.

I could see why someone like Daniel wanted to possess her. Not me, though. I had beautiful women daily; last week I'd slept with a supermodel and a movie star.

In my past, I'd fucked some of history's most sought-after women, some holy and some whores.

Helen of Troy was said to have been so beautiful that two men went to war after she left one for the other. History, however, failed to mention that I fucked her till she couldn't walk straight and played the two men off each other.

It was all a game to me. Death and destruction were a few of my many talents, and if I could get laid in the process, then I wasn't going to say no.

I was lost in my thoughts when I realised Emma and Tess were subtly looking my way. I tuned in to their conversation.

"Tess, look at him, just *look* at him. Oh my God, I want his hands all over me. I want to climb him like a tree." I smirked to myself and continued to listen.

"Emma, you're so bad. You're like a horny kid, get a grip of yourself. He's attractive but, Christ, have some self-control. What about the guy you were going to tell me about, the one who gave you his number?"

"He was cute, and I liked him, but just look at him, Tess… Look. At. Him."

I wasn't looking, but I once again felt Tess's gaze upon me as she tried to sneakily study me.

"Yeah he's okay, but come on, Emma, what about the guy you had an actual connection with. Tell me about him?"

She appeared immune to my good looks and my powers. *Let's see what we can do to change both those things before I send her back to her ex*. After all, he wanted her, and in return, I'd get his eternal soul. He could have her... but not before I had my fun with her.

I pushed myself from the booth and headed in the direction of the bar. "Excuse me, is this seat taken?"

10

TESS

I HEARD THE SMOOTH, deep voice on my right and looked up to see where it came from.

It was the guy Emma had been eye-fucking all night—the one I'd awkwardly made eye contact with.

"Sorry?" I honestly hadn't heard what he'd said. I was in a world of my own.

"I'd just asked if this seat was taken? Could I join you?" His voice was like silk.

Now that he was here, standing in front of me, I could see why Emma was interested. He was the epitome of handsome.

He was in his early thirties and I'd guess he was around six-foot-three with amazing tanned skin. He wore an expensive-looking black suit, and it fit perfectly to his athletic frame. It had to have been tailored—it fit that well.

A black shirt completed the look. It wasn't fully fastened, the top few buttons left open revealing what looked to be a very muscular chest with short black chest hair—I wondered if it was as soft as it looked.

His wavy hair was also jet black and was styled perfectly

to frame his face. A chiselled jawline was covered with black stubble, and his eyes… wow. Up close they were incredibly dark, almost black, but I could have sworn I saw red in them, like a flame flickering.

I realised I was staring at him and hadn't actually said anything. "No, it's not taken," was all I could manage.

Get a grip of yourself, Tess.

He was trouble. Someone that hot *had* to be trouble, I knew it. I was over drama. I wanted an easy life and I had a feeling this guy was *not* that.

"Thanks," he said while pulling out the stool next to me and sitting down. As he sat, the most amazing smell hit me. It was earthy and smoky, like burned sandalwood.

He held out a hand to me. "I'm Luke Albright, pleasure to meet you."

I looked at his hand for a while trying to decide what I should do; I eventually shook it. When I touched him, it was like sparks ignited inside of me. The contact was like fire, and I immediately met his gaze.

His eyes were now fixed directly on me. I felt like he was staring directly into my soul, like he was searching for something.

I broke the contact and went back to my drink.

"You are?" he asked. I realised I hadn't responded when he introduced himself.

Shit, I don't want to get involved in whatever he's after.

"Busy," I replied, not making eye contact. *That ought to do it.*

"Red." I could tell he was looking at me when he said it.

"Sorry?" I asked, meeting his gaze once again.

"Well if you aren't going to tell me your name, I'll have to come up with one of my own. Red." He was so self-assured. My harshness had not deterred him in the slightest.

"Luke, was it? I don't mean to be rude, but I'm not interested. I'm here to have a quiet drink with my friends, and that's it."

He flashed me the most brilliant smile—not the reaction I was expecting.

"Red, I'm not hitting on you. I saw you sitting alone and just thought we could talk, nothing more than that." He was still smiling at me.

"Yeah I'm okay, thanks. I've got my friends here." I motioned to Emma, who was now behind the bar and getting a tray of drinks.

"You can't sit around all night waiting for the bar staff to be free. I'm here ready to keep you company, all night if I need to, Red." His face was serious.

"So, you just want to talk to me? I don't buy it, Luke. A man like you must be after something."

There was something about him; I was drawn to him in a way I'd never experienced before. Like a pull, an invisible thread joined us. It made me uneasy.

"A man like me?" He queried.

Shit.

How the fuck do I tell him that I mean someone as hot as him?

"Look, you're a good-looking guy, expensive suit, self-assured, and confident. There's no way you just want to talk." Honesty was the best idea in this situation. I hoped.

"Trust me, Red, I just want to talk, nothing else. You have my word. Give me ten minutes, and if you aren't enjoying our conversation, I'll leave you alone."

"Emma, could I get two glasses of Johnnie Walker Blue, thanks." He motioned to the bottle on the top shelf of the bar.

He'd just ordered the most expensive whiskey the bar sold. I knew how expensive it was as Daniel had ordered some at a bar in London once. He was trying to show off to some friends, and a round had set him back about two hundred pounds. I remember telling him that it was extravagant—I'd paid for that comment when we'd got home.

Emma poured the drinks and placed them both on the bar in front of Luke, casting a look at me as she did. I couldn't tell whether she was pissed off or happy, but then she flashed a smile, and I knew.

Luke slid one of the drinks over to me. "There you go, Red, enjoy." Was he really giving me a sixty-dollar drink? Talk about flashy.

I looked at him while pushing the drink back towards him.

"Red, take the drink. Consider it an icebreaker. You're drinking whiskey already. Trust me you'll appreciate it." He pushed the glass back over to me.

"Thanks," I said, picking up the glass and taking a sip. It was like nectar. I closed my eyes as it warmed my throat. It was expensive for a reason. When I opened my eyes again, he was staring at me intently.

"Good?" He already knew the answer from my reaction. I noticed his full lips smirk. I nodded, embarrassed at my own response.

Shit, Tess, he's playing you, don't get sucked in.

I put the walls back up, and we continued talking. I was happy to chat with him, but that was where it ended. Nothing more than conversation.

He was funny and charming, and I was actually having a good time. He asked questions; I answered. It felt like he was studying me and searching for an answer that he just couldn't find. It was unnerving, but I didn't feel afraid. He intrigued me.

He ordered us more drinks. His ten minutes had long gone, but I didn't ask him to leave. The time passed by quickly as we talked.

I'd noticed an attractive woman had been casting glances at Luke all evening. She was maybe early forties. As she passed us on the way to the toilet she gave Luke a long, lingering look. I wasn't surprised she was staring at him; I imagined he got it all the time and was used to it by now. He seemed unfazed and I wondered if he'd even noticed her.

On her way back to her table, she made a slight motion to approach him. I could have sworn that she dipped her head in a sort of bow towards him. Luke noticed her and waved a hand in her direction, then said, "Not tonight, please. I'm busy."

What the hell was that about? I watched her sulk back to her table, likely to relay the story to her friends, two other women who were seated at the front of the bar. All three now looked to watch Luke and me. He was oblivious, still carrying on the conversation.

"That was weird," I said, interrupting him mid-sentence.

He looked at me, following my eyes to the three women at the front of the bar. All three continued to stare—until he fixed his gaze upon them; they immediately looked at the table and played with their drinks.

"Work," he said dismissively, going back to their previous conversation.

It was more than that. I could sense it. He was hiding something. It didn't matter, since I wasn't planning on anything more than tonight. I wouldn't see Luke again.

It niggled at me, though.

"Red, you still with me?" he asked, studying me. It was like he was trying to look directly at my soul.

I shivered at the thought.

"Are you cold?" With that, he reached over and rubbed my arm. His hand on my skin ignited something within me. My gaze shot up to search his face for a similar reaction. His eyes gave him away. His face remained the same, but his eyes betrayed him. He'd felt it too. We just stared at each other as he removed his hand from my arm.

What was going on? Who was this man that made me feel such intensity at the slightest touch? He seemed shocked at the feeling—he was struggling to form words.

So, not so self-assured after all.

"You two need anything else? The bar is closing soon." It was Emma who broke the uncomfortable silence that existed between us. She stood staring, waiting for either of us to say anything.

I answered first. "No thanks, Em, we're all good here," I said with a smile. "Well, Luke, I'm pleasantly surprised. I've enjoyed chatting with you. Thanks again for the drinks." I motioned to the empty glasses still in front of us.

"You've very welcome, Red." He picked up his glass, finishing the last of his whiskey. "Could I get your number? I'd very much like to see you again." His self-confidence had returned.

"See now, Luke, that wasn't the deal. You said it was just talking, so I'm not giving you my number."

As nice as the evening had been, my original assessment of Luke stood. He was trouble, and I didn't need that. I'd get hurt.

By this time there were very few people left in the O'Malley's. I noticed a very attractive couple leaving with another man who had been seated with them at the other end of the bar. They all seemed very pleased with themselves. Luke followed my eyes to the threesome, and he smiled as if he was in on some sort of joke.

He turned to me. "Then how about we go out somewhere. Continue our conversation. Drinks or food?" He was determined I'd give him that.

"No, I'm sorry. I didn't expect it to go anywhere, and

despite having a lovely time I can't see you again." I looked away when I answered. I had to—if not the pull between us was going to make me change my mind. *What the hell is it?*

"No pressure, Red, it doesn't have to go anywhere. Just drinks," he pushed.

I couldn't, I had to leave. If I didn't, I'd agree to meet him and I knew deep down he was no good for me. I stood from my barstool, and pulled on my jacket.

"Sorry, Luke. It was lovely to meet you. Enjoy the rest of your night." With that, I walked away to the door of the bar.

"See you soon, Red," he called after me, certainty in his tone.

I turned to look at him one last time. He held a hand up to me in a wave, his smile bright on his face. I turned and left the bar.

I'd spent all day thinking about Luke and previous the night. All we'd done was chat at the bar, yet I couldn't get his face out of my head. Why did he have that effect on me?

It didn't matter; I'd refused to give him my number or agree to see him again.

Emma was furious with me. Apparently, I was mad to refuse such a man. She'd scolded me plenty for my rejection of Luke, but I knew it was the right thing—despite my whole body screaming it wasn't.

Emma had texted to ask me to go to the bar; she apparently needed to chat. I'd been distracted by Luke last night, so she hadn't had a chance to catch me up on her news.

I made my way to the bar. I was there about ten minutes after she texted as it was close to my place.

I pushed open the door, not paying much attention as I

made my way to my usual seat. I stopped dead about halfway there.

My seat was taken, by Luke.

He turned to look at me, with a huge smile on his face.

I was frozen to the spot. I couldn't move.

"Come on, Red. I got you a drink."

11

LUCIFER

IT HAD BEEN a few days since I'd seen Tess at the bar.

She really was a remarkable woman. When I looked at her, when I searched her, there was nothing. Most people would think that was bad; it was, in fact, the exact opposite. It didn't happen often, and I was intrigued. Who was she, and why couldn't I read her?

Was she aware of what she was doing? I didn't think so. The look she gave me when I searched her was one of puzzlement. She was bewildered as to why I was so interested.

The last time I'd felt this was several decades ago. A witch had been paid handsomely to cast a spell on a young man, who was the subject of a deal I'd made. The spell had meant that I was unable to read him, similar to how it was with Tess. He was aware of his spell; I didn't get that impression from Tess. How was I to know, though? I couldn't read her.

This was going to be interesting. Not being able to rely on my powers meant I'd have to use my natural charm and charisma. I wasn't worried—I'd seduced people for centuries. Despite her initial hesitancy, I knew she was drawn to me.

I'd felt it—I knew she had to. That moment when my hand brushed against her soft skin; it was fire, burning hot. It was desire. I desired her, and she felt the same. I hadn't needed my powers to be sure of that—I knew it.

I was keen to see her again; I wanted to learn more about her and see if I could figure out what was going on. Was she under a spell? Was she simply immune to me and my powers? Why did I feel nothing when I looked into her soul? Well, not nothing—I felt a great deal of things, but that was just me, not my powers. They were out of play when it came to her.

I'd had a few demons surveilling her ever since we'd found her. After the initial fact-finding and discovery of her location, I'd told them not to let her out of their sight.

They hadn't. They knew where she was at all times and reported back accordingly.

I'd decided that today we'd bump into each other again. She'd still refused to give me her number or agree to meet me after I'd returned to the bar to see her. With that in mind, we'd have to accidentally meet each other, and I could work my charm to disarm her some more.

I could home in on the location of all my demons if I wanted to, like a built-in tracker system. On this occasion, I very much wanted to see Tess again and find out what she'd been up to.

I established that Conrath was the closest to her and focused on his location. I portaled to the closest point.

"Update please, Conrath." He was a lower demon but had always been useful in these sorts of matters. Efficient and subtle. Someone like him usually wouldn't be on my radar, but he'd proved himself over the years.

Conrath detailed what Tess had been up to since I'd last seen her at the bar. She'd been to work, couple of ad photoshoots. I got the impression this wasn't where her true passion lay; she preferred more candid photography. *That* was what she was about.

He went on to tell me about more trips to the bar to see Emma; the two had spoken about me apparently. Emma had told her she most definitely should have given me her number. She'd said Tess was crazy to have passed up the opportunity to spend more time with me. I had to agree with Emma. Smart girl, that one.

The gym and self-defence classes had been a big part of her life since arriving in New York, and he confirmed she'd attended them—her routine was pretty rigid, other than her job. Conrath pulled out a few photos to show me her grappling with a large man. There was a slight pang of jealousy in my gut.

What was that about?

I shrugged it off. It had been a long time since I'd felt it. Not since my casting out. A *long* time.

I wondered if I was feeling "put out" at her rejection, and whether that was the cause. She'd rejected me. Yet, here she was, another man with his hands all over her.

I had to double my efforts. It would soon be *my* hands all over her, that I was sure of.

She'd done little else to write home about.

"Where is she now?" I asked him, since I wanted to go find her. I was drawn to her, and I didn't understand it.

"She's grabbing a coffee from across the road and then heading to Central Park to take some photos. I saw her leave her condo with her camera." He was good. He'd maintained a visual on her, but she would never have known he was there.

Having read the dossier, I knew she spent a lot of time in the park, either running or taking photos. I'd seen plenty of surveillance shots of her there, in several different spots.

I turned my attention to the coffee shop across the road, waiting for her to emerge. It seemed like forever since I'd seen her and I wanted to see her. I *needed* to see her. The feeling was new to me, and I was sure it was because she was a mystery. That had to be the reason I was feeling like this. It had to be.

Then she stepped out of the shop. She wore tight leggings and trainers; a hoodie completed the look. Her hair today was in a messy bun on the top of her head. Even casual, she was stunning. I focused on her natural beauty.

Conrath was right; she had her camera around her neck, coffee in hand. She made her way towards the park.

"Conrath, you and the others can take some time. I have this." I wanted her alone and didn't want anyone else's eyes on us.

"Yes, sir. Let me know when you want us to resume." He bowed and disappeared back off into the shadows.

I made my way behind her. She would never see me—I was careful of that. I watched as she walked—her backside was so pert. I desperately wanted to wrap my arms around her, cupping her ass before lifting her up against me.

She carried on sipping her coffee, snapping any shots that inspired her on the way.

I needed to know what this power was she held over me. It had begun as me trying to get one up on Mr. Turner. I hoped it would end that way; the journey, however, was likely going to take a different path from the one I had envisioned.

I continued to follow at a distance, watching and waiting for the perfect opportunity. It had to be natural; she was clever and would see right through me if I wasn't careful.

I watched her from afar while she took photos of the many people in the park. I thought I'd position myself within the crowd. I was ready.

Okay then Tess, it's about time we bump into each other again.

TESS

THE LIGHT BREEZE tickled my face as I walked through the park. I'd already been to my favourite coffee place to pick up a quick bite.

The park was busy today—it always was, more so on the weekend though. I made my way through the crowds of people and found an isolated bench. I sat down and took out the large blueberry muffin. I loved them from the coffee shop; they were made fresh every morning, and they were massive.

I sat on the bench, sipped my drink, and ripped off chunks of muffin while I watched the happenings before me. Central Park was always so full of life, and I loved it—never a dull moment.

The park was full of amazing photos just waiting to happen, and I needed to update my portfolio with some edgier shots.

I'd unknowingly captured a couple of proposals in the background of some shots I'd lined up. They were completely accidental. I managed to catch up with the couples so I could share the amazing images with them. The looks of pure joy on the couples' faces made my heart ache. They were overjoyed, and I'd captured it completely accidentally.

As beautiful and emotional as they were, though, they lacked the edge that I was after for my portfolio.

I was trying hard to impress the more prestigious clientele and needed more variety in my shots. I'd had it in my old portfolio, but I couldn't use that now. Daniel would recognise those shots, so they were useless. If he did an image search, he'd find me. I'd had to start from scratch.

During my time in the city, I'd built up a good body of work, but I needed to branch out.

I knew there was a scavenger hunt happening that day that started at Bethesda Terrace, so I made my way over there. As I reached the terrace I saw the start of the treasure hunt; it was really busy. I made my way over to the fountain and perched on the edge of it, then scanned my surroundings for shots.

I was looking in the fountain when I saw some clouds reflected in the still water. With some editing and tweaks they'd make great photos. A little farther down in the reflection, I could see a couple arguing. They weren't shouting and screaming at each other, but I could tell they were in the middle of a fight. I knew the signs all too well.

Daniel had had a way of arguing in which anyone looking at us would never have guessed he was ripping into me. I hated the altercations, because I always knew how they would end when we got home. Thankfully that was now in the past.

It would make a good shot, but I just couldn't bring myself to take it.

I carried on discreetly watching them for a while before he stormed off and she soon followed after.

I looked to see if I could spot them in the crowd, but

they'd gone. I hoped she'd be okay and I'd been wrong about them.

I turned back to the fountain and focused on the start of the scavenger hunt.

As I lined up a number of shots, I thought I saw a familiar face—Luke from the bar. I lowered my camera to scan the scene before me, but he wasn't there. He'd either walked away, or he'd never been there to begin with. I raised my camera to look through the shots I'd taken.

There he was. The last shot he was there. Staring directly at my camera with a broad smile across his face. The pull to him that I'd felt in the bar tugged at my insides.

Where was he?

I scanned where I'd just been photographing. I knew he was here, but I couldn't see him. Looking back at the photo, I once again focused on his handsome face. He really *was* beautiful. I zoomed in on the image as I continued to study him, lost in the photo.

"Red, you only had to ask. I'd be willing to pose for you anytime." His smooth voice came from right in front of me.

I looked up from the shot of him on my camera to the real-life version, and he grinned down at me. I felt like I was suddenly mute; I literally couldn't say anything. He moved next to me so he could see the screen on the camera and the zoomed-in version of his face.

"Looks like you've captured my good side. You take a good photo, Red." He looked from the camera to me.

I still had no words for him; all I could do was look up at him like a lost puppy. What the hell was going on? Why did he literally make me weak at the knees? *Pull yourself together, Tess, for Christ sake.*

I finally managed to speak. "It's, Luke, isn't it?" There was no question of me not remembering him, but he didn't have to know that I'd been thinking about him.

"Ouch, Red, you mean you've forgotten me already?" He held a hand over his heart, but there was a playful smile on his lips. His full, pink, glistening lips. "What are you up to?" he questioned, again looking at my camera. I turned it off, so his photo was no longer visible.

"I thought that was pretty obvious," I said snarkily back at him.

"Well obviously, but is this business or pleasure?" he continued, apparently unphased by my coldness.

God, he's persistent.

"Both. Just taking some personal shots and some for my portfolio," I answered him honestly.

"The photos of me are for your own private collection, aren't they? If you want, I could pose properly for you?" he said with a wink.

I rolled my eyes and began to move back towards the entrance to the park. He followed me.

"Don't leave, I'm sorry," he said, jogging to catch up to me. "So you're a professional photographer?" he asked, now by my side again.

"Yeah, something like that. Why?" I turned to look at him when I answered, studying his face.

"I have an event coming up for my company. Would that be something you'd be interested in doing? It will mainly be taking photos of guests." He was deadly serious.

"A job? With your company?" I was suspicious, to say the least.

"Yes, Red. It'd be a fair amount of work, lots of important guests to photograph. I'd need your actual name and number, though, so I could pass it on to my assistant. Either one of us would be in touch to discuss the details," he said with a smirk.

I'd give him his due, he was smooth and persistent, but it

was absolute horseshit, and we both knew it. He wanted my number, and that was it. There was no job.

"I don't think so, I'm sure there are a million other photographers you could use,"

"Come now, Red, are you really going to pass up such a lucrative opportunity? Trust me, it'll be worth your while." He dug into his pocket and pulled out an extremely expensive-looking business card. He passed it over to me, and I glanced down at it. It was matte black and contained a phone number embossed in silver—nothing else. I'd never seen a business card like it.

He was definitely persistent. And mysterious. I thought it best to try and change the subject.

"What brings you to the park today, Luke?" The change wasn't lost on him.

"My place isn't too far away, and I often find myself here. Mostly I come to clear my head and watch the people. I just don't have a camera." He motioned to the equipment hanging around my neck. "I find it therapeutic, watching people. I've become very good at reading them," he said confidently.

"Really? Do you think you're an expert?" I probed.

"I've picked up a few insights, Red. You can test me if you like?" He smiled, clearly sure of himself.

"Test you?" I asked. He was looking directly at me, waiting for a response. "Fine, those two," I said, motioning to a couple on some benches not far from where we were. I saw his eyes fall on the pair and he grinned.

"Too easy," he replied.

"Come on, then, Mr. Big-Shot, tell me about them," I pushed. Sitting down on one of the seats close by, I looked at the couple. Luke sat next to me and dropped his arms across the back of the bench.

"They're having an affair. You can tell by their body language."

I fixed my gaze on the couple. "Both are wearing wedding rings," I said, nodding my head towards the couple.

"Good spot, Red, they are indeed married, just not to each other." He moved closer to me so his leg was now pushed against mine and his head had leaned in towards me. "See, the man keeps glancing around, like he's on the lookout for something," he said as his arm now came around me on the bench.

The pull I felt to him morphed into butterflies that grew more intense. The contact of his body ignited a burn inside of me. This slight contact between us had me feel sparks I'd never had with anyone before.

"See? She is trying to be close to him, but he's uncomfortable with it." He was watching the couple intently, studying them just like he'd studied me in the bar.

He was right. She was tracing her fingers up and down the man's arm, stroking his muscles with her perfectly manicured fingers. He did seem uncomfortable with it, continually looking around like he didn't want to be seen in public with the woman.

"If they're having an affair and he's so nervous, why would they be out in public?" I asked. He might have been right, but I wanted to know more of his reasoning.

"Well now that's trickier. My guess is that they thought it might excite things more. Bring more to the relationship. I'm assuming this will be the first and last time they go out like this. It'll be back to hotel rooms and nights away." His leg was still pushed against mine, and I could feel how muscular it was.

Breathe Tess; it's just his God damn leg.

I raised my camera to snap the couple. At this point, the woman had leaned in for a kiss, and the man moved away quicker than the speed of light. I captured the hurt that spread across the woman's face. She stood facing him; I couldn't make out what she was saying, but he must have responded with something bad, as she slapped him across the face and stormed off. I had the whole thing on my camera. I was sure they held raw emotion that I could use. It'd definitely be a boost to my portfolio.

I looked up to find Luke gazing at me, watching me, a sexy smile on his face. He leaned over and tipped the camera so he could see the images.

"You have an eye, Red. You've captured something beautiful," he said, studying the screen on my camera.

I thought it was odd to call the shots beautiful. They conveyed anguish and sorrow. But the more I looked, the more I realised he was right. They did have beauty in them.

"You have to take the job, Red. Now I've seen your talents, I insist. So how about that number?" He definitely wasn't taking no for an answer.

13

LUCIFER

I'd "bumped" into Tess in the park yesterday. Now I wanted her to meet me for a date. It wouldn't be easy, though. She really was something else. I'd never experienced anyone like her before. She was a breath of fresh air; I had to work with her and put some actual effort in. It didn't come easily. It had been a long time since I'd been challenged and had to rely on anything other than my powers, natural good looks, and charm.

She'd reluctantly agreed to give me her number, and her name. She wasn't immediately forthcoming with the information, but I figured she realised work was work. I'd sent her a text with a few vague details about the job I wanted her to photograph. Of course, it was all bullshit. There was no job; it was all done in order to get her number. I was just playing the game.

I'm pretty sure that she was also aware that it was all an act, but she'd gone along with it. She'd also replied to my texts, although it was all business and there was no hint of anything else in them.

My texts, on the other hand, were filled with flirtation. It wasn't subtle, and she wouldn't have missed it. She was simply choosing to ignore it and not respond.

When I'd met with her in the park the other day, I didn't expect her to stay. We had in fact spent about an hour, walking, taking in the surroundings, me trying to coax her out of herself.

I'd had people looking into why she was immune to me, but so far no one had come up with anything. I'd personally ruled out that she was under a spell. She was private, but I didn't get that she was intentionally trying to hide something from me—not something that big anyway.

Plus, magic leaves a trace. I would have been able to sense it the more time I spent around her. I got nothing—no trace of magical essence anywhere near her. Whatever was blocking my powers, it wasn't as a result of a spell or something that had been done to her. She had to have been born with it. That led me immediately to her father. It must have something to do with him. I knew from her dossier that her mother was human. Her father, however, was unknown. Whatever it was that made her special, it came from him.

In the park, she had seemed impressed by my skills reading the couple, having eventually agreed with my assessment. I'd watched her as she studied them, desperately trying to make it some sort of happy situation. Despite everything she'd been through, deep down, she still looked for the good in people.

On our first meeting in the bar I'd thought she was attractive. The more I saw her though, the more the attraction increased. I was sure it was because she resisted me—once I had her everything would be back to normal. I wanted to spend time with her and put the effort in; it would make the reward even sweeter. Like I'd earned it.

It was taking longer than I had anticipated, though. I was immortal, and I had all of time before me, so this little detour wouldn't hurt in the grand scheme of things. It was a welcome distraction, if I was truthful, something out of the ordinary.

I was sure that once I'd fucked her, the mystery would be shattered and I could hand her over to Daniel without hesitation. Normal service would resume.

I wanted to get things moving. Just texting wasn't enough. It was time we spoke again. I dialled her number. It had crossed my mind that she might not answer, possibly send me to voicemail.

It rang several times, and I was just about to hang up, when she answered and I heard her sweet voice.

"Mr. Albright, what can I do for you?" she answered. Her tone was solely professional, very different from when we'd just met in the bar.

"Please, Red, call me Luke. I was wondering if you'd had a chance to peruse the information regarding the job?" I had to lead with work—anything else and she'd shut down on me.

"You know my name now, so you can call me it. You don't have to stick with Red," she responded.

"I know that, Red." It suited her.

"Fine. Regarding the information, I have had a chance to look at it, and everything seems doable. Shouldn't be a stretch. I am available on that date too." She seemed excited; it was a shame it was all completely fabricated. I'd have to make it up to her.

"Excellent, Red. Now when are you next free?"

"What do you mean? I've told you I'm available on the date." I could sense uncertainty in her voice.

"Well I wanted to meet up, perhaps take you to dinner so we can go over some of the finer details."

"You can send everything via email, there's no need for us to go out," she responded coldly.

"Now, Red, that's not the way that I do business. There

are certain things that I insist on. This is one of them." She remained silent, and I imagined her weighing everything up in her head, probably biting her lip and trying to decide.

Silence.

"Red, it's just dinner to discuss business. I know you wouldn't normally do business in this way, but evening is the only time I'm available. I have a lot going on at the minute and my days are full." I tried to sound sincere, but I wasn't sure if I'd managed to pull it off.

"What about a videoconference?" she questioned. Was she this way with everyone, or was it just me?

"Evenings are best for me. It's the only time I have free in the next few weeks. We both have to eat, so it would kill two birds with one stone. I'll pick somewhere nice; you won't regret it. Trust me."

She hesitated, and I didn't need my abilities to sense she was having an internal battle with herself.

"Fine, I'll meet you to discuss the job," she finally responded. "I'm free tomorrow evening, if that's any good?"

It didn't give me much time to prepare, and I'm sure that was her plan. I was not deterred, though. I had all of Hell at my disposal and knew we could arrange a spectacular night.

"Tomorrow night works for me, Red. I'll be in touch to let you know the details." I hung up quickly before she could change her mind.

14

TESS

"TESS, you need to get to the bar now," Emma squealed over the phone at me. She was excited—not in trouble. I was clueless why she was screaming at me though.

"Woah there, Em, chill out and tell me what's going on." I was trying to be calm, but I could just hear gasps and squeals from the other end of the line.

"No, I can't, you have to come to the bar now," she nearly screamed at me before hanging up.

She was such a drama queen sometimes; I didn't have time for this. I had my business meeting with Luke tonight and was trying to sort things out. I'd updated my portfolio with the shots from the park, those of the couple having an affair. Even though it was a good shot, I couldn't help but think about when he sat so close to me and made me tingle.

I suspected it wasn't a business meeting, but I couldn't really pass up potential work. Plus, despite my best efforts to control myself, I wanted to see him and spend time with him. In all honesty, I wanted him in every sense of the word. I knew it wasn't smart; I couldn't help the attraction though.

I made my way from my condo. As I walked to the bar, I

flicked through my emails and found he'd sent the details over for tonight's business meeting. I read over the email; they were sparse to say the least. All it said was that I had to be ready for 8 PM and that he would send a car to pick me up; all I had to do was send him my details.

Nope, that wasn't happening. I didn't want him knowing where I lived—not yet, anyway.

I thought it quicker to text, as the email might get lost.

I'LL MEET YOU AT THE RESTAURANT. WHERE ARE WE GOING AND WHAT TIME SHOULD I BE THERE?

I quickly fired off.

I continued walking, nearing the bar while I thought about what I was going to wear. I wanted to look professional, but I also wanted to look hot. I mentally scanned through my outfits in my head when my phoned pinged.

RED, IT'S NO TROUBLE FOR ME TO SEND A CAR. TELL ME WHERE TO PICK YOU UP.

He was persistent, but I already knew that.

THANKS. HOW ABOUT THE CAR PICKS ME UP FROM OUTSIDE THE BAR?

I didn't think he could refuse that; he was allowed to be chivalrous, and I was allowed to be mysterious. Everyone wins.

I was outside the bar when my phone pinged again.

BE OUTSIDE THE BAR FOR 8 PM. A CAR WILL BE THERE TO PICK YOU UP. I LOOK FORWARD TO DISCUSSING BUSINESS WITH YOU.

Although he said he wanted to discuss business, I didn't believe it for a second... yet I was still willing to go.

I pushed the door of the bar open and made my way in. As soon as Emma saw me she let out a squeal and ran over, hugging me and bouncing up and down.

"Oh my God, Tess, it's so beautiful, did you know about it?" She questioned.

"Em, what the hell are you talking about?" I was genuinely lost.

She motioned over to a huge, fancy-looking box on the bar, which had already been opened; I imagined she'd done that. "What is it?" I asked her.

"Just go see, I can't even..." she trailed off while grinning broadly.

I walked over to the box on the bar and noticed that it contained a stunning green fabric. I was unsure what exactly it was so I reached in and pulled whatever it was out. I knew Emma had already looked—she couldn't not. I held the item up and realised it was a dress. It was beautiful, and I just stood gawping at it, mouth open and everything.

"How amazing is it? Oh my God, Tess, you would look unreal in it," Emma squealed once more.

I was more blown away with the dress the more I studied it. It was sleeveless with a V-neck bodice, and straps that crossed over an open back. The silky green fabric fell full length with a split up one side. It was beautiful, like a fairy-tale dress.

I was lost, though—what did this have to do with me?

"Em, what's going on?" I asked, a bewildered look on my face.

"Oh right, yeah," Emma said, thrusting an envelope into my hands. She'd clearly already opened it, despite it being addressed to me. I glared at her.

"I swear I didn't read it... well I didn't read *all* of it," she said.

I pulled out a beautiful card and opened it to see a note written there.

Red,

Saw this dress and thought of you. It's the same green as your eyes, so you have to have it.

I thought you could wear it tonight. If not please keep it for another time.

See you soon

Luke

He bought me a dress? What the fuck? It wasn't just any dress either, but a gorgeous, sexy dress at that. I was gobsmacked. No one had ever bought me something like that before. I stood open-mouthed for a good five minutes before I heard Emma speak.

"You have to wear it. It's so beautiful. The man has taste," she said as she ran her hands over the silky fabric.

"I can't wear that. It's supposed to be a business meeting!" It was totally inappropriate. The more I looked at the dress, the more convinced I was that I was about to go on a date, not to a meeting.

"Of course, you can. He sent it to you—he obviously wants you to wear it. I suppose it depends where you're going?" I knew she was asking out of curiosity, but I couldn't tell her because I didn't know.

"I don't know. He's just sending a car here to pick me up, other than that I don't have any details." The more I thought about it, it was actually weird. I'd be completely isolated and alone. I hadn't realised, as I'd been too distracted by his hotness, but now I was thinking clearly. Emma must have realised I was freaking out.

"Don't worry, I can track where you are. As soon as you get to wherever you're going message me the details, and I'll stay available all night if you need me. Don't let this stop you." Her words were calming, but I still felt uneasy.

Time was ticking, and it was too late to cancel. She was right, I was overreacting, and she'd know where I was.

"Right, well I better go get ready, I suppose," I mumbled to myself.

"How are you wearing your hair? What about your make-up?" She stared at me, waiting for an answer. I had no clue, so I just shrugged my shoulders.

Emma rolled her eyes at me. "Come on, let's go. My shift has finished, so we'll go get you ready." She dragged me out of the bar, box tucked under her arm.

Back in my bedroom, Emma brushed her fingers through my hair, loosening the curls she had just made. She swept it all over my right shoulder and began pinning it into place. The look was elegant and classic; I thought it would complement the dress. I still wasn't sure if I was wearing it though.

She looked at me. "Gorgeous. Now let's get some make-up on. Not too much, though, just enough to make your eyes pop." She studied me, deciding what she should do. I was glad she was here, in all honesty. She was amazing at this sort of thing. I, on the other hand, was not. I wasn't a "tomboy," but I wasn't exactly a "girly girl." I had a handful of easy hairstyles I could do and had absolutely no clue about make-up. I'd tried to follow a few basic online tutorials once and ended up looking like I'd walked out of a cheap brothel. I mostly just stuck with mascara and that was about it.

She began working, and I zoned out. I should have been paying attention, but I was too busy thinking about tonight.

"It'll be fine, you know?" she said, clearly picking up on my anxiety. "Not every guy is like Daniel," she said, giving my shoulder a reassuring squeeze.

I smiled at her as I admired my reflection in the mirror. She'd done wonders—I looked amazing. She had indeed made my eyes pop with a slightly smoky colour, though it wasn't too much. My skin was flawless, but not caked in make-up. I looked glowing; red lips completed the make-up. I would never have dared to do a red lip, but it worked.

"Go try that dress on now!" she demanded, pushing me to my closet.

I slid the dress up over my thighs, and the material was so soft and silky. Like nothing I'd worn before. It really was luxurious. I studied my reflection in the mirror. The dress fit perfectly. How did he know my size? It was more than that, though; it fit all of my curves exactly, like it had been made especially for me. How the hell? I turned and twirled, looking from all angles. I'd never worn anything like it.

I walked back into my bedroom, and Emma gasped. "Oh my God, Tess, it's perfect, like it was made for you." She looked like she was about to burst into tears.

"I can't wear it, it's too much," I said to her.

"Tess, you are wearing that fucking dress, end of discussion. Now let's choose your shoes and accessories." She took my hand and dragged me back to the closet.

I was ready—black heeled shoes, a pair of silver earrings, a silver bracelet, and my silver necklace completed my look. Emma had tried to persuade me to ditch my necklace and wear another, but I never took it off. I'd bought it when I first moved to the city. It was a long, thin, silver pendant, and engraved on it was the day that I first landed in New York. The date my new life started. I couldn't take it off. It was a reminder of everything that had gotten me to that point.

Emma had packed all of my "essentials" into a black clutch for me, and I'd grabbed my portfolio. It did spoil the look of the outfit, but I had to take it. Emma had rolled her eyes at me, but hey it was a "business meeting," so I had to be prepared.

We waited inside the bar for Luke's car to pick me up. All the bar staff had wolf-whistled at me when I entered, and I politely told them all to go fuck themselves while flipping them off. Emma had gotten me a shot of tequila. Dutch courage, she said. Then I saw the car pull up. *Oh shit.* my stomach was churning. I was so nervous.

I walked out to the car, expecting him to be there. He wasn't, but the driver got out and opened the car door for me. "This way, Ms. Adams, Mr. Albright will meet you at the restaurant." I nodded at the driver in thanks. I was disappointed he wasn't here to meet me. I shuffled into the back of the car.

We drove through the city, and I noticed we were heading towards Hell's Kitchen; I knew there were lots of nice places over there, way out of my budget though. With that, we pulled up. I went to open the door to get out of the car, when the driver was there opening it for me. "I'll take that for you, Ms. Adams," he said as he grabbed my portfolio. I thanked him; it would make things easy getting out of the car.

"Follow me," he said, then led me to the front of a magnificent-looking building. I followed him through the most plush lobby I'd seen and up some stairs. "This way," he said, gesturing for me to walk through an open door.

I entered into a huge room with high ceilings and a stunning crystal chandelier. I carried on walking, taking in my surroundings. It was all dark, lush walls and wooden accents.

Then I noticed the table-just one. This enormous, spectacular room dwarfed the lone table. I gulped as I realised this was just for us. Luke and me.

Then I spotted him—he was on the phone and hadn't noticed I'd arrived. I studied him for a moment; he truly was handsome.

"Mr. Albright," the driver said from behind me. I jumped a fucking mile and turned to look at him. He gave me an apologetic look.

When I turned back around, Luke's eyes were on me. They traced up and down my body, taking in all of my curves in the dress he'd bought for me. His eyes met mine, and I could have sworn I saw a hunger in them and a lust, there for everyone to see.

"Wow, Red, that dress looks perfect on you," he said, standing up from his seat at the table and making his way over to the chair opposite his.

I raked my gaze over his body, as he had done to me. Another perfectly tailored black suit hugged his form, this time coupled with a crisp white shirt that made his tanned skin glow. His black hair—as always—framed his face perfectly. I was about to actually swoon.

He pulled the chair out for me. "Will you join me, Red?" He motioned to the seat. I made my way over, my hips swaying as I did due to my heels. He didn't miss it, and I saw him bite his lip. Wow, I seemed to have quite the effect on him. I sat on the chair, and he pushed it in for me. His driver handed him my portfolio, and Luke dismissed him. He then made his way back to his seat, my portfolio in his hand.

"This is amazing, Luke," I said, gesturing to the set-up. "Do you do all your business like this?"

"Let's not bore things with business," he said, placing my portfolio on the floor.

"I knew it was bullshit. There isn't a job, is there?" I questioned, looking him in the eyes.

"Not presently, but there could be in the future," he said without skipping a beat.

"I knew it."

"You knew, yet you decided to come anyway. Let's just enjoy the evening, shall we?" he said, then smiled. "I've ordered us both the tasting menu with the wine pairing; I hope that's okay with you?"

I normally wouldn't let anyone take the lead, order for me, tell me what I was doing. But I was his guest. "That's fine, thank you," I replied.

We studied each other for a while, neither saying anything. He exuded power—I could feel it. It both drew me in and terrified me at the same time. He was the epitome of self-assuredness and confidence. Maybe that was what made me want him. The butterflies in my stomach continued to flutter as we took each other in.

"Tell me, Red, what are you thinking?" He leaned forward in his chair, placing his elbows on the table and interlocking his fingers.

"Just that you're rather sure of yourself," I replied honestly.

"Normally, Red, yes… but not with you. Why is that, do you think?"

"Maybe it's because I'm not interested," I lied. "I think you just like the chase, and that's what draws you to me."

"Not at all. You're different, special. I can't quite put my finger on why though." After he replied he searched me, as if he'd be able to find it in my appearance.

Luckily, the first course arrived, as well as an accompanying wine. The waitress practically fawned over him. One had visited the table about four times already; he dismissed her every time.

"What does your company do, Luke?" I asked.

"My company deals with acquisitions, procuring things,"

he said with a smirk, not providing anything else. "Tell me, Red, how long have you been in the States? What made you leave your home?"

We continued eating and drinking throughout the evening, the conversation following with more mundane topics.

Another course of food and wine arrived, which gave me chance to think about my answer. *Be vague, you don't need to tell him your life story, not yet anyway. Be cool.* "I've been here a little over two years now, and I love it. I couldn't imagine being anywhere else." I didn't want him to know all my reasons for leaving. "My mum died, and a relationship broke down. There was nothing to tie me to London anymore, so I thought a fresh start would be a good idea. I've never regretted it once."

He looked at me. I thought he was deciding whether he should probe further. He clearly decided against it and sipped some more wine and placed another exceptional morsel of food into his mouth. He licked his lips, and I watched him. I thought about his lips… kissing them, biting them.

"Red? You okay?" he asked, breaking me out of my dirty thoughts.

Shit, he'd caught me watching him. My cheeks flushed red from embarrassment.

"I think the wine is going to my head, "I lied, hoping he'd bought it. The look on his face told me he didn't. His smile told me he knew *exactly* what I was doing.

At that, the over-zealous waitress returned. She had been so attentive to him all evening. Not to me, though, just Luke.

He ignored her and she hurried away. "Only one more course left," he said. "I've very much enjoyed our time together. You really are something." There was sincerity in his voice, and the look on his face embarrassed me. I quickly looked away and began playing with the napkin on my lap.

We stayed in silence for a while until the staff brought us the final dish and wine pairing—the waitress still fawned. It was coming off as a bit pathetic. Apart from this waitress, all the staff had been so attentive all night—nothing was too much trouble. I imagined that Luke was used to it. He seemed unfazed by everything that was going on. He couldn't have been oblivious to the attention he was getting from the waiting staff; I certainly wasn't. There were twinges of jealousy in the pit of my stomach, but he was here with me, and that felt good. He'd never once looked at them, always keeping his focus on me. Tonight, I felt like the centre of his universe; he only had eyes for me.

"Red, I'd really like to see you again. No pretences though, no business meetings. Just me and you on a date. What do you think?" he said. I had no clue what time it was, in all honesty. I'd been having too much of a good time to care.

"I'd like that. Your company hasn't been as bad as I expected," I quipped. *Can't have him being complacent.*

He laughed. "I'm glad it wasn't a total waste for you." His smile lit up his face.

A waitress returned and informed Luke they were about to close and asked if he wanted them to keep the place open later for us. Who was this man that a super exclusive place like this would stay open, specifically for him?

"That won't be necessary. I have a meeting early in the morning, so we should be calling it a night," he said, standing from his chair and fastening one of the buttons on his jacket. My stomach dropped. I genuinely didn't want the night to end.

He made his way over to my chair, pulling it out to let me stand. I did so and made an attempt to move my legs, but the alcohol had made me wobbly, and I stumbled in my heels.

Thankfully he grabbed me around the waist and pulled me to him to stop me falling.

We were face to face, his hands still on my waist, looking at each other. Our faces were inches apart. His touch sent shockwaves through my body. The butterflies that were in my stomach had multiplied, and my breath hitched. The closeness was intense. I inhaled deeply, trying to gather myself, but that just made things worse as I was hit with his amazing smell—burned sandalwood.

He made absolutely no moves on me. He stayed still, his hands still on my waist, watching me. It felt like we were frozen, neither of us making any attempt to move.

The tension was broken when his driver made his presence known with a small cough. Luke's eyes moved to look at the driver, and he let go of my waist. I ached when he broke the contact. I longed for his touch again, for his closeness, his body against mine.

He held his arm out for me to grab on to. "In case you need it." He grinned. I clasped onto it, as my legs were still a little wobbly, now not just from the wine.

He escorted me back to his car, and his driver set off. The car headed back through the New York streets. "Where can I drop you off, Red?"

"Just the bar is fine thanks," I replied, trying my best not to sound drunk despite feeling it.

"I'd rather drop you at your place, so I know you're safe." He did seem genuine, but the bar was fine. He shrugged his shoulders. "Up to you, Red."

I thought it best to try and say as little as I could on the journey home to avoid embarrassment. I was drunk, and God knows what the hell I'd say if he questioned me. Knowing me, I'd probably tell him how I wanted to ride him like Seabiscuit. Best to keep quiet.

"Here we are, Red," he said, motioning out of the window

to the bar. He exited the car and made his way round to open the door for me, offering me his hand to help me step out of the car. I was genuinely thankful for his help. My level of drunkenness and the slit up to the thigh of this dress had me wondering if I was going to flash him when I stood. Thankfully, with his help I managed—it wasn't graceful, but I managed.

He continued holding onto my hand. "Red, I really have had an amazing night. One of the best I've had in a long time. I very much look forward to seeing you again," he said, lifting my hand up to his mouth. His full lips brushed against my knuckles before he placed a gentle kiss on the back of my hand.

I was holding my breath. I couldn't help it. Everything in me had stopped functioning from a combination of the alcohol and what his touch did to me. He didn't wait for a response; he let go of my hand and climbed back into the car.

He put the window down and leaned over. "Until next time, Red," he said smoothly as the car drove off. I watched it drive away until I could no longer see it.

I'm fucked, I thought to myself.

15

DANIEL

I WAS PACING up and down, pounding the pavement outside the London bar. Why the fuck wasn't the prick answering my calls? This was the sixth message I'd left. Neither he nor any of his people were getting back to me. I wasn't stupid enough to think that the number he had given me was his direct line, but I expected *some* sort of fucking response.

He was the fucking Devil—I knew he'd be busy, but I wanted an update, since I was growing ever-more impatient. What was taking so fucking long? My anger was growing inside my chest. I was always angry—ever since she'd left I had been—but now it had gone up a notch.

That useless dick had told me he could get this done; he was overly confident that it was achievable. If that was the case, what the fuck was the hold-up? What was he doing?

It had been three weeks since I'd made the deal. I'd get Tess, and he'd get my soul. Of course, I was working on a plan to get out of it, but now that didn't look like it would be a problem, as he was clearly struggling with his end of the bargain.

I'd had no luck finding anything, but he assured me it

wasn't a problem for him—that it could be done, and done quickly. So why the fuck was I still waiting? Had a stupid little girl like Tess really managed to hide from the Devil? I doubted it very much, so what was the delay? The thought of not having Tess made my chest swell with rage.

I should have had her by now; she should have been with me. If she had been, I would have ended her. Watched the life leave her body. Until she was gone and I could be at peace—both of us could. I'd thought about how I would do it, how I'd end her life. I settled on strangling her; that way, I could watch her. I could see her struggle and fight until her very last breath, and she, in turn, could watch me. She would know that she was mine. If I couldn't have her, then no one could. My face would be the last thing she saw. The thought of it made me hard. It was good that my jeans were fairly tight, or everyone outside the bar would be able to see me pitching a tent. There was still a visible bulge, though, for anyone who did take notice.

I was stressed, and now I was turned on. I had to go somewhere to sort that out. *I know just the place.*

Soho in London was known for its risqué vibe, and that was why I spent most of my time there. I was very sexual, and London was perfect for me. Especially this part of the city.

I'd cheated on Tess several times during our relationship, just one-night stands, no repeat fucks. She was mine, but I'd needed more than she could give in that regard. I'd often visit strip clubs, and whenever I was away on business I'd always hook up with someone. She never knew about it though; it was none of her fucking business.

I made my way to one of my favourite upmarket strip clubs. The girls were always decent, and they had all the right moves. I paid and made my way to the bar, then ordered a double tequila. Drink in hand, I walked over to a seat at the front of the main stage.

It was busy tonight, mostly men, though I did spot the odd woman or two.

The lights dimmed, and a spotlight fell on the stage. *Here we go*. A long leg appeared from behind a red curtain, adorned with fishnet tights, suspenders, and high heels. The leg was slowly followed by the rest of the woman. Early twenties, blonde, slim figure with the most incredible fucking tits. She wore a short black skirt and a white shirt, her hair was pinned up in a bun, and she wore glasses. *Sexy secretary*, I thought to myself. *I wish my secretary looked like that; I'd have fucking ruined her if she did.*

The dancer made her way to the front of the stage and began her performance, slowly peeling off layers while she worked the pole. She undid the bun, shaking her long blonde hair free. She grasped the pole dipping back over so she could see me. Winking, she lifted back up, spinning around. She made her way to the edge of the stage, on her knees. She touched her breasts, then moved to the fastening, freeing them and throwing her bra to the side. Fuck me, her tits were so amazing. I wanted to bury my head in them.

She gyrated while cupping her tits, squeezing them together as men threw money at her. I continued to watch the show. It wasn't the best I'd seen, but she did a good job. My dick was still hard, pushed against my jeans. *I ought to do something about it.*

A few dancers had approached me offering private shows, but no one had really caught my eye.

I finished my drink and scanned the crowd for a waitress to fetch me another. That was when I saw her. A tall, busty redhead. A poor version of Tess, but she'd do. I caught her eye, and she strutted over to me.

She was about to start with all of the small talk bullshit, so I cut her off before she had the chance.

"Private dance, how much?" I didn't need to woo her or be polite. She was there for my fucking pleasure, so I could speak to her however I wanted.

"How about we start at fifty-pounds for ten minutes and go from there? I'm sure you'll want more," she said in her best seductive voice. I didn't care about any of that shit; I just wanted her to dance for me. I wasn't bothered about her pretending to like me.

"Fine," I said sharply, standing up from my chair. She made her way through the crowd of people to a long corridor. Several doors branched off from the passage, and I knew each would lead to a private room. We made our way to the last room, and she ushered me inside.

The room was dark, with two plush red chairs in the centre and a small table nestled in between them.

"Do you want a drink before we get started, sweetheart?" she asked.

"No, let's just get on with it," I said, taking a seat. I held onto the sides of the red velvet chair.

She made her way to a sound system positioned on another table and pushed play. Music filtered through the speakers in the ceiling, and she made her way over to me. She placed her hands on my thighs, pushing my legs apart. She swayed, going from standing to crouching down, her head directly in front of my crotch. Then she pushed her arse out and straightened her legs. Letting go of me, she moved her hands up her body, running them over her breasts and through her hair.

She moved, so she was facing away from me, her rear now in my face. She moved her hands from her hair to the clasp of her bra and removed it, throwing it across the room. Still swaying her curvy hips, she turned so I could see her tits.

I'd seen better.

She squeezed them together while she continued to dance. She again turned around and backed onto my crotch, grinding against my hard cock.

I grabbed hold of her thighs and slid my hands up to her hips. She immediately moved forwards away from me.

"No touching, sweetheart, or we'll have to stop," she chastised.

I can do whatever the fuck I want, who does she think she is? I thought to myself. As if agreeing to her request, I held my hands up in the air and she began dancing again.

She still had her pants on, but they were see-through. She walked towards me, again placing her hands on my thighs and shoving her tits in my face. I remained still—for now. She backed away and laced her fingers through the top of her pants. Bending forwards with straight legs, she removed them, so her arse was bare before me. She stepped out of the underwear and turned to me, again swaying in my direction.

Once in between my legs, I grabbed hold of her, tightly.

"We've talked about this, sweetheart, you aren't allowed to touch," she said, looking directly at me.

"I can do whatever the fuck I want with you. I've paid for you," I spat at her.

The colour drained from her face when she realised I had a tight grip on her behind; she couldn't get away. I held firm despite her struggles. "You can't," she said desperately.

"I can, and I will," I said, standing up from the chair. The more she struggled, the harder I got. I enjoyed the fight. Tess always put up a good struggle. She'd known how to play.

I easily overpowered the woman, still holding onto her, and then I ground my crotch up against her. She tried to break free, but her hands were pinned by her sides, and my arms were around them, gripping her tightly. I was sure she'd be bruised with my fingerprints. I grinned down at her.

Next thing I knew was searing pain—the bitch had kneed me in the balls, forcing me to let go. Maybe she had fight after all. She ran towards the door, and I made a move to follow but I noticed she'd stopped. The exit was blocked.

Her exit was blocked by a beautiful blonde-haired woman —the dancer stopped dead in her tracks. The woman stared at her and stroked her hair. I couldn't hear what she'd said, but there was no mistaking how her eyes glowed. They were red—blood-red. I'd never seen anything like it.

Immediately the dancer calmed, and the pair both made their way back over to me, the blonde woman guiding her. She looked like she was in a trance.

"Sit," the blonde said to me while motioning to the chair. *Who the fuck does she think she is? I'm not taking orders from her.* I made no attempt to move.

"Daniel, I'm not here to cause you problems. Now sit down please, we have business to discuss."

What business could we possibly have to discuss? And how does she know my name? I sat, I was intrigued now, *who is this fucking woman?* I'd entertain her for a while, likely not long though.

She turned to face the dancer, who was standing next to her, still in some sort of trance. The blonde woman's eyes glowed again while she spoke. "I have this, young one. Go back to your business and mention this to no one." The dancer—still naked—walked from the room.

"The cameras?" I said, nodding to the CCTV on the wall.

"Taken care of, Daniel, no one is coming," she said smoothly. Good for me, bad for her.

Once we were alone, the woman made her way back over to me and sat on the other chair by the table. I studied her. She was beautiful—not my type, but I could appreciate beauty. "Who are you, and what the fuck do you want?" I said. She'd just ruined my fun, and I wanted answers.

"Now, Daniel, I don't think there is any need for that tone when I'm here to help you." She was perfectly calm. Not the least bit put out by my aggression.

"I don't know what the fuck you think I need help with, but I don't need anything from someone like you," I spat.

What the fuck??

I tried to get up and leave this crazy bitch behind, but I couldn't. My legs weren't working. I told my body to get up, to stand and exit the room. To ditch this woman, but I couldn't. My arms were fused into position. My whole body was frozen. My eyes locked on the woman—had she drugged me? What was happening? I willed myself to move, but my body was no longer responding to what my brain told it to do.

"What have you done to me, bitch?" I could still speak; everything else had gone.

"Now, now, Daniel. There is no need for such language. As I said, I'm here to help you. Once we're done, I'll release you. The effects aren't permanent," she assured me.

"I'm going to fucking kill you when I break free from this. *No one* does this to me." I was fucking livid, and she was going to feel it when I was free.

"You could try," she said, smiling. "If I were you, though, I'd save your energy; you have bigger problems on your hands."

What the hell was she talking about? I didn't know this woman, so what could she possibly know about me and my problems?

"Oh yeah, and what exactly is that?" I questioned.

She placed her hands on the table between us as a smile formed on her lips. "By helping you get Tess," she said without skipping a beat. My eyes widened. How the fuck did she know Tess? What did she know of me wanting her?

"Don't worry, Daniel. I know all about your deal with Lucifer. I'm going to help you, no tricks or games, and your soul will remain yours. Your deal with him will be void."

How the fuck does she know all of this?

I couldn't speak, but not because she'd done anything to me. Just that I didn't know what the fuck to say.

"He hasn't been completely honest with you, Daniel. You have to expect that from the original sinner. He likes his games more than anyone," she said smoothly.

"What are you talking about?" I hissed.

She threw a large envelope onto the table towards me. In an instant, whatever she'd done to me broke, and I could move again. I looked between her and the door, trying to decide what to do.

"Don't run, Daniel, I could stop you in a heartbeat. Anyway, we have a mutual problem that needs addressing," she said, motioning towards the package on the table.

I leaned forward and picked up the envelope. I opened it and peered in; they were photographs. I plucked them out and there was a substantial amount. As I focussed on them, I saw Tess. They were recent. I looked up in amazement at the woman, who was watching me with a knowing smile.

"How?" I said, gobsmacked. Was this a trick? I continued to scan through the photos in my hands. She looked so fucking good. There was photo after photo. Tess in a bar, in a restaurant, in a park and the gym. I sat, shuffling through all the images until I stopped dead in my tracks.

Are you fucking kidding me??

It was Tess, with another man. Not just any man, though. My blood boiled in my veins. Tess was laughing and joking with the fucking Devil himself.

16

LUCIFER

I'D ENJOYED my date with Tess. She gave me a run for my money in the snark department. Smart and sassy, she wasn't afraid to say what was on her mind. Maybe that was because she wasn't aware I was the Devil. People tended to tell me whatever I wanted to hear if they thought it would benefit them.

I hoped that I could see her again, and soon. These new feelings had taken me by surprise. The moment I caught her in the restaurant and her body had pressed against mine, I ignited. Flames felt like they licked at my entire body, and the desire to have her intensified. I'd have to hurry up and fuck her; the feeling was too much. I'd never had to wait for a woman before—they usually threw themselves at me.

But she was different. She was making me work, which I was sure was why I wanted her so much. It had become a need now, and I needed her. I needed to feel her naked body pressed against me. I needed to know what she tasted like. I needed her legs wrapped around me while I buried myself deep inside of her.

Fuck, I needed her badly. I was sure once I'd conquered

her I could move on. It was the anticipation that was getting to me.

Unfortunately for me, though, Tess would have to wait. Duty called, and I had to return to Hell.

From my place in New York, I portaled back to my inner circle of Hell. This circle was mine, and mine alone. No one had access or could enter unless I invited them. The innermost circle of Hell was my home. I had places to stay all over the world, but this, this was home.

It could be a lonely existence, but this was my punishment. I hadn't chosen this life; it was a direct result of my own actions. I'd been furious for so long, but I had learned to make the best of it, and now I was content. I had a job to do, and I did it well.

Today I'd be checking in on the new arrivals, which meant a trip to the first circle of Hell, Limbo.

Dante was right when he wrote about the nine circles of Hell; he just got the finer details a little jumbled.

Limbo was a holding area of sorts, where new souls arrived. It was the first circle, and other than my own, it was probably the calmest, which was saying something. Souls there would be assessed and examined. It was here that their primary sin would be established. Souls would commit many different sins over the course of their lifetime, and it was the job of Limbo to determine which sin drove the behaviour; in most cases this was a simple task.

There were seven sins into which souls were sorted: pride, envy, gluttony, lust, anger, greed, and sloth.

Each sin had its own circle of Hell. Each circle was led by one of my most trusted. Demons and fallen angels had both earned their places as circle guardians. Bee and Levi led two of the busiest circles; I'd never had any issues from either of them. They were not only loyal to me, but loyal to Hell.

That had not always been the case with others. Over the

years I'd found it necessary to rearrange guardians, for several reasons. It had been some time, though, since that had happened. My current team was strong. Hell was thriving, despite the best efforts of some.

Within each of the circles, there were several levels. The level a soul would reach would be dependent on the degree of sin they had displayed in their lifetime. The more intense the sin, the worse the punishment would be. It was an effective system that had worked for millennia.

Once a soul's primary sin had been established, it was a case of finding their worst fears and arranging a suitable eternal punishment. The leaders of the circles and their teams were creative with the everlasting pain caused to the souls they were tasked with guarding. Never a dull moment.

Arriving in Limbo, I saw a familiar sight. New recruits. No two the same—old, young, men, and women. I didn't discriminate. As I made my way through the cells, I was joined by Abaddon.

Abaddon was the guardian of Limbo and had been since the beginning. He revelled in the role, and I'd never had reason to question his loyalty. He was always eager to please. Abaddon was the second line of defence for Hell. As Limbo was the first circle, it was closest to the gates and therefore needed extra protection. He was the demon for the job.

All souls entered Hell through the gates. Huge and fiery, they were guarded by hounds, spells, and so much more. The gates were there to keep the souls in as well as others out. Once through the gates, you'd reach Limbo and Abaddon.

As a result, Abaddon had to be worthy of the task, and he had to look the part. As he never left Hell, he had no human form. Just his demonic side, and it was spectacular. He stood around eight feet tall with wild flaming eyes. He was skeletal, but he had a huge hulking frame. He always wore a long cloak and hood which made him look even creepier—the perfect introduction to Hell.

"What have we got today, Abaddon?" I asked the giant guardian.

He nodded his way to the holding cells. "A lot of low-level sinners in this batch," he said in a disappointed tone. He liked the more sinister ones—the worse the sin, the better for him. He enjoyed breaking them down before sending them on to their new homes.

"Things are going well though; the gate is stable and there's very little activity trying to get in or out," he rasped. His voice was gravelly and low, like something from a nightmare. It was another thing that made him the perfect guardian for Limbo.

"Anything good?" I asked; he wasn't the only one who liked to have fun with the new recruits.

He nodded, a smile broke across his skeletal face, and he led me to a cell. Inside was a small, meek-looking man who was cowering in the corner. I raised my eyebrows as I studied the man, then turned to look back at Abaddon. He continued smiling and gestured for me to enter the cell.

"Don't let appearances deceive you, Lucifer, he's got quite the chequered past," he said while we looked at the figure in the corner of the room. "He's a serial killer. Multiple victims over several years. Sadist too, got off torturing his female victims before he killed them," Abaddon said, tilting his head towards the man, who still hadn't looked up from the floor.

I entered the cell and immediately felt myself change. The cells were all warded, and my natural form was released as I stepped in. There were no chains or bars; the wards were enough to keep the souls in, meaning I and the others could come and go. Only the souls would be trapped.

I made my way over to the man. "Stand," I commanded. As if torn from some form of trance, he turned to face us, and when he did, I saw it: pure fear. That was what his victims would have felt knowing they were about to die. He would have no such reprieve.

"Why are you here?" I asked. He shook his head, not wanting to answer, instead looking down at his bloody, dirty feet.

Abaddon punched the man in the stomach, and he doubled over, coughing up blood. "This is Lucifer, Prince of Darkness, and you will answer his questions," he spat at the man.

"Look at me," I commanded. The man, now collapsed on the floor and still coughing, raised his head to look at me. He shakily stood, and I took a step towards him—he immediately flinched. It was then that I noticed he'd pissed himself. Probably from the fear; it was common.

"Tell me, why are you here?" I repeated my question.

"M-M-Murder," he stuttered, "but I, I…" he trailed off.

"Come on, out with it. I don't have all day," I said. There was much to do while I was here and I couldn't afford to waste time.

"I, I repented my sins before God. I repented. I'm forgiven, this is a mistake. I shouldn't be here," he pleaded.

I looked from the man to Abaddon, who was now looking at me. We both laughed and laughed hard; it took the man by surprise. Apparently he hadn't been expecting this response from us.

"You are exactly where you should be. Murder is a sin that cannot be forgiven," I informed him.

God did have his little jokes. Some sins could be repented for, your eternal soul would be wiped clean, and you would be able to escape the depths of Hell. Murder, however, regardless of how much a person repented, couldn't be forgiven, despite how much people begged him.

"No, your soul is mine for eternity," I coldly said. I

watched as the man once again sank to the floor, now sitting in his own blood and urine. He sobbed, a sound I'd heard many, many times before.

I turned and made my way back out of the cell, making my way to another; there was much to be done in Hell before I could see her again.

TESS

EVER SINCE MY date with Luke, he had been all I could think about. This was so unlike me; I had my shit together after everything that had happened with Daniel. But Luke, he consumed my every thought. What the fuck was going on with me?

I'd arranged to meet Emma for a coffee, as I hadn't seen her since the date and she was desperate for all of the sordid details. She'd be disappointed that I hadn't slept with him.

I walked up to the coffee shop and decided to wait outside for her; she was always late. I don't know how she kept her job at the bar. Jerry had a soft spot for the two of us —he was a lovely guy.

I pulled out my phone and noticed I had a text from Luke. When I opened it I couldn't help but smile.

RED, IF YOU'RE FREE TONIGHT, I'D LOVE TO TAKE YOU FOR DRINKS. I HAVE WORK TO ATTEND TO BUT CAN PICK YOU UP AT THE BAR AROUND 9 PM?

Hell yes, I was free tonight. I wanted to see him so badly.

However, I didn't want to come across as desperate, despite the fact I was. I quickly fired off a reply.

YEAH, THAT'S FINE, I'LL SEE YOU AT 9 PM.

I was grinning from ear to ear studying my phone when Emma grabbed me and shouted, "Boo!" I jumped a mile.

"Sorry, babe, didn't mean to frighten you," she said unapologetically. "What's got you looking so happy?" she questioned, leaning over and trying to look at my phone.

I ignored her and entered the coffee shop. Emma found us a table, and I made my way to the counter to get drinks. She'd want a flat white; she was a creature of habit. As it was mid-afternoon and I'd already had a million cups of coffee I thought it best to get a tea. I was British, after all—I had a reputation to uphold.

I gathered the drinks and made my way over to where Emma was. She was eyeing me up as I walked over.

"You didn't get laid," she said, seeming disappointed.

"Jesus, Em, I haven't even got my coat off yet," I chastised.

She was still eyeing me as I removed my coat and sat down on the chair opposite her.

"No, I didn't get laid. He was very gentlemanly and didn't push things," I told her.

I could see that under her thick blonde bangs she was raising an eyebrow at me. "He could push anything against me if he wanted to. God, Tess, he's fucking hot," she said, waving her hand in front of her face as if trying to cool herself down.

I envied her sometimes. She really was so carefree and didn't give two fucks about what people thought of her. If she wanted something, she'd go after it. Men, mainly. She hadn't had a relationship since I'd known her. She'd dated plenty, slept with more. I knew it would happen for her, but she was just having too much fun at the moment.

"Come on, tell me everything," she said. I'd have to literally relay every detail to her; she'd know if I was holding back.

"Well we've only been out once, so I'm not really sure what you want me to say?" I responded.

"Everything, the works. Don't be a fucking tease," she said as she lifted the cup to her mouth. After she'd swallowed, she started up again. "He sent a dress to the bar for you, which by the way is so romantic. Then he took you to one of the city's most upscale restaurants; there is no way nothing at all happened. Now go."

I proceeded to fill her in on the events of the night, how he wasn't in the car that picked me up, and how he was waiting for me in the restaurant. In our own private dining room. Her eyes widened, and she hung on my every word. I told her all about what he was wearing and how unbelievably hot he looked. She feigned swooning but I knew how she felt about him. I knew she'd seen him first before he ever showed interest in me. She was happy for me, though; she'd urged me to go for it.

"So, when I tried to get him to look through my portfolio, he admitted to me that there was no job. He'd just wanted to take me out," I said.

"Well no shit, Sherlock," she snorted. "I can't actually believe you thought there was."

"Alright, alright," I said. "Let's move on, shall we?"

I described the food, wine, and that everyone bent over backwards for him and his every need. Hell, they'd offered to keep the restaurant open for him. She didn't seem surprised by this. Emma had dated a few high-powered professionals and had told me similar stories in the past, not to the same extent though. I felt Luke was in his own category.

"We talked, Em, and it was so easy. I felt calm with him. But…" I hesitated. "But there is something I can't put my finger on, like he's trying to figure me out. Searching me for something he can't quite find?" I sounded crazy when I said it aloud.

"Tess, he's getting to know you. Asking questions is part of that. How do you expect to things to progress if you won't open up?" she said, looking at me.

I didn't mean that, though. It wasn't his questions—it was the way he looked at me. Like he was searching my soul, my very being. Like I was a puzzle to him, one that needed solving. I nodded in agreement with her; it was easier than arguing at this point.

"Just enjoy spending time with an absolute hottie, okay?" I again nodded in agreement.

"So, I know you didn't have sex with him, but did you at least shove your tongue down his throat?" She grinned.

"Jesus, Em, no. But I've agreed to see him again tonight," I said with a shake of my head at her.

She stood up, immediately pulling on her coat and throwing mine at me. "Right come on, back to yours. We need to make sure you look absolutely fuckable." She had a deadly serious look in her eyes.

I shook my head at her, pulling on my coat and following her towards the door.

"Trust me, Tess, you need to get laid," she said loudly. So loudly, that a group of guys sat having coffees near the door all turned around to stare at us. All grinned up at me.

"Calm down, boys, not by any of you," she said, grabbing my hand and pulling me through the door. By this point, I was so embarrassed my pale skin had turned the brightest shade of crimson.

"Fuck, Em. That wasn't at all uncomfortable," I said, hiding my beetroot-red face.

She turned to face me. "Tess, I know that having sex with Luke will be amazing, exactly what you need to get you out of this slump you've been in since you got here," she said. It sounded harsh, but I knew she didn't mean it like that. Other than my one-night stand, it had been ages since I'd had sex.

"How do you know it will be amazing? Can you tell just by looking at him?" I said cynically.

"Of *course,* you fucking can, and deep down you know it, too," she said, pulling on my hand in the direction of my place.

I knew she was right.

LUCIFER

MAKING my way back to my inner circle, I was approached by one of the many demons who lived in Hell.

"Sir," he said, dipping his head to a bow. "Mr. Turner has been very persistent with his requests for an update. He has left several messages since you made your agreement," he continued.

He carried on standing there, waiting for my response. He wanted to know what to tell the boy. After all, that was what Daniel was, a mere boy.

"How does he seem?" I questioned.

"Sir?" he said, confused.

I wanted to know how Daniel was feeling, if I was getting to him. I'd have to listen to his messages before I worked out my response.

"Do you have the messages?" I asked. With that, he handed me a phone, and I began to scroll through the voice-mails. There was a substantial amount. With each message left, he became more and more agitated. It pleased me to think of how annoyed he was now. *Imagine how he'll feel when he finds out I've fucked her before I handed her over.*

I handed the phone back over to him. "Tell him that things are progressing as we expected and that we will contact him in due course to arrange the handover," I said dismissing the demon. He bowed again as he left.

It was a short response, which I knew would increase his rage. He could continue to squirm for all I cared; I was having way too much fun trying to bed Tess.

Now I'd completed my tasks for the day I was back in my inner circle. It was a tenty-four-seven job, but everyone needed breaks. Hell would continue without me for a bit; I could always be reached in case of emergencies. I had a direct connection with Hell. If something were happening, I'd feel it. At least, it had worked like that in the past.

Now, though, it was time to return to the mortal realm. I portaled back to my New York place.

Tess had agreed to meet me that night for drinks, and I'd be picking her up in a couple of hours. I looked forward to it; it was refreshing to spend time with someone I couldn't manipulate. Everything she did was her, and there was no one whispering in her ear. She wasn't influenced by my powers in any way, and that made her harder to read. Everything she said and did was unexpected. She was a breath of fresh air.

Making my way through the condo, I stripped, then stepped into the bathroom. Hell was grimy and hot, so I needed to wash the day away and prepare. I turned on the huge waterfall shower and stepped underneath. I let the hot water run down my body, washing away the smell of sinners.

My thoughts once again turned to Tess and her perfectly curved figure. Her pert breasts that bounced when she walked. He full lips that I wanted to devour. I grew hard thinking of her; I definitely needed to get her out of my system.

I palmed my erection, all the while fantasizing about her. Wishing it was her hands around me, pleasuring me. I thought of her taking me in her mouth and me lacing my fingers through her auburn hair. I continued my steady, rhythmic strokes, focusing on Tess's face in my mind. The water continued to fall over my body as I braced my hand against the side of the shower. Thinking of her made me climax quickly.

I knew that I'd last longer when I finally got to have her. I'd make her come all night if she gave me the opportunity. I'd fuck her so hard and make her feel so much pleasure that she'd forget Daniel was ever in her life.

This dalliance with Tess was just a brief encounter in my long, immortal life, but I was enjoying her company. I'd had "relationships," if you could call them that, in the past. With both humans and demons. Nothing serious, though. I got bored easily, and few could keep my interest.

I'd hurt many over the years; but that had never been my intention, though it was always a side effect.

I could be cruel, and sometimes I used people to get what I wanted, especially in the earlier days. Some of these had come back to bite me, but it was done now, and nothing could be done about it.

More recently, though, I had engaged in infrequent hookups, as that was easier. These days there were more and more willing participants who didn't want anything from me other than sex. How times had changed. Long gone were God's good old days where sex was meant for marriage only and everyone else was cast out as sinners. God had had to rethink that one recently.

I'd never used my powers to influence anyone into bed with me; they did that of their own accord. They were drawn to me, and they wanted me in ways they'd never desired anyone else.

Tess, though, was making me work hard. It just meant the payoff would be all the better. I was enjoying the chase.

I dried off, heading towards the closet to pick an outfit. Mostly dark colours—I was the Prince of Darkness, after all. I had a reputation to uphold. Plus, it always helped to blend into the shadows when I needed to.

I heard my phone buzz and found a message from Tess.

YOU HAVEN'T SENT A DRESS THIS TIME. WHAT SHOULD I WEAR?

I could tell she was teasing, though she was also asking what would be appropriate.

SOMETHING SHORT.

I immediately got a follow-up text.

SMOCK IT IS, THEN, SEE YOU SOON.

I was sure I'd still want to fuck her even in a smock.

I headed towards the door to make my way to the car. She still hadn't told me that she lived in the Upper East Side. I doubted it would be long before I saw the inside of her place, and her bedroom.

TESS

WE'D BEEN at the rooftop bar all evening; it was possibly the fanciest bar I'd visited in the city. Luke was given the best table in the place, obviously. I'd quickly gathered that this sort of treatment was a regular occurrence for him. It was, however, all very new to me and was taking some getting used to. I was beginning to wonder who this man really was.

The evening had been spent chatting, laughing, and drinking. Not too much alcohol though, especially not after last time. I felt unusually comfortable in his presence, but there was still something that lurked in the back of my mind.

I thought I sensed a darkness in him. Maybe I was just paranoid after Daniel. Emma had told me so many times that not every guy was bad. I had to trust him, since he'd given me no reason not to.

As I scanned the bar, I noticed that there were several pairs of eyes not so subtly watching us. More than likely, watching Luke.

It was no wonder, as he looked immaculate, again. Today he wore a deep plum-coloured suit with a black shirt. His shirt was left unbuttoned, showing a smattering of his black chest hair. I wanted to see what else was under there too.

Emma had helped me get ready, thankfully. Today she'd styled my hair in a high ponytail and done minimalist make-up. I'd really have to take notice of how she did it so I could recreate it myself. We'd decided on a little black dress—not as short as he'd requested, but it hugged me in all the right places. A pair of heeled boots and a leather jacket finished the ensemble. I looked good, but I knew, all eyes were on Luke.

"How do you cope with all of the attention?" I asked, gesturing to the eyes on us.

"I don't notice it, to be honest," he said.

"Are you serious? How do you not notice it? Ever since I met you, there hasn't been a single minute I haven't seen someone fawning over you. People are drawn to you."

"Not you though?" he quipped. "You apparently seem immune to my charms." If only he knew the effect he had on me, the fact that I was hotter than hell at the thought of him touching me. Jesus, sometimes when he looked at me, I felt my nipples harden like bullets.

"Thanks for an amazing evening, Luke. I've really enjoyed myself. But I should be heading home, since I have an early start in the morning." I actually didn't want to leave, but I had to make a living.

He stood up and held his hand out for me to take. "Come on, I can drop you off at the bar," he offered.

"Would you mind dropping me off at my place?" I asked. It was scary, but I decided I was okay with him knowing where I lived. He looked at me with surprise. Then, smiling, he led me out of the bar to his waiting car.

I gave his driver my address, and we made our way through the still-bustling city. We continued chatting as we pulled up outside of my condo building. He stepped out of the car and made his way round to help me out.

"So, this is me," I said, loitering on the pavement. I wasn't going to invite him up. I knew Emma would be screaming at me to take him upstairs and ride him senseless, but I wanted to wait. I wasn't really sure why, though, if I was honest with myself.

I could tell that he was waiting, so I tried to say my goodbyes.

"When can I see you again? Soon I hope?" he asked. He'd caught on that this was it and he wouldn't see the inside of my condo, or my pants.

"Text me," I said, turning away from him and making a move to the doors of my place.

As I walked away, I was grinning from ear to ear. I was determined not to look back—if I did, I'd cave. I felt his soft hand grab mine and tug me back towards him. It wasn't forceful like Daniel used to grab me, more a gentle pull.

Now that I was face to face with him, he snaked his free hand behind me, pulling me into him; he left his hand on the small of my back. His face was mere inches away from mine. It was then that I realised I had been holding my breath. *Exhale*, I thought to myself, *or you're going to pass out like some fucking damsel.*

He was looking deep into my eyes; I could feel his hot breath against my face. His breathing was fast, and so was mine. My heart hammered in my chest, and I'm pretty sure I was trembling with his closeness. *What the fuck is happening?*

I studied his face, drinking him in. His lips were full and shiny; they called to me. I'm pretty sure I had been staring at them way too long when I felt him squeeze my hand, which I hadn't realised he was still holding. I looked back up to his eyes, and I could see it—he wanted me. I could also feel it in his hard cock, which was pushed up against me.

I wanted him too—I wanted him more than anything—so

I licked my lips and parted them slightly. A sort of encouragement for him. It was all the invitation he needed.

I expected his lips to crush against mine, for him to devour me, but it was the opposite. He was tender and soft, though there was a definite need to it. It was hot, and my body tingled from head to toe. His touch brought me to life; I was ignited. His tongue gently stroked mine, and he nibbled my lip before he pulled away.

I was panting like a dog when his eyes met my gaze.

"Soon then, Red," he said, releasing me and making his way back over to the car. I was still, frozen on the spot, but I smiled at him as he got in the car and drove away.

I forced my legs to move and made my way back up to my place. Luke's kiss had had quite the effect on me, and now I was horny. It was a kiss, how the fuck had it brought me to my knees? Who was I kidding, it'd been so long since a man had touched me I probably could have got turned on just by him holding my hand.

I was feeling hot; at this rate, I'd never get to sleep, and I really did have an early start in the morning. *Cold shower*, I thought to myself and headed to the bathroom. After about ten minutes, I was cooled off and clean—well, my body was, not necessarily my dirty thoughts. *Stop it, Tess*, I thought, if not I'd have to stay in the shower for another ten minutes.

I pulled on a pair of pyjama shorts and a vest top, then brushed my long hair, giving it a quick dry and pulling it into a bun on the top of my head.

My thoughts began to drift back to Luke, and his dark, desire-filled eyes. *Stop it, Tess, you horny bitch.*

I went to check the multiple locks on the door to my condo before I headed to bed. This had been a regular routine for me for as long as I could remember, long before I moved here, when I still lived in London.

My bedroom was a decent size. There was a large

window in the room, which was surrounded by long teal curtains. I checked the fastening on the window, as I did every night, and pulled the curtains closed.

I flopped onto the generous king-sized bed. It was overkill, way too big for one person, but I had instantly fallen in love with it when I went to the store. Plus, I liked to starfish. I sank into the marshmallowy mattress, pulling the plain white bedding back and throwing the various blue scatter cushions on the floor.

I began applying coconut oil onto my skin. As I did, I thought about Luke's strong hands rubbing it in for me.

Jesus Christ, Tess, STOP IT.

I climbed under the soft white bedding and let myself drift off thinking of Luke's handsome face.

"Hey, Red, I had a feeling you wanted me to come up." Luke was seated on the end of my bed. He wore black sweatpants and a tight-fitting black t-shirt. That wasn't the outfit he'd had on earlier in the night.

"Of course, I did, I'm only human," I replied mischievously.

"Tell me what you want." his voice was low and husky.

I wouldn't tell him; I'd show him. I got on my hands and knees and crawled over to him. "Everything you've got," I purred, trying to sound seductive.

Once I reached him, I straddled his lap, placing my hands on either side of his shoulders. I was looking down at his face, which in this light was unmistakably filled with lust.

His strong jaw and slight black stubble made him look irresistible. Dark, hungry eyes focused on me, and I could see he was waiting. Waiting for permission.

I wasn't ready to submit just yet.

I leaned into him so we were almost touching and brushed my lips along his stubbled jawline to his ear. "Hands to yourself, Luke," I whispered, nipping his earlobe. I heard his breath hitch, and I smiled, pulling away.

I moved from his ear, I trailed kisses along his jaw. I could smell him, but it wasn't aftershave—it was his skin. That smoky scent that I found intoxicating.

I made my way to his soft lips, brushing my own against them. I kissed his bottom lip slowly before taking it between my teeth and biting hard. He let out a deep moan, and I swear the noise nearly pushed me over the edge. I pulled my face back, looking again into his eyes. They were now impossibly dark, with just a hint of fire. They were beautiful.

He was showing amazing restraint; his arms were still either side of him on the bed. I'd have thought he was unaffected by my closeness, but the massive bulge in his trousers told me otherwise.

I grabbed the bottom of my vest and pulled it over my head. I let my hair down and it fell over my back and breasts. Grabbing his face with my hands, I pulled him even closer. I kissed him and tried to get as close to him as I could.

Again, his body didn't move, but I could feel the twitch in his trousers. I pulled away breathless. Opening my eyes, I saw it: want, need, and desire. His eyes were on fire; he wanted me that much.

"Are you ready, Red? Is this what you want?" His voice was low and rumbled through my chest, causing me to tingle everywhere.

I was ready, so ready. I wanted him in every way imaginable, and for the first time in a long time, I wasn't scared to hand myself over to someone completely. "Yes," I said. Even I could hear the conviction in my voice.

In an instant, his hands were under my thighs, lifting me like I was a feather. He stood holding me while he kissed across my collar bone and neck. My skin was alight where his lips had touched me.

He turned and threw me onto the bed; it was clear he was in charge now. I wanted nothing more than to submit to him. He pulled off his t-shirt, showing his naked torso.

I was staring. No, I was gaping, mouth open and everything. I bit my lip, hard. His frame was athletic with perfect muscles and beautifully tanned skin. He looked like he'd been chiselled from stone. He was like some sort of demigod. Trimmed dark hair covered his chest, trailing down his stomach and beyond.

I was still open-mouthed as I took every inch of him in.

He untied his trousers and slid them down, revealing muscular legs that I wanted to lick. Fuck me he was beautiful, every inch of him.

"Enjoying the view, Red?" he growled.

"I am." I nodded in approval. "You're a bit too far away, though." I surprised myself with my forwardness.

He was on me in an instant, a blur. I didn't see him move, but I felt his lips on mine. His hands either side of me on the bed caged me in, allowing him to assault my mouth with his own. He was passionate, kissing me like our lives depended on it.

Then he stopped.

I opened my eyes, which I didn't even realise I'd closed. He was inches away from my face, but before I could ask why the hell he'd stopped, he moved to my neck and began to nibble and bite. The pleasure it caused was intense, like he'd just found a direct line to my clit.

He carried on biting and sucking down my neck until he reached my breasts. He licked and kissed them with such intensity; no one had ever given them this sort of attention. My nipples reacted in the only way they could, by going rock hard beneath his touch.

A hand cupped one of my breasts, and he pulled and tweaked my nipple with his fingers. The other nipple was in his mouth whilst he tugged and grazed it with his teeth.

"Oh Christ," I moaned loudly.

"Christ has nothing to do this, Red." I heard the laugh and felt the smile play on his lips.

He adjusted himself and, using his spare arm, moved his hand to the waistband of my shorts. His fingers were nimble, and he removed them in a heartbeat.

I was now completely naked in front of him. Normally I'd have felt really self-conscious about it, but in all honestly, I think I'd lost all of my fucking senses.

"You are beautiful, Red," he said as he stopped to admire the view.

At that moment, I wanted him with every fibre of my being. I was angry that he stopped and that he was no longer touching me. He clearly saw this in my gaze. "Don't worry, we're not nearly done," he promised, returning his attention to my breasts. This time, though, his other hand roamed between my legs.

I was ready for him, and he knew it.

His fingers brushed against me, and I shuddered. I felt him smirk. "Oh, Red, it's going to get so much better than that."

Before I knew it, two of his fingers plunged inside of me, working their magic, stroking rhythmically. He continued to graze and pull on my nipple at the same time. *Fuck, at this rate I won't last five minutes.*

He continued to move his fingers in some sort of magical rhythm, finding all the right places and making me moan and gasp.

Shifting his body, he buried his face between my thighs. Then, he moved his hand from my nipple to hold on to one of my hips while his other continued to stroke me from the inside out. His tongue began to lick circles around my clit, moving to nibble and suck it.

His touch set me on fire; everything was so hot.

I moaned his name as I felt the pressure and intensity within me growing. He sensed it too, and he concentrated all of his movements, building and building.

"Let go, Red," I heard him growl. It was a command, and I definitely wasn't going to argue with him. I'd never experienced anything like it; wave after wave hit me and he still didn't stop.

"Luke, please," I begged. It was so intense, I thought I might spontaneously combust.

He didn't stop; instead, he increased his tempo. I felt it again, surely not. No one had ever made come like this before. Another wave overtook my body, and I flung my head back, trying to catch my breath. He rode this one out and released his grip on me, allowing me some relief from the pure pleasure he'd just provided.

I managed to regain my faculties and looked him in the eyes. "Wow, that was amazing. You were amazing," I gasped.

"I'm not finished with you yet, Red," he said with a smile while removing his boxers. His gaze never left mine, and his eyes still looked like they were on fire.

I woke with a start; it was pitch black in my room. Turning on the lamp, I surveyed my surroundings. I was alone, but I was struggling to catch my breath. The sheets on the bed were soaking… and so was I.

"Holy fuck," I said to myself.

20

LUCIFER

AFTER LEAVING Tess at her condo, I'd returned to my own place. I was disappointed that she'd chosen not to invite me up. I thought I was getting somewhere, and in all honestly, I needed the release. One that didn't come from my own hand.

My pursuit of Tess was taking up a lot of time; I couldn't remember the last time I got laid, and I definitely needed something.

I was eager to gauge her feelings for me. Did I have any effect on her at all? Or was I going to have to up my game? She was really making me work for it.

My powers hadn't worked in person, but I wondered if I could use any of my other powers to gather intel. I thought I'd try and enter her subconscious; it was a neat trick and often led to good results. Well, it had in more open subjects.

I lay on the bed in my place and searched for her. I was thinking of her and only her. The red glow of her hair, the curve of her hips, the fullness of her lips—I focused and continued to search the abyss.

Then she was there; I wasn't sure whether I'd be able to

link our minds, but I had to try. Thankfully, this part of Tess was open, and I managed to connect easily.

She was sleeping—dreaming, it seemed. Time to make myself known to her. I'd never steer things into a certain way; I would follow her lead. It was her dream, after all. *Let's see what she really wants.*

I was surprised how forward she was; she knew exactly what she wanted, and she didn't hesitate to go for it. Very different from Tess in real life. God, she was even sexier when she was forward.

It was clear that she was definitely interested in me, there was no denying that from the content of her dream. I didn't do anything, just sat back and let her take the lead. That was until she wanted me to take charge.

When she woke, it snapped me out of the link, and I knew we were both feeling the same desire and the same want. It was an itch that we wanted to scratch.

I wasn't sure if I wanted her so much because she was making me work for it, or if something deeper was happening, but I was getting further drawn to her. I didn't understand it, and I needed to. I would have to find answers. There were a few loyal demons looking into it for me, but I needed something else—I needed a witch. A witch that could get to the bottom of the mystery that was Tess.

Witches had both been useful allies and a burden to me over the years. Most were dedicated, but a few had strayed. I'd check in with Bee; she'd have some names for me. I needed someone loyal that wasn't a blabbermouth—witches liked to brag, and I didn't need that.

I'd initially suspected witchcraft was the cause of the void I felt with Tess, but now that time had passed I had grown less convinced.

Witchcraft could be traced, and there was none in Tess's past. I'd be able to put a trace on her; check for past use of magic. If none was present, a witch might be able to help me find out about her father. I was sure that he was the key to everything.

There were so many unanswered questions.

Now, though, I was just pleased to know that she wanted me. I was glad. I was used to getting what I wanted. People threw themselves at me daily, but here she was, holding me off.

But now I knew we wanted each other.

I sat and wondered where things would go. I clearly just needed to fuck her, and I'd be free. I was sure once I had experienced her, I'd be free of this feeling. Then I could hand her to Daniel and carry on with the business in Hell.

21

DANIEL

As I'd stared at the photos of Tess and the fucking Devil, I'd been seething. When I finally managed to tear my eyes from them, I had expected to see the blonde woman smiling at me, but she'd gone. I'd been alone in the room—I wasn't sure how long I'd stayed, staring down at the photos and envelope. As I'd leafed through them, I'd found a card with an address—nothing else just an address.

After our meeting at the strip club I'd spent a great deal of time considering the woman's words. I had thought long and hard, and if there was any way I could get one up on that bastard and leave with my soul intact, I had to take it. Tess would be mine, and I'd be free, with my soul still my own. It was a fucking no brainer.

So, a week or so later, I went to the building—an affluent, high-end apartment block in Mayfair. I waited, though I wasn't really sure what I was waiting for. All I had was the photos and the address, so once I had gotten there I wasn't sure exactly what the hell I should do. She hadn't given me a name, so I wasn't sure who to ask for. I couldn't approach the guard in the lobby; what was I going to say, *"Hi, I'm looking for a blonde woman who knows the Devil?"*

I became aware I was being approached. A tall, thin man with black hair and a pale complexion stood before me.

"Mr. Turner, she's been expecting you. Please follow me," he said, turning around to walk away.

I didn't move, I just stood still, eyeing the man. He didn't turn to look at me; he simply said, "It's your choice, Mr. Turner."

I hesitated. I knew I was going to follow him, but I didn't want to give the prick the satisfaction. Eventually, I followed him into the lift and watched as he placed a key into the control panel. The lift began to move, and we made our way past all other floors. We continued on past the last numbered floor; we were heading to the very top of the building, which I assumed was a private penthouse. Only accessible by key so to keep everyone else out.

The doors opened to reveal a very decadent living area, all reds and golds. Very opulent. The lanky man moved out of the lift and gestured me to one of the huge red leather sofas.

"Please wait here," he informed me before skulking off.

I didn't sit; instead, I made my way over to the window and the small table that was next to it. There was a decanter with amber liquid and some glasses. I helped myself and stood overlooking the city.

"Daniel, it's a pleasure to see you again." The words were spoken from behind me, and were delivered in a silky tone. I turned to face the voice I recognised from the strip club. Fuck me, she was a beautiful woman. Today she wore a tight black suit. She had nothing on underneath the suit jacket, so I could see the outline of her perky tits. Her long blonde hair flowed in waves over her shoulders and down her back.

I was gawping, but I couldn't help it. There was something about this woman.

"Please, sit," she said.

I did immediately. She'd asked politely, but I moved the moment the words had left her mouth. It was as if she commanded it, and my body reacted without thought.

She sat on the chair next to the sofa where I sat. I studied her further, taking in everything about her. She was powerful. I could feel it; everything about this woman was impressive. I fucking hated the feeling, the sensation of being overpowered, by a woman no less. Who the fuck was she?

"Who I am, Daniel, is of little importance. What does matter, though, is whether you've made a decision?" she cooed as if reading my fucking mind.

I shook my head, trying to dislodge her from wherever she had taken up residence. She had to have been in my head. I didn't like her having the upper hand; I was in charge. Always.

"A decision?" I questioned.

"Yes, a decision. Are you willing to take what is yours and screw the Devil over in the process?" She smiled calmly.

"Before I decide, what do you get out of all of this?" I asked. I genuinely wanted to know what I was getting into.

"Daniel, we already know that you have decided to accept my proposal. I will, however, tell you my role. I want Tess dead. I know you intend to kill her, and I want her gone for good." She was matter of fact in her response, like she was talking about something far more mundane than me killing my ex-girlfriend.

"How am I supposed to do that if she's with the fucking Devil? I'm pretty sure he'd snuff me out before I got anywhere near her." The realities of the situation were dawning on me—Tess was involved with the Devil, so killing her now would be trickier. If he wanted her, then I'd never be able to get to her.

As if she sensed the sudden realisation I'd had, her features softened. "That's not a problem for us, Daniel, we have many resources at our disposal."

"Us?" I questioned, "Do you have a team working for you?"

She let out a small laugh—her demeanour never changed from calm and collected. "My children's reach is far and wide. I also have a few tricks up my sleeve," she purred.

What the fuck was this crazy bitch talking about? Children? She couldn't have been older that thirty, what could her babies have to do with anything? And tricks? We didn't need tricks; we needed a fucking miracle against the Devil.

"Look, lady, I'm not sure what your plan is, but count me out," I said, attempting to stand on my heavy legs. I looked down to see why I was struggling to get to my feet. There was a whoosh of air that rushed past me, and the woman was standing in front of me.

How the fuck did she do that? In the time that it took me to stand up, she'd crossed the room in the blink of an eye and now stood face to face with me. She was so close I struggled to focus on her.

"It's one of my tricks, Daniel," she said seriously.

"What the fuck was that?" After the words left my mouth, I realised she'd already answered my question. How did she answer before I'd even asked it? What was going on? Was I drugged? The booze I'd helped myself to must have been spiked. I shook my head, hoping it would help me find my bearings.

As if reading my mind, she made her way to the window and poured herself a glass of the amber liquid, then took a long sip. She had her back to me, as she looked out of the window—she finished the drink and set the glass back down.

"You're not drugged, Daniel, and there's nothing wrong with the cognac." She motioned towards the bottle.

"Who the fuck are you?" I spat. I was pissed off and in all honesty, a little fucking scared.

"You might want to sit," she said, and I sat immediately, almost like it was an involuntary action. I hadn't told my body to sit; it had again followed her command.

"Daniel, I'm not human. I'm a vampire," she said matter of factly, still looking out the window onto the London skyline. "I'm offering you the opportunity to become like me. I will give you immortality, and power you've never experienced. All I want is Tess, dead. Does that sound like something that would interest you?"

I laughed hard; I couldn't help myself. Was this bitch crazy? A fucking vampire? I carried on laughing, all the while watching her back as she continued looking out of the window.

"You are one crazy bitch, lady. Thanks for the laugh, but I'll be heading off now."

I was watching her and I still didn't understand what happened. She was there, and then she wasn't. It all happened in a blur. She had been standing with her back to me, and the next thing I knew she was behind me. Her hand wrapped around my throat, pulling it to one side. Something sharp pressed against my neck and I felt her warm breath against my skin. I was still sitting on the chair, but now I was held down.

I tried to move, to struggle against her, but I couldn't. This scrawny little tramp was stronger than me. What the actual fuck was happening right now?

"I'm a vampire, Daniel," she purred again, this time directly into my ear from behind me.

"How? What?" were the only words I could manage. To be honest, I was surprised I managed to form any words.

She released my neck, but I couldn't move. I was frozen; still, I strained to hear anything, but there was just silence. Then I saw her out of the corner of my eye, rounding the side of the sofa and coming to stand in front of me. She was silent when she moved, and there was no noise from the stilettos she wore.

I tilted my head up as she stood in front of me; it was the only movement I could manage. Then she straddled me and placed her finger under my chin, further tilting my head back. As I looked into her eyes, I noticed they were now glowing bright, blood red.

In that moment, I saw them. Two perfectly white, pointed fangs that were nestled below her full top lip. She must have noticed me staring at them, because she licked her lips and then licked one of the fangs, leaving her tongue pushed against the bottom. I saw a drop of blood leave her tongue where it met her fang. She was obviously making a point, showing me how sharp they were.

Oh shit.

I was fucked.

"Why do you want Tess dead? Who is she to you?" I questioned, not sure what else to say. Tess had never mentioned anyone like this woman—what was her connection to Tess?

"I want Lucifer, that's all I've ever wanted. I, therefore, want Tess gone, no longer a part of his life." I could feel the rage in her, and things began to click into place.

Lucifer was to her what Tess was to me, an Achilles heel. She wanted him at any cost and would do anything to get him. We were the same; we'd do anything for the ones we loved.

She edged her face closer to mine and looked directly into my eyes, and it felt like she was talking to my very soul.

"The choice is yours, Daniel. Join me and become a vampire. Take what Lucifer is hiding from you, or continue as you are. Weak and insignificant, never able to find Tess again." She lowered her voice, again whispering into my ear, "Time to make a decision."

This woman was powerful, and I wanted it. I wanted to exert that same power over Tess, have her quake and beg before me. There was no question in my mind; I was taking this chance. I was already in over my head, why not add another deal to the mix?

"What's your name?" I asked the woman before me. She held all of the cards, and I didn't even know her name.

"Lilith," she said alluringly, still straddling me and looking deep into my soul.

"Well, Lilith, I accept your offer," I said with as much conviction as I could.

With that, she moved in a blur, and I felt the prick of her fangs sinking into my neck.

2 2

TESS

I'M COOKING AT MINE TONIGHT. I'LL SEND A CAR TO PICK YOU UP AROUND 8 PM. SEE YOU THEN, RED.

IT WAS A TEXT FROM LUKE. He was going to cook for me, and at his place? Now I was nervous; I hadn't been to his place before, but I wanted to. I was nervous, but it felt good— butterflies at the thought of seeing him again.

I LOOK FORWARD TO TESTING YOUR CULINARY SKILLS.

I added a winking emoji to the end of the text; I wondered if he was cooking or whether he'd be getting someone to do it for him. There was something sexy about a man that could cook.

It had been a month since we'd met in the bar and we'd spent a lot of time with each other. I was enjoying myself. He affected me more with every meeting.

I knew that going to his place might lead to something. Sex, it might lead to sex. After my very steamy dream, I clearly wanted it, but was I ready? It had been a long time since I'd given myself completely to anyone the way I wanted to give myself to Luke. Daniel had been the last, and look how that turned out. I'd given myself to him in that way at the start of our relationship, when he was loving and gentle and not the monster he turned into.

The one-night stand I had just after moving to the city wasn't the same; that was just sex. And not very good sex either.

This thing with Luke was something different.

Get a move on, Tess. At the rate I was moving his driver would be waiting outside for me. I showered and headed to my closet to pick an outfit. If this was going to be the night, I need to have amazing underwear. I decided on an emerald-green lace bra with matching lace shorts; it was sexy, but not too much. I pulled on a pair of dark blue jeans and a black silky camisole top. I left my hair in loose curls and applied simple make-up—not as glamorous as when Emma helped me, but she was working today, so I was on my own.

I didn't look too shabby. Black heels and my leather jacket finished my ensemble. I spritzed myself with my favourite perfume and grabbed my bag. I studied myself in the mirror. *"You can do this, it's just dinner and possibly sex,"* I said, giving myself a pep talk.

With that, I left my condo and headed down to find the car Luke had sent waiting for me. As we weaved and manoeuvred through the city traffic, I realised we were heading to Chelsea. *Is this where his place was?* It was an affluent area, and the buildings were unreal. Of *course*, he lived somewhere like this; I don't know why I was surprised.

We pulled up outside a gorgeous, industrial-looking building. Luke's driver opened my door for me, and I followed him. He opened the entrance door for me and urged me to go through. He didn't follow me in, though, and I saw him disappear down the corridor.

I called out hello, but there was no answer. I could hear loud classical music playing through the massive high-ceilinged space. I was only in the entranceway, but I knew it was going to be grand. I took my jacket off and hung it on the coat rack. I wasn't sure what to do, as he wasn't there to greet me. I decided to leave my shoes on; I had no idea if that was the right call.

The place was breathtakingly beautiful. I was taking in every inch of it as I rounded a corner into a vast living space. I was glad Luke wasn't there waiting for me because I stood open-mouthed and whispered *"fuck,"* mostly to myself.

The living area was probably bigger than my entire condo. It was double-height, so it immediately felt huge. A frosted glass wall spanned the entire right-hand side of the room. I couldn't make out what was behind the frosted glass and assumed it must be some private balcony. To the left was a massive fire that was roaring, kicking out a fair amount of heat. Two huge black sofas had been placed on either side of the fire with a sleek white table in the middle. It was decorated minimally, but it was so stylish. A large modern chandelier hung from the ceiling, though it wasn't on. Instead the room was lit with the fire, some smaller lamps, and lots of candles.

Romantic, I thought to myself, swallowing hard. He was definitely pulling out the stops.

I carried on through the space, following the amazing smell to where I presumed the kitchen was. As I turned, I saw him with his back to me, stirring pots and pans on the massive stove in front of him.

I stood admiring his muscled back for a little while. His perfectly crisp, white shirt stretched across his broad shoulders. The sleeves were rolled up, showing his lean forearms. His firm backside was contained in black trousers, but I could still see its perfect form. He must have been aware I was there, as he turned with a huge grin on his face. He walked over to me and placed his hand on the small of my back, pulling me to him and planting a warm kiss on my cheek. I tingled at his contact; he was something else.

"Would you care for a drink? I have the best 1787 Bordeaux," he asked, pointing to an old-looking bottle on the counter.

"Yes, thanks," I said. I had absolutely no clue about wine; my knowledge was limited. If I was ordering wine, it would usually be house white or house red; I wasn't going to admit my naiveté to Luke though.

I watched as he poured the wine into an exquisite long-stemmed glass. Then he walked over, handing it to me. He watched me with anticipation as he sipped his own drink. He cupped the glass, bringing it to his lips seductively. I wished I was the glass—or the wine, I really didn't care.

Realising I'd been staring at him too long, I looked down at the glass and took a sip of the rich red wine. It was bold and fruity but so incredibly smooth; it was the most amazing wine I'd ever had. My eyes fluttered closed with the taste, and I let out a little moan. I opened my eyes again to see him fixated on me.

"Good?" he asked, already knowing my answer.

"Exceptional," I replied, trying to regain my composure. He continued to watch me as I took another sip.

"I hope you're hungry." He grinned at me as he moved around the kitchen with ease. It smelled amazing.

"Wow, you really are the full package aren't you?" I teased. He laughed and carried on stirring and chopping. "Your place is amazing. How long have you been here?" I asked.

"A while now," he replied. "I have homes all over, as I travel a lot for work. I'll give you a tour of this place after we've eaten." He gestured to beyond the kitchen where I hadn't yet seen.

My heart raced at the thought of seeing his bedroom. *Get a grip, Tess, you're not a stupid fifteen-year-old girl.*

I snapped from my thoughts as he appeared in front of me, holding his hand out for me to take. I held onto him, and again the sparks ignited as soon as our hands touched. He led me to the living room and headed to a huge table that was set for dinner. I'd somehow missed it when I entered; I wasn't really sure how, as it was imposing. He pulled out a chair for me, setting my wine on the table. Then, he disappeared off to the kitchen.

He returned with two plates of restaurant-quality food. It smelled absolutely divine, and I studied the meal before me— beef Wellington with mashed potatoes, roasted vegetables, and a rich-looking sauce on the side. The beef Wellington was cooked perfectly, medium-rare, just how I liked it. How did he know?

"I hope it's okay? I wasn't sure how to cook it so took a chance." He grinned.

"It's perfect, thank you," I said, cutting into the amazing meal. Every single morsel melted in my mouth; it was unreal. Just as good as the meal we'd had at the restaurant.

We laughed and joked while eating, and we stayed there talking after we'd finished our plates.

"Dessert?" he asked.

"You've made dessert as well?" I loved dessert and definitely had a sweet tooth.

He stood and took our plates away, heading to the kitchen. While I waited for him to return I studied the room and sipped my wine—it really was a good wine. I tried to peer through the frosted glass doors but couldn't make anything out. I jumped when he placed a plate in front of me.

"Shit," I squealed. "You frightened me."

He just laughed and made his way to his seat, placing his own plate down. The dessert was so fancy looking. A perfect pastry tart, with soft white mousse, and it was topped with a mango which had been rolled to look like a flower. "Did you make this?" I was gobsmacked.

"Wait till you try it," he said, raising his eyebrows in a smug way, as if I was about to taste heaven.

I took a piece of the tart on my fork and slipped it into my mouth. The different flavours and textures hit me all at once and made my eyes go wide with shock. Crisp pastry, smooth vanilla mousse, and a tangy yuzu curd hit me with a sensation I wasn't expecting. I jerked my head in Luke's direction, as if now understanding what he was talking about.

"I have many talents, Red," he said, his voice dripping with sensuality. I felt my stomach tighten.

When we'd finished eating, we chatted for a while, before he once again got up and held his hand out for me. This time he led me to the sofas, placing my glass of wine on the table in front of me. He'd been continually topping it up through the night, so I was completely lost as to how much I'd drunk. I didn't feel drunk though—it was probably the food cancelling it out.

While he was clearing the plates, I decided to kick off my shoes and curl up. I was so comfortable.

He returned, carrying his glass and another bottle of the wine. Placing the bottle on the table, he sat on the same sofa, at the other end though. He draped one arm over the back and held his wine glass in the other. His legs were crossed, with a foot resting on the opposite knee. He looked regal, like he was sitting on a throne. I was staring again—it wasn't lost on him, but he didn't say anything.

I, however, was less graceful. My feet were tucked underneath me as I made myself at home on the marshmallow-soft sofa. I wouldn't do that just anywhere, but around him it didn't seem weird. We sat like that for a while, comfortable in each other's company, chatting and laughing. I was having a really good time.

"So, do you want the tour now, Red?" he said, standing and placing his glass on the table in front of us. He moved towards me, once again holding his hand out for me to take. An invitation, willing me to go with him.

I took it, and he pulled me up to him so we were facing each other, very close, very intimate.

We stared at each other for a while before he breathed. "You've obviously seen the living area and kitchen. Through there is the pool."

"Sorry what?!" I said in astonishment. *Did he really just say pool?* I had to have misheard him.

Still holding onto me, he brought me through the frosted glass doors, the ones I thought had led to a balcony. When we stepped through my eyes scanned the space, taking in the long pool that stretched nearly the entire length of the floor. It was breath-taking.

"Wow, this is amazing," I said, gesturing to the pool before me. "I have to go to the gym and share a pool with usually no less than ten other sweaty, hairy men," I laughed. It was no joke, though.

"You like it?" he asked, searching for my reaction.

"It's perfect," I said with a huge grin.

"Care for a dip then?"

23

LUCIFER

She looked taken aback by my invitation. "I don't have a swimsuit," she said with genuine disappointment in her voice.

"That's okay, we don't need them." I grinned as I began to unbutton my shirt. As I slowly undid the buttons, she stood still, watching my every move. I slid the shirt off, letting it crumple to a heap on the floor. I unzipped my trousers, and allowed them to fall before stepping out.

She was still looking—never once did her gaze leave me. I now stood in my boxers in front of her. I let her admire the view for a while before I stepped towards the edge of the pool and dove in.

Resurfacing, I turned to find her still watching me. "Come on in, Red, the water's lovely."

She remained at the side of the pool and looked hesitant, like she was weighing things up in her head. I continued to tread water, waiting for her to join me. I knew she would; I just had to wait for her, like with everything else.

Then she took the hem of her top and lifted it over her head, revealing a green lace bra that made her eyes stand out more than they already did. She'd already taken her shoes off when she decided to curl up on my sofa, so she just had to unbutton her jeans and remove them. I continued to watch her as she slid the jeans down her long legs and then stood up straight.

Fucking hell.

She had on matching lacy shorts, and the lingerie made her body sing and mine scream. The colour looked bold against her ivory skin, which I knew would be so smooth. The style accentuated all of her curves, and I could see her nipples were hard through her bra. Now *I* was staring.

At that moment, she was the most beautiful creature I'd ever laid eyes on. I shook my head as if to shake away the feeling that engulfed me; *fucking get a grip of yourself.*

As I looked up at her face, she was grinning at me, and then she gracefully dove in. You could tell she swam regularly; she was toned in all the right places. I watched as she swam under the water, only resurfacing at the other end of the pool. She turned to face me as she smoothed the water from her hair, still smiling—she looked genuinely delighted.

"You approve?" It was clear she did from her face.

She swam over towards me. "How the hell could I not?" She paused for a moment before carrying on hesitantly, "I imagine all the other women you've brought here approve as well?" She was jealous. I smiled to myself knowing that I had her.

"I've got a past, Red, everyone does, and I'm not ashamed of it. What about you? What about your past?" I tried my best to steer the conversation away from my sexual history—shit, if we got onto that, we'd be here for weeks. Probably months, fuck maybe even years.

I could tell she was uncomfortable with the question and I already knew everything anyway, but I was curious to know how much if anything she was willing to share. Did she trust me enough to tell me?

"I've been single for a few years now, taking some time after my last relationship." She paused for a while, and I continued to watch her. "It was abusive," she said quietly.

I swam over to her. "I'm sorry, do you want to tell me about it?"

She took a moment, and then proceeded to tell me about Daniel: how when they'd first met he was sweet and loving, how everything was great that first year. How she didn't even realise she was being isolated from the people she cared for until it was too late, and how he became aggressive and angry with her. How he hit her for the first time. Rage filled my body; I was looking forward to that fucker ending up in Hell, and I'd take a personal interest in his eternal punishment.

She must have sensed my anger, as she reached out and stroked her finger down my cheek. "Don't you dare feel sorry for me. It happened, and now it's done. Without it, I wouldn't be the person I am today." With that, she again took off under the water. I continued to watch her as she swam lengths.

I moved to the edge of the pool so I could get a better view. I had my back to the wall with my arms outstretched on the tiles outside the water. I watched her elegantly glide through the water, tumble turning at each end of the pool and continuing on. She was so graceful, even in the water. I wondered if maybe her father had been a merman. I'd have to mention it to the witch that I was going to ask to look into Tess's origin.

Lost in my thoughts, I hadn't realised she was swimming towards me; I snapped my eyes to her as she reached the side of the pool next to me. She placed her arms outside of the pool, crossed in front of her, her breasts pushed up against the tiles. Resting her head on her arms, she turned to face me and smiled. She closed her eyes, clearly very content in this moment.

I continued to study her perfect skin and face; my eyes travelled under the water to her legs and her perfect ass. As I continued looking up, I noticed a scar on the side of her ribs, near her bra. I knew what it was from.

"Stare much?" I heard her say, a smile evident on her face.

I leaned my hand across to her, and reached my fingers out, as I gently brushed them against her scar. "What's this from?" I questioned. Would she tell me?

She let out a sigh before answering, "I had a collapsed lung. They had to put a chest tube in, but the wound got infected. Hence the scar. It's faded a lot; sometimes I forget it's there." She paused before looking away and carrying on, "I'll always have a permanent reminder of my time with Daniel though," she said softly.

I absentmindedly continued to caress her side and the scar, hoping she would feel comforted by my touch. "I'm sorry that happened to you," I said, turning to face her.

Her breathing quickened; I could feel it as I continued stroking her side. I didn't want to break the contact. I could feel our excitement grow, the neediness of it—it had nothing to do with my powers. My touch was having quite the effect on both of us.

Fuck, my touch was gentle, not overtly sexual, but here we both were acting like we never had sex before. *Well, maybe my touch isn't that innocent*, I thought to myself.

I edged closer to her and moved my hand from her side to under her chin so I could take in all of her. I leaned forward, placing a gentle kiss on her lips. To my surprise, she parted her lips and kissed me back. Soft and tender. I licked her lips with my tongue before searching her mouth. Her tongue met mine, and the two stroked and danced against each other.

I deepened the kiss; it was hotter now, needier. With that, she turned her body to me, wrapping her arms around my neck and her legs around my waist. *Oh fuck*, she felt so good.

I cupped her backside with my hands, pulling her to me as close as I could. I wanted there to be no distance between us. I wanted her so much in that moment. Who am I kidding? I'd wanted her that much since that first moment in the bar. I wanted her more than I wanted anything in all of my years. I needed her.

I pulled my mouth from hers, and breathed heavily. My eyes focused on hers. She was watching me, waiting for my next move. But this had to come from her; I needed her to want it as badly as I did.

"Are you ready, Red? Is this what you want?"

Please, let her say yes.

TESS

IT WAS WHAT I WANTED, with every *fibre* of my being. I wanted his hands roaming over my body, his mouth nipping and licking every part of me. I wanted everything about Luke in that moment. I had done since I first met him, but I'd been too scared to admit it to myself. Now I wasn't scared; I was ready.

I could tell that he wanted me too—I could feel his hardness pushed up against me. My legs remained clamped around his waist as I squeezed onto him.

I looked into his eyes and kissed him gently, nipping at his bottom lip. I nodded.

"I need you to say it, Tess," he panted.

He'd used my name, and it sent shivers directly to my core. "Luke, I want you," I breathed huskily. It didn't even sound like me. The voice was all desire and need.

At my words, he walked through the water with my legs still wrapped around him; I clung on, knowing I was safe. He was heading away from where we'd dived into the pool, to the opposite end of the room. I expected him to put me down when we arrived at the stairs, which stepped up gradually out of the pool, but he still held onto me, kissing and grazing his teeth along my jaw. I had my back to wherever he was taking me, so I had no choice but to trust him.

He pushed us through large frosted-glass doors, all the while licking and sucking my neck. My head fell back at the sensations he was creating inside of me.

He stopped walking and placed me gently back on my feet in the middle of the room. We were in a plush marble bathroom with a massive bath to one side; a stack of fluffy towels was piled next to it. He walked over and picked up two of the towels, and wrapped one of them round me; he was so tender. He rubbed and dried my body with the super-soft fluffy fabric.

Using his own towel, he quickly rubbed his hair, which now hung around his face in perfect black waves. He threw the towel into the corner of the room and tugged mine from my hands, throwing it into the same spot.

Stepping back towards me, he tipped my head back with his fingers and placed a kiss on my lips. He snaked his hands around my back and squeezed my backside while kissing me deeply. His tongue searched my mouth with fervour.

I got lost in how long we were there kissing, both adrift in the pleasure of it. My hands were draped around his neck so I could hold on and steady myself from the pleasure. His hands remained securely on my arse, pulling me to him and crushing our nearly naked bodies together.

I let out a little squeal when he once again hoisted me up. I could feel him smiling through our kisses at my surprise. My legs once again wrapped around his chiselled back, like they instinctively knew what to do—like they belonged there.

He moved with purpose, and I felt my back against another set of glass doors—I flinched at their coldness. His hands gave my thighs a comforting squeeze as he continued his deep kisses.

He pulled away, looking deep into my eyes, watching me greedily.

We were in a bedroom, I could tell, but I couldn't process any of the details. All there was, was him.

Luke.

This man who had swept into my life and made me feel things I hadn't felt in a long time. Crap, things I'd never felt with *anyone*. Not even in the beginning with Daniel. These feelings were all new, and I wanted more.

He gently laid me on a massive bed and moved back to admire me.

"Fuck, Red," he growled. He actually growled the nickname I'd affectionately come to love.

I propped myself up on my elbows, looking him up and down. He returned the favour, scanning my body from head to toe. He was drinking in every inch, every curve of my body.

Then he moved, slowly and with purpose. His hands were on the bed as he crawled up towards me. The muscles in his strong arms flexed with every movement. He stopped at my ankle, kissing and nipping, slowly making his way up my calf, my thigh, still grazing me with his teeth. Farther up, across my stomach, my chest, stopping to kiss each breast before continuing. Up to my neck and my chin until his whole body was above me.

Once there, he crashed his mouth onto my already swollen and flushed lips. It was a needy, desperate kiss, and one of his hands moved, gently brushing against my hardened nipple. My back arched instinctively towards him. Holy crap, that was hot.

He deftly moved his hand round my back, unclasping my bra and pulling it off. He'd freed my breasts from their confinement. My nipples pebbled against the hot air of his breath. He grazed his teeth across them, and I tried to stifle a moan.

"Louder, Red, I want to hear you," he said, smiling up at me.

He continued to tease and suck my breasts, and then I felt him move lower, brushing featherlight kisses against my ribs, my stomach, and farther still until he grazed the top of my lacy shorts.

He moved his hands lower to either side of my shorts, slowly pulling them down my legs and throwing them to the floor. He kneeled up, looking at his handiwork, revelling in my nakedness.

"Red, you're exquisite," he breathed. His need was evident in his boxers; he really did like what he saw.

Then it felt like he moved in a blur. He was nibbling the insides of my thighs with his teeth, grazing them, licking them, making his way to my core. His tongue pushed against my clit, and I moaned loudly.

"Good girl," he growled against me.

He continued his attentions, licking, swirling, and sucking—it was Heaven. Then without any warning, his fingers plunged inside of me, and I gasped. He stroked, moving his fingers in and out, all the while never removing his talented mouth from my clit. *Fucking hell,* this was unbelievable. He knew exactly what he was doing.

He found a particular spot that felt unreal, and as if he could sense my pleasure concentrated all his movements on it. I felt my muscles clench around his fingers, willing him to be farther inside of me. My back arched and my hips thrust against his hand and mouth.

I could feel it building and building; it was a need. I needed him to keep going—I was so close. "Please, Luke," I moaned while grabbing onto his hair, holding on tightly.

He upped his tempo; I was going to come. I clenched around him as I crescendoed into the most amazing orgasm I'd ever had.

"Oh Christ," I moaned loudly.

"Christ has nothing to do with this, Red." I'd heard him say that before. In my dream, my very intimate dream. *What the fuck?* I propped myself up on my elbows so I could see him. I was dazed and breathing heavily from the pleasure he'd just elicited from me. I looked at him, and he grinned at me—it was a coincidence, it had to have been.

I watched as he backed off the bed. He stood at the end, studying me intently. He grasped either side of his boxers and slipped them down before stepping out of them. I took him in, every inch of his athletic body. He was unreal, like no man I'd ever seen before.

"Stare much?" He smiled, using my own words against me. I couldn't respond—words evaded me, and I continued to stare. He leaned forward on the bed, crawling up on all fours until he was above me. His body engulfed me but there wasn't actually any contact between us.

His face hovered over mine. "Ready for another round, Red?" he asked, voice sounding gruff.

I lifted up to capture his mouth with mine in a needy, desperate kiss. I was ready; I ached for him to be inside of me. He leaned into me so I could feel his hardness pushed up against me. We both moaned at the contact of our naked bodies.

Then he pulled away, breaking our kiss. His hands pushed me back as they made their way to my breasts. His fingers lightly grazed them on their way lower down my body till they found their goal. He pulled my hips towards him in a fluid motion, never once taking his eyes off me.

He was watching me, likely wanting to see my face when he entered me. He moved slowly and with purpose as he pushed inside of me. Slowly, too fucking slow. I wanted him, needed him to fill me with everything he had. I tried to move my hips to take all of him, but his grip was too tight. He watched, not saying anything as he continued to slide into me until I felt his hips against mine. My breath was gone; oh my God I felt so full.

At that moment, I felt complete, like something had awakened inside of me.

"Look at me, Tess." I heard him growl out the command. I didn't even realise I'd closed my eyes again. I opened them, finding his dark eyes, which looked like they were burning like embers. Not just with desire, but like actual fucking embers.

"Is that all you've got?" He knew I was mocking him, but he grinned that knowing smile as he slowly pulled out of me and repeated his actions, slow and rhythmic. His hands once again found my breasts, pulling and tweaking my nipples as he watched my every reaction.

He increased his tempo, and I clenched around his length.

"Fuck. Keep doing that, Tess, don't stop," he rasped.

I didn't—I kept squeezing tightly, as he pounded into me. Over and over again, still attending to my breasts. Then he was kissing me, desperately, biting on my lip, hard. I gasped as his bites timed with his thrusts.

My arms went to his back, and I dug my nails into his flesh, raking them down while still gripping his shaft with everything I had. I was close, literally about to explode from within.

He sensed it, again kissing me desperately, pushing me farther and farther. Then I was gone, driven over the edge into a state of ecstasy. My body convulsed involuntarily when wave after wave of pleasure overtook me. He carried on until I could feel he reached his own climax, thrusting deeply into me as he panted loudly.

He collapsed on top of me, breathing heavily into my neck. His hot breath elicited goosebumps on my sensitive skin.

He moved to lie next to me and pulled me to him, resting my head against his chest and wrapping me up in his strong embrace. I smiled against his body, feeling content.

In that moment I felt safe. I snuggled up against him as we both fell into a comfortable position. My eyes felt heavy, and I quickly fell asleep in his embrace.

25

LUCIFER

I FELT something heavy on my arm, wondering what it was. I opened my eyes from the deep slumber I'd fallen into. Bright auburn hair was spread across my chest, and I smiled. Tess was still asleep, curled up in a ball half sprawled over my chest and arm, the rest of her spread out on the bed.

I couldn't see her face from where she was sleeping, but I knew she would be just as beautiful as she had been last night. Since she had been the moment I first saw her.

My thoughts drifted back to the events of the previous night. How she'd willingly given herself to me in every way. She opened up about her life, let me into her past, and let me into her. The sex was unreal. I'd had a lot of sex, but she was exceptional. It felt so different with her—it felt like home. Which was fucking crazy.

Having her once wasn't enough. I'd wanted to keep going —I'd wanted to go all night—but it was clear from her snuggling into me that she was tired, so I relented and let her sleep.

I'd thought once I'd had her, once I'd quenched my thirst for her and satisfied my need, I'd be free of the feeling. I thought I'd be able to move on from this woman who was a complete enigma to me, move on from the feeling that had me tethered to her.

From that first moment that I'd seen her in the bar, I was drawn to her like a moth to a flame, bemused by her lack of apparent interest and desire to brush me off.

I'd convinced myself once I'd had sex with her that it would be over, but the complete opposite had happened.

I wanted her more.

I wanted everything about her.

This was a unique feeling for me; I'd had connections with a few people, but nothing to this same level. I'd never experienced someone like Tess in all of my years. It was more than sex—was I falling for this woman?

I knew I wanted to make her smile and laugh, to make her happiness my number one priority and keep her in a state of bliss. Most importantly, though, I wanted to protect her, keep her safe. Safe, and away from that asshole who'd hurt her, who'd tortured her and made her feel less than worthy.

One thing was certain; my deal with Daniel was void. I couldn't hand her over to him now, not ever. I would kill him myself before I ever let him lay a finger on her.

I needed to speak with Bee immediately. I sent her a link asking her to join me at my place as soon as she was available. Linking was something I was able to do with my demons and other fallen. Angels and werewolves were the only other creatures I was aware of who could do it. It was a form of mental communication. I knew it wouldn't be long before Bee turned up at my place but, I wanted to leave Tess to sleep—she'd earned it.

I gently slid out from under her. She let out a little moan in her sleep, and the desire to wake her up and fuck her all over again rocked me to my core. I could not get enough of this woman. She rolled onto her back, exposing her breasts, her hair falling away from her face. I was right; she was just as beautiful as she had been last night. Her lips seemed fuller today, probably still swollen from the kissing and biting.

I watched her for a while longer before remembering I'd summoned Bee. Pulling on a pair of black bottoms, I made my way to the kitchen to make a coffee.

When I arrived, Bee was already there, perched on the countertop and waiting for my entrance. "Coffee?" I offered.

"Strong, four sugars, milk." It always amused me that she took her coffee like that. I'd expect her to take it black, but she had a sweet tooth, hence the sugars. "What's up?"

"Tess is here, in the bedroom, so let's just try and keep the volume down can we?" I really didn't want Tess hearing any of our conversation—it would have taken a *lot* of explaining. Bee made a surprised face before nodding in agreement.

"I take it you summoned me in relation to Tess, then?"

I moved around the kitchen, making coffee and avoiding the question. Which was stupid, because that's the only reason I'd requested her to come to my place. *Come on, Lucifer, pull yourself together*, I chastised myself.

"I need to know where we stand on reneging on an agreement." It was a fact and not up for discussion.

She said nothing and instead studied me for a while, placing her hands on the counter and leaning her body back. She looked relaxed, but I could tell she was anything but.

"Depends on the agreement," she finally said.

"You know good and well what I'm talking about, Bee, don't be obtuse." She was pissing me off.

"I'll have to check with the other side, as you know all too well this has never been done before. We've *always* completed our obligations. This would be completely new territory."

She was right; I'd never backed out of an agreement before. Therefore, I didn't know the issues—or should I say *complica-*

tions—that might arise. Of course, we'd need to consult the other side. They'd take this as a sign that I wasn't fulfilling my duties. God would definitely have something to say about it.

I hadn't realised Bee was looking at me intently, studying the face she had known for so many years in bewilderment.

"What is it, Bee? It's not like you to hold your tongue." It was true, she'd always been one hundred percent open and honest with me about everything. It was extremely annoying.

"Why are you doing this? What is she to you?" There was no malice or contempt in her question, just genuine willingness to know the truth.

I sighed, raking my hand down my face. The face I'd worn since the dawn of time. I wondered at these new feelings I was experiencing, unsure of how best to explain it all to her.

"She's special, Bee. I don't know what it is, but I don't want to hand her over. Even if she doesn't want to be with me, I can't let him have her. I can't allow him to end her." It was all I could offer her; I had nothing else that made any sense.

She waited for anything else I could give her, but I had nothing. I didn't understand it all myself. Hell, I didn't understand any of it.

"I need your help with another matter. I need to find a loyal witch. Someone who specialises in family ties and origins. She's blocking me and is immune to my powers, and I need to know why. I think it has to do with her father. Can't be her mother, she was human. Whatever is going on with her stems from whoever her father is."

"You're telling me that she's completely unaffected by you? Nothing? No reactions at *all*? It's been years since someone has been able to resist. Wait, is this why you want to negate the contract?"

"Partly. I thought that it was just her immunity to me that

made me want her more, and I was sure once I'd fucked her that I'd be free of her, free of whatever the fuck is going on, but…" I stopped myself from saying the last bit, unsure of how to say it.

"It made you want her more?" Bee answered for me. I nodded at her. What the fuck was I doing? I was the leader of Hell, father to all demons, punisher of sinners—and I'd been brought to my knees by a woman.

Bee broke the silence which had filled the room. "Leave it with me. I'll see what I can do about the agreement and the witch." She'd be loyal to the end, and I was thankful for it. "I'm still waiting for my coffee though," she said with a laugh, lightening the mood.

"Shit, sorry." I finished making the drink and passed it over to her.

"Thanks. Look, while we're on this whole subject, I've got bad news. I thought it would be more of an annoyance, but now, knowing everything you've just told me, I think we might have a serious problem."

"Is it Hell, or something to do with Tess?" I asked.

"We can't find Daniel," she replied immediately.

"I'm sorry? What do you mean we "can't find" him?" Had he just disappeared off the face of the Earth?

"We had men watching him in London. They'd been able to keep tabs on him fairly easily, and then all of a sudden he vanished. No one has been able to find any trace of him. He's been off our radar for four days." She seemed skittish saying the last part aloud, and for good reason.

"*Four days?*" I bellowed furiously.

"Hey, don't be like that with me. I only found out last night. The demons trailing him thought he would show up, so they waited to mention anything about it. When they realised he wasn't going to, they didn't know what to do."

She was right; it wasn't her fault some of my people couldn't do their jobs.

"Tell me everything," I said in a softer tone.

"He hasn't been back to his apartment; we've had people stationed at all his go-to places, but nothing. He's gone, Lucifer," she said, shaking her head.

He couldn't be gone; he had to be hiding somewhere. Maybe he'd gotten protection, a spell or charm. Perhaps he was already dead and stuck in Limbo. That would solve a lot of problems.

"Have you checked Limbo? Has he already joined us?" I queried hopefully.

"First place I looked last night after I was informed of the news. He's not there. We know for sure that he hasn't gone upstairs, so that means he's still in this realm somewhere, albeit very well hidden."

"What about his work?" I knew he was obsessed with his job, the high-pressure environment boosting his ego.

"Nothing. Like I said, we have people stationed everywhere, and there are no signs. His apartment has been empty for several days, and it doesn't look like he's packed any of his belongings to take a trip. Everything is like he left it. We have eyes everywhere, and everyone has their ear to the ground to find out any info we can. We'll find him, Lucifer," she said confidently—she was a loyal soldier and a good friend.

"Thank you. I appreciate the hard work you've put into this." I knew I'd have to go to London, to his apartment, so I could see what I could find. "Up for a trip to London?" I asked.

"I'm ready when you are," she replied, hopping down from the countertop.

"I need to check everything myself and get a feel for what

he's been up to," I told Bee. I knew the slimy bastard was up to something; hopefully his place would hold some answers.

I walked over to the counter, placing my drink down. "Give me fifteen minutes, and we'll leave. You wait here while I speak with Tess." I looked up to see her smiling, looking past me.

I turned to see what she was looking at, only to be met with Tess in one of my t-shirts and some of my boxer shorts. She looked between me—half-naked—and the woman in my kitchen. She smiled at both of us, but it didn't reach her eyes, I knew she wasn't happy.

Shit.

26

TESS

I STRETCHED out on the bed, feeling for him and finding only emptiness. I was expecting to see him next to me, but I couldn't feel him. I brushed my hair off my face and opened my eyes to search the bed for him, but I was alone.

I sat up and realised I was still naked from the night before. I blushed at the thought of the incredible night we'd had. Emma was going to be so proud when I told her everything. And insanely jealous too.

I pulled the sheet up over my chest as I sat thinking of the previous night. It was incredible, effortless, and so unbelievably hot. Usually, the first time with a new partner was clunky and awkward, figuring out each other bodies, likes, and dislikes. Mediocre at best.

But last night was something else, and I was shocked. He was so at ease with my body and I with his. I felt content at his touch. He was so generous, which I wasn't used to. Daniel was in and out, little care given to my needs, as long as he came that's all that had mattered.

Luke, though, was all about me and my pleasure. He'd

been so attentive to me and made me come like I never had before.

He knew exactly what he was doing. I suddenly felt sick. *Is this what he's like with everyone?* If he was that confident with my body, was it because he'd had plenty of practice? I felt jealous, jealous of those before me. I didn't want to think about him with other women.

I shook my head, attempting to shake the thoughts away. I realised that he had definitely been there when I'd fallen asleep—I remember snuggling up to his chest. I didn't normally fall asleep so easily, but I'd felt so at ease in his presence—I was also exhausted from the many orgasms Lucifer had bestowed on me.

The feelings I was experiencing for Luke I'd never felt before; I was comfortable being completely myself. Goofiness and insecurities included. I felt that he was someone special and the thought of where things could go excited me. *Calm down, crazy, it's only been a few dates.* I tried to rein myself back in, but it was proving very fucking hard.

When we'd come into the bedroom last night, I was too distracted to take in my surroundings, a little too focused on other things. Now, though it had my full attention, all I could say was Jesus Christ.

Luke's bedroom was immense. Bigger than most New York apartments. The bed I sat in was larger than any I'd ever seen, and I wondered to myself what size it was. Much bigger than a king-size. I'd have to ask him.

The bedding was all black. I hadn't noticed last night, again since my attention was elsewhere. It was luxurious and soft—the rest of the room decorated in white and gold, very regal and plush. As I took everything in, I realised it was all very high end, as was everything with Luke.

I wrapped the sheet around me like it was a towel so I could move around the room. I made my way off the bed, which felt like descending Everest. Wanting to see the view from there, I headed over to the massive floor-to-ceiling windows that covered one side of the room.

As I got closer I realised they were doors which led onto a balcony. I slid the handle and stepped out, making my way to the edge of the railing. As I took in my surroundings, I was in awe of the view. You could see the river and Madison Square Garden; this was prime real estate right here. I blew out a breath thinking about how much this place cost—it had its own pool, for God's sake.

Just then I heard a raised voice; I thought it was Luke, so I made my way back into the bedroom. As I strained to listen, I could hear his voice, and another, a woman's voice. *What the fuck?* Had he really left me alone in his bed to go and chat with another woman?

Calm down, you crazy bitch; I chastised myself. It could be anyone; it could be his mother, for all I knew. *Oh shit, what if it's his mother? Pull yourself together, Tess.*

I thought that I'd venture out to where the voices originated from, maybe not just wearing a sheet though. I made my way through to the bathroom, which I remembered was beyond the glass doors.

As I pushed through them, I was once again left catching flies, mouth gaping open from surprise. I really need to learn to control that. I remembered the marble and bathtub from last night, but I honestly hadn't taken in the finer details. Marble tiles from floor to ceiling covered the bathroom, and the bath was sunk into the floor—it could probably fit about six people. My mind wandered back to the enormous bed and wondered if Luke was into orgies and needed the space.

Don't be stupid, I told myself. *That would be crazy.* I hoped I was right, and my imagination was playing tricks on me. I continued to scan the room, finding a shower enclosure which occupied the end of the room nearest to the pool. It had a large waterfall shower overhead, as well as several other showerheads attached to the wall. I wasn't exactly sure what they were for, unless they were for all your solo masturbatory needs—showerheads could be very useful in dry spells. I'd used my own on many occasions when the mood took me.

I made my way over to the twin sinks and vanity; a mirror spanned the entire length of the unit from the back of the sinks up to the ceiling.

I studied my reflection in it, half expecting to be met with a bird's-nest hairstyle and panda eyes. To my utmost surprise, I found neither. The little make-up I had applied had held up well with my eyes still looking bright; my skin had a glow to it. Getting laid and having multiple orgasms clearly agreed with me. My hair was a bit wild, but I could sort that easily.

I freshened up using the things available in Luke's bathroom, noticing some toothpaste and mouthwash. I used both; I would most definitely need it—no one could escape morning breath.

I raked my fingers through my hair, smoothing it as best I could. I decided to try and fashion it into some sort of bun wrapping it on itself. It wasn't perfect, but it would do.

Not too shabby, I thought, peering at myself in the mirror. I looked presentable enough. I made my way back into the bedroom and began searching for my clothes. I looked for a while before I realised I'd left them near the pool when I stripped out of them last night. *My underwear should be here, though.* I carried on looking but found nothing; *where the hell did they go?*

Shit, now what am I supposed to do?

I noticed a recessed doorway; I thought it might be Luke's closet. Hopefully, I could find something in there to wear. My hunch was right, but the size of it was unexpected.

There was row upon row of designer suits, various button-up shirts, and more shoes than Macy's. There had to be something casual somewhere.

I headed over to some drawers and pulled them out to find boxer shorts. I pulled out a pair of black ones and stepped into them. It was a start. Moving on to the next drawer, I found more boxers. I was sure he didn't need that many pairs. Did he only wear them once? Moving on, I finally found some t-shirts, all black. I picked one up and slipped it on. The makeshift outfit would do for now until I could make my way back to the pool and gather my clothes. It was better than a sheet.

I made my way out of the bedroom and slowly edged towards the voices, trying to listen in as best I could. Luke was definitely one of them, and the other belonged to a woman. I was sure it was a woman now. *Don't overreact, it could be anyone*, I said to myself, trying to calm my anxieties.

As I walked the smell of freshly brewed coffee hit me, and I realised at the same time that I was starving. My stomach grumbled loudly. Shit, the last thing I needed was my stomach giving me away when I was trying to be stealthy.

Rounding the corner, my eyes met a muscular and naked back. I noticed there were light scratches; I may have been a little rougher last night than I'd thought.

He was only wearing a pair of jogging bottoms that hugged his hips. He was so sexy. One hand was leaned against the countertop, and he held a cup in his other. I smiled at the sight of him.

Then my eyes fell beyond him and his delectable back. They fell on a woman, a stunning woman with black hair and a killer body. I continued smiling, trying my best to make it believable, but in all honesty I was livid. I knew it was ridiculous. I had no hold over him; we'd been on a couple of dates

—we'd had sex once—but I couldn't help my possessiveness. It took me by surprise.

She smiled back at me, and it was at that moment that Luke turned; he saw me and smiled broadly. He said something, but I was in a world of my own and hadn't taken it in. "Sorry?" I mumbled.

"This is Bee; she works for me, has done for years. She's my most trusted advisor," he said, making his way over to me, planting a gentle kiss on my lips. "Coffee?" he asked.

"Please, just milk, thanks," I replied, "Nice to meet you, Bee." I flashed her a sickly, sweet smile.

"The pleasure is all mine, Tess. Oh, and don't let Levi hear you say I'm your most trusted. You know how he can get," she laughed. Luke joined in with her, and I felt like I was missing the joke—of course, I was, I didn't know who they were.

"How long have you two known each other?" I questioned.

"As long as I can remember," Bee answered while Luke nodded in agreement.

There was definitely something between the two of them, but I couldn't quite figure out what it was. Were they friends and colleagues, or did they have any other history between them? I could try and figure it out on my own, or I could just ask him after she'd gone.

Luke made his way over to me, passing me the coffee he'd just made. "Thanks," I said, smiling. He was so handsome.

"Red, Bee is here because there's been a problem with an item in London. I'm afraid I've got to leave for a few days," he said, studying my face and searching for my response.

Fuck, I thought to myself. This was it, I'd read too much into it, made something out of nothing. I'd created something that wasn't there. He'd gotten what he wanted, and that was it. How could I have been so stupid? Obviously someone like him didn't want someone like me.

I composed myself, trying to sound as nonchalant as possible when I said, "No problem." Inside I was screaming.

"You could come with me if you like?"

Did he seriously just ask me to go to London with him? Really? The look on Bee's face was not lost on me—surprise and shock, only for a second though. He clearly hadn't told her about it.

"You want me to go to London with you?" I had to check that I wasn't going crazy and hadn't imagined the whole thing.

"Yeah, it'll only be for a couple of days, and then we'll be back. Bee is coming too, since we have business to attend to. That shouldn't take too long, though, so I'll be free the rest of the time," he answered, still leaning against the countertop, his muscles taut.

Fuck, I couldn't go back there, not while Daniel was still in the city. So much had happened. I was a different person now, but I couldn't risk the chance of bumping into him, especially not with another man. Daniel would likely kill both of us. I had to come up with a believable excuse.

"I have a few jobs that I can't get out of," I lied. "I'll just catch up with you when you get back though?" I continued.

"Of course, I look forward to it, Red," he said with a smirk.

Maybe I'd overreacted—Bee *was* just a colleague and friend. It was *me* he wanted to spend time with. I sipped my hot coffee, but the warm feeling I was experiencing had nothing to do with my drink.

27

LUCIFER

BEE HAD MADE her excuses and left Tess and me alone. She'd been surprised at my invite—in all honesty—so had I. I'd only asked her to come because I knew she wouldn't. That wasn't to say that I didn't want to spend time with her, I really did, but it was more that I couldn't look for Daniel if she was with me. As expected, she had declined my invitation by saying she had work she couldn't get out of. It was a lie, but I didn't push it.

As soon as she saw Bee in my kitchen, I knew that she'd start to question things, and herself. I didn't want her to feel like that, so I'd asked her to come with us, since I figured that would at least reassure her that I wanted her with me.

My invite had thrown her, I could tell. She put on a good show, but I could see she was shocked. I had started to be able to read her, although this was just our connection and nothing to do with my abilities. I had spent so many years around humans I had been able to pick up their tells and subtleties. She was on edge.

I made us some breakfast, but that wasn't what I was

hungry for. If I wasn't going to see her for a couple of days, I needed to be close to her again; I needed my fill of her.

Three hours later, I finally said goodbye to her. I could have spent all day exploring every inch of her body, but I had pressing matters to attend to. I kissed her gently as she left my place, telling her I'd be in touch as soon as I had an idea when I'd be back.

As she left, I watched her ass sway.

"Perv," she said, grinning over her shoulder at me. I smiled as she disappeared from sight.

After she'd gone, I linked Bee to tell her I'd be ready in thirty minutes. That would give me a chance to get showered and changed. Sure enough, half an hour later, she was in my kitchen.

"Where's Conrath?" I asked. I'd wanted him on this; he'd been useful in the search for and surveillance of Tess, so I trusted him. Clearly, the others on the job before him weren't up to the task. I'd be having words with them soon enough.

"He's outside Daniel's apartment building waiting for us," she answered.

I portaled us both to Daniel's building. Bee could portal, but there was no point in us both doing it. Different demons all had various ways of getting around. Some had to use the old-fashioned methods, but as Bee and I were fallen, we could use portals. Portaling did sap Bee's strength a little though, and I needed her at one hundred percent in case we ran into any complications. I was unaffected, since I had more power than she did—as much as it pissed her off.

As we got to the building, we saw Conrath outside, and he moved to join us. "Sir," he greeted me, dipping his head slightly, showing his respect while not trying to gather too much attention.

"What have you got for us?" I asked, eager to get the matter sorted out.

"He hasn't been home for several days. His work colleagues haven't seen or heard from him, and neither have any of his neighbours. No social media activity or posts, which is very unusual for Mr. Turner," he relayed.

"What was his last known location?" I asked him.

"His apartment. He headed out and seems to have just vanished," His face was contorted, not his usual self. I could feel his irritation needling at him. He wasn't impressed by his fellow demons' work on this one. "It is possible that something could have happened to him. I've checked the hospitals, and he hasn't been admitted. He may be dead."

"No," Bee interjected. "If he were dead he'd be in Limbo, but we've checked thoroughly. I knew it was unlikely, but I checked with upstairs, and he hasn't gone up there either." She was always so conscientious—it must have been hard for her to do that. She had complicated feelings about our previous home.

I dismissed Conrath; Bee and I could handle this one, and I wanted him to continue the search.

We portaled directly inside—I was happy to go inside uninvited. If he was there, I didn't care if he was offended by our sudden intrusion.

As expected, it was empty.

His apartment seemed very sterile to me; there was no heart to it—little decoration. Lifeless and stark.

We made our way to the kitchen. Fruit on the countertop had started to decay, and the empty dishes that had been left in the sink had begun to smell. Bee and I exchanged a look of disgust. It appeared he'd left in a hurry.

The living room search proved fruitless; there was a large L-shaped sofa with a huge television fixed to the wall. He had a variety of game consoles and games—it definitely came across as a bachelor pad. I couldn't imagine Tess having ever lived here, and there was no trace she ever had.

"Lucifer," I heard Bee call from another room. Making my way to find her, I entered Daniel's bedroom.

She'd pulled out a drawer to find a large supply of condoms, more than he would ever need. I rolled my eyes. He was a fucking prick.

We continued to go through his drawers and found a large stash of bondage gear: ball gags, whips, restraints, varying-size butt plugs. I wasn't surprised by this find, and in all honesty, I'd expected it.

Then my blood started to boil at the thought of him using them on Tess, her being tied up and at his mercy. We knew he had none, considering all he'd done. I clenched my fists into balls, and my nails dug into my flesh. My jaw had clenched without me realising.

I'd make that fucker pay.

My anger passed as quickly as it came. I had to focus, concentrate on the task at hand.

We made our way to the last room, his office. Bee sat down behind the computer and began tapping away. She was very tech-savvy and definitely enjoyed this side of things. It wasn't long before I heard her say she was in.

I continued looking around the room, searching for any type of clue I could find.

"Nothing," she sighed, frustration clearly evident in her voice. "Just work, and a huge amount of porn. Most of it very… unsavoury," she continued. "There's a folder on Tess too, nothing major: photos of them together, previous searches, copies of the restraining order. He searches the internet at least once a day for her."

"There has to be something here. I can't believe he just disappeared without a trace."

I made my way over to the desk where Bee was seated and leafed through the documents. Nothing really worthy of note: bills, bank statements, various work documents. Then as I moved one piece of paper, I found a large brown envelope. It looked out of place amongst everything else.

I picked it up, opening the top and tipping the contents onto the desk—then stopped in my tracks. They were photos, at least fifty I'd say, and staring up at me was my own face. Tess and I together, laughing and joking.

Bee stood from behind the desk and came to join me, then looked through the photos. "Shit," she breathed. "These are recent, Lucifer."

She was right; they'd been taken in the last few weeks. There were photos of us walking in Central Park on the day she was taking pictures. Shots of our night at the rooftop bar. There were photos of nearly every time we'd been out in public together.

As I spread the photos out across the desk, I came to the last one, me kissing her softly outside of her apartment.

I was raging. I could feel the heat of Hell's fire bubbling through my veins, and I was all too aware my eyes had gone red. It was becoming hard for me to maintain my human form. At times, I couldn't hold myself back, and I was getting close to that right now.

Bee was continuing to scan the photos, then she looked up apparently sensing the shift in me. "This wasn't Daniel. Before he vanished he was in London, so he couldn't have taken these. We know he never left the country."

"So who the fuck took them?" I bellowed.

TESS

As soon as Emma found out I'd spent the night at Luke's place, she was on her way over. We'd decided—or should I say she'd decided—we needed drinks and gossip. She'd want to know every single detail, and she'd be able to tell if I was holding back; she always could.

I was pulling on some comfy leggings and an oversized tee when I heard Emma's familiar knock. Constant banging, she was very impatient. I made my way to the door, then undid the numerous locks I had on it. As soon as I opened it, she bounded in nearly knocking me over.

"Oh my God tell me all about it, he was amazing, wasn't he? I bet he had a huge di—"

"Wow, Em, calm down," I managed to butt in before she could finish. "We've got all night. I'll tell you everything, just let me close the door first, so the whole floor doesn't know about my sex life."

"I'm just so pleased you finally *have* a fucking sex life. Oh, and I brought these." She held up a large bottle of tequila and some margarita mix. I didn't say anything; instead, I moved to the kitchen and opened one of the cupboards, pulling out the same two bottles.

"It's going to be a good night," she said, laughing loudly.

I made us some margaritas and got all the food ready for later so I could throw it in when we were drunk, hungry and had the munchies.

Pizzas and nachos were prepped and ready to go. I was a good cook, but I knew that this occasion called for quick, easy food. We'd want to spend most of the time drinking and chatting, not cooking.

Once that was sorted we moved to the living room and put on some music as background noise. It was one of my favourite rock stations, not so much Emma's thing, but she didn't grumble.

She flopped down onto one of the sofas, nearly spilling her drink in the process. "Shit, sorry," she mumbled, licking the spilt drink off her fingers. "I'm just so excited. Tell me everything. I mean *everything.*"

I told her all about how he said he would cook for me and that he sent his driver to pick me up. She whistled, wide-eyed when I told her where his place was.

"Wait till you hear this…" I paused for dramatic effect, and she rolled her eyes at me. "It has its own pool—not the building, his actual place has a pool in it."

"Are you fucking kidding me? I knew I shouldn't have let you have him," she said, laughing.

"Em. His place was unreal; his living room was bigger than my entire space." I gestured towards my comfy living room. I carried on with all of the details, describing his place and the food that he'd cooked, and the amazing wine. She proceeded to Google it and found out the wine was about five hundred dollar a bottle. *Fuck, I think we polished off about four bottles.*

"Tess, as impressive as all that is, you know fine well that I wanna know about the good stuff. Every. Single. Detail," she said, wiggling her eyebrows at me.

"Right, let's get some food and more of these and we'll get to 'the good stuff,' as you put it."

The pizzas were ready, and our drinks had been topped up, so I was all set to spill all of the details to Emma. I wouldn't hold back—I couldn't—not from Emma.

"So you slept with him, how did it start? Did he make the first move or did you?"

"Well things got a little heated in the pool, and then everything just sort of progressed from there. Before I knew it, we were naked in his bedroom, getting down to business." Thinking about it was getting me a little hot.

"So come on, I need the details," she begged.

I proceeded to tell her about how he'd gone down on me and that it was incredible, and then after that we'd had sex. I told her how he'd been so gentle to start, but that he soon became more needy and rough. How I'd clung onto him for dear life as he made me orgasm again. She looked pleased.

"I'm so fucking pleased for you. I honestly thought you were a fucking born-again virgin. It's been far too long since you've been laid," she said, laughing and making the sign of the cross over her chest.

I laughed along with her. "Honestly, Em, it felt unbeliev-able, like it was meant to be."

"Thank you for all the details, but I think you seem to have forgotten the most important one," she said, putting her palms together and then slowly moving them away from each other, a smirk on her face.

"Let's just say I wasn't disappointed," I said while moving her hands even farther apart.

Her eyes widened as she mouthed *fucking hell.*

"It wasn't even that though, Em. He just knew exactly

what he was doing, what to touch and when." I shivered at the thought of his touch, and Emma laughed.

"I like him, Emma. I really like him," I said quietly.

"That's amazing. What's wrong, though? You should be over the moon, so what's with the face?" She looked concerned.

I carried on the story about how Bee was there when I'd woken up, and she was with a half-naked Luke in his kitchen. How they'd apparently known each other years and that she worked for him. I told her about how the pair of them had gone to London together, and that he'd asked me to join them. My mind wandered back to Bee though. I just wasn't comfortable with her, though I was sure it was probably just my own insecurities.

"You have to trust him, Tess, especially since he's given you no reason not to. Plus, he wouldn't have asked you to go to London with him if there was something between the two fo them. No one does that," she said. I knew she was right, but ignoring the voice in my head was hard. The one that told me I wasn't good enough.

I went back to the kitchen to fetch us more margaritas; by this point, we were well on our way to being wasted. It was a good night; we laughed, joked, ate, and continued to drink and drink. The margaritas were going down too easily.

I told Emma how he'd messaged me to let me know that they got to London okay and that he missed me. She let out an "awwwww" while also pretending to gag with her fingers down her throat. I threw a cushion at her, which hit her on the head and caused her to fall back on the sofa.

He'd also said that he couldn't wait to see me again and that as soon as he was back, he'd be over to see me. I believed him, because I felt exactly the same way.

But there was just something I couldn't quite put my finger on. I thought I'd worked through so many of my issues since coming to New York, but clearly I still had a way to go. I wouldn't let my insecurities ruin this for me. I decided to ignore the feeling, bury it as deep as I could. I needed to; I wanted to give this a chance. A real chance.

"Come on," Emma slurred. "More margaritas." She moved to refill the pitcher.

We drank and laughed until the early hours when Emma crashed out on the sofa and began snoring loudly. I placed a blanket over her and headed to my bedroom.

I managed to brush my teeth; I knew if I didn't, my mouth would feel like death in the morning. I climbed into my huge bed... well, I had thought it was huge until I saw Luke's. I'd have to ask him where he got it—oh and if it was for crazy orgies. Maybe I wouldn't ask the last bit.

I decided to send Luke a text.

HPE YOU'RE BUSNESS ISS GOING WELLLL, MISS YOU. LOKING FARWARD TO SE YOU SOON XXXXX

My phone buzzed with a response—I hadn't expected him to immediately reply.

YOU'RE DRUNK. GET TO BED, RED, AND SLEEP IT OFF X

How did he know I was drunk? I then realised my message was littered with mistakes and it was 3 AM. Didn't take a genius to figure it out. I was looking forward to seeing him again. I'd show him just how much I'd missed him.

29

LUCIFER

After the developments in London, I needed to speak with the team in Hell. As a result, I had created a portal to take Bee and me there immediately and arranged a meeting with the guardians.

Now in my inner circle, I paced, wondering where the fuck that little prick was. I was going to end him myself; I didn't care about any possible consequences. Once that was done, I'd enjoy punishing him for eternity. I was going to personally oversee that. Maybe I'd make him watch me and Tess fuck for the rest of time. That ought to piss him off.

It was hot in Hell, as usual. My inner circle, however, was different from the rest of Hell. It was my home. As a result, it was smaller than the other circles and situated in the most secure part of Hell. As with all of my places, my home in Hell was plush and luxurious.

It was just like any other home, save for the unusual location.

I made my way to the bathroom, wanting to rid myself of the memories and images from Daniel's apartment. I felt grubby, mainly from finding his bondage gear and the vast amount of sick porn he had on his computer. Normally I wouldn't care, but the thought of Tess being involved with this scumbag made my skin crawl.

I was showered, clean, and dressed, ready to make a plan with those I trusted most. We had to sort this mess out, and I wanted it finalised quickly so I could move on, whatever that looked like.

We'd arranged the meeting in Limbo, and all eight of the guardians would be there—none of them would dare refuse a request. Not even Bee or Levi. They were friends, but they knew how things were.

Most people thought Hell was underground. It was a common misconception, but I could understand where the confusion had come from. The heat, the rock formations, and of course, the burning red glow. It wasn't all fire and brimstone, but that was definitely part of it.

In order to reach Hell you'd have to go through the gates, and those were underground. Rather than leading to the centre of the Earth, though, they led to the realm of Hell. The pearly gates were up in the clouds and led to the realm of Heaven. Most people, therefore, thought Heaven was up in the sky and Hell was underground—not quite.

The gates to Hell were actual flames. When a soul entered for the first time, they would have to walk through them; this would lead them to the realm of Hell. They would experience the literal pain and discomfort of the flames; it only got worse from there. It was a baptism of fire, and most souls *should* only enter once.

I say most souls, as we had over the years experienced escapees. Those who had slipped through the cracks under sloppy guardianship. We always found them, though, and it had never ended well.

Demons who entered Hell, however, would suffer no ill effects. To them, it was just like walking through any other set of gates. Demons were free to come and go as they pleased. Many did just that, but there were some, like Abaddon, who never left the realm. That was his choice and the choice of a few others.

Demons who came and went would have to be sworn into the Legion of Hell. Without that allegiance to Hell, they wouldn't be permitted entry. Disguised angels had attempted to breach the gates a couple of times but never made it through; their fealty was to the Celestial Army.

The gates were well protected; Hell Hounds stood watch as well as spells and incantations. Many other hidden protections were in place too, and only a few knew of those. There was a need for such measures in case anyone tried to bring us down. A couple of angels had, over the years, attempted to rid the world of us, but it was impossible. Both sides needed to exist for balance. I knew that better than most—after all, God Almighty himself had created us.

I made my way through Hell to the meeting. It was very different now from what it was in the early days. We'd made it into our home, and each circle was different from the others, but the cavernous rocks, heat, and blazing blood-red sky was the same no matter where you were.

I reached Limbo to find all of my guardians ready and waiting for my arrival. Good. They were prompt. I was glad I didn't have to reprimand anyone. I was saving all of my aggression for one purpose, and he would feel every last bit of it.

As I entered and made my way to the head of the conference table, all rose from their seats and bowed their heads. Even Bee and Levi. It was expected of them; although they were all-powerful, I still commanded the respect of all those below me. It was a necessity. I'd been challenged many times, but I was still here, standing as the Master of Hell.

"Ladies, gentlemen, thank you all for coming. While we

are all together, I'd appreciate an update on your circles. Are we having any issues?"

One by one, the guardians updated me on the affairs relating to their circles. They informed me of their current numbers, problems, and things that appeared to be going well. Everything wasn't running smoothly, though—just like everything else.

"Levi, while I'm here I'll join you to handle some of your more problematic inhabitants as we discussed. Is that agreeable to you?" I asked the giant man to my left.

"Thank you, my Liege, that would be most useful." He tipped his head in thanks.

"I'm aware some of you are requiring more help with your circles; let me know what you need, and I'll look into some recruitment. We'll have to see what we have to work with, of course." Not everyone could be trusted with torturing souls. It was a skilled role, and some weren't right for the job.

It was about time I got to the point; I'd called them here for a reason, and that was to tell them of everything that had happened over the last couple of months. Although they had no say in the matter, my actions could affect them if things took a turn.

"I'm sure you all know why I've called you here. It's true that I intend to renege on a deal." No one said anything, but a few exchanged side glances with each other. It was a big deal —since the beginning, nothing like this had ever occurred. "The deal was to deliver a girl to a Mr. Daniel Turner; I do not intend to carry out this request, as I want the girl for myself." I thought it best to be as vague as possible, since I didn't want them knowing any more than I needed them to. I trusted them, but my own personal business was just that. Personal.

I didn't want anyone perceiving me as weak. For all they

knew I wanted Tess for sex and sex only. In all honesty, I didn't actually know why I wanted her, I just did. More importantly, I didn't want *him* to have her.

I waited, wondering if anyone would question me or make any comment. Instead, there was only silence.

"We do, however, have another problem," I continued. "It appears Mr. Turner has vanished." I detailed to them what we had found in London—in particular, the pictures of Tess and I together, although not what we were doing in the photos. They didn't need to know that.

"Who do we think would do this? The angels?" asked Mammon, the guardian of Greed. He was a demon who had been in his post the least amount of time compared to the others, only six hundred years or so. In that time, he had proved himself worthy of the role. He hadn't been overly qualified in the beginning, but Levi vouched for him, and that went a long way with me.

"That, we have yet to establish, but I want everyone on this. Keep an ear out for any information you may become privy to. If you hear anything at all, no matter how trivial, I want to know *immediately*."

"It must be someone who knows what they're doing," Mammon continued, rubbing his black-stubbled face. He was in his demon form, so his mottled, black-and-red skin was on show. He had wild black hair which sprouted from all directions of his head.

All demons looked different, and just like humans, they all had their own little quirks.

Mammon was an oni demon. He was large in stature, bigger than Levi. All oni were large in size, even the women. He had one large horn that protruded from the top of his head, though others of his race had two, sometimes three horns. As he continued rubbing his cheek, I was more focused on the large tusks that jutted out from his mouth. He was right; it was someone who knew what they were doing. "I take it he's not dead, or we wouldn't be having this conversation," he finally continued.

"No, Bee has looked into both sides. He's still out there somewhere. Whoever is helping him has hidden him from us; therefore, it must be someone with the skills and knowledge to pull this off. I was unaware the photos were being taken." I clenched my jaw. It had *royally* pissed me off that I hadn't sensed we were being followed and spied on, especially since I'd been too focused on other things.

"We need answers on this, and quickly. If you come up with any theories, contact me immediately. I will take the link straight away," I told them.

"Yes, my Liege," they all said in unison with a dip of their heads. I waved my hand to dismiss them, and they all dispersed except for Levi.

"I hope you've got something good for me in your circle, Levi. I've got a lot to release and intend to unleash actual Hellfire." I wasn't joking. What better way to unburden some of my rage than visiting those souls who were here to be punished?

They would suffer today, that was certain.

30

TESS

WE WERE MEANT to be at the bar about 9 PM. It was now 10:30 PM, and we'd only just left my place. His poor driver had been waiting in the car all of that time—I genuinely felt bad.

Luke had been early. He'd knocked on my door at 7:30 PM to pick me up for the night. I'd had every intention of leaving straight away, and I was ready to go. It had been clear from the look on his face, however, that that wasn't going to happen any time soon.

As soon as I'd opened the door, he'd pushed me against it kissing me passionately. He slid my jacket down my arms and his hands found my arse. Before I'd known what was happening, he'd hoisted me up. My legs had instinctively wrapped around his waist. *What is with that?* It was like they had a mind of their own.

He'd pushed the door closed behind him and moved us to my bedroom before he threw me on the bed. "I've missed you, Red," he growled. "I intend to show you just how much."

We'd spent the last two hours reacquainting ourselves with each other's bodies. It'd felt so good; *everything* about him felt so good. He'd been right; he had shown me just how much he'd missed me. I'd been floating on a high of orgasms, unsure if I'd ever fully stop my legs from shaking.

I'd apologised to the driver as soon as we'd gotten in the car, though he'd politely told me there was no need to. With that, we'd set off. Luke placed his hand on my knee, slowly moving his hand farther up my skirt. I clamped my legs shut as I glared at him.

"Spoilsport," he said with a pout.

He moved his hand and laced it with mine and gently began to stroke my thumb with his own. It was the smallest thing, but it made me tingle. This tiny little gesture tugged at my heart. What the hell was going on? I was sure he was doing it absentmindedly, but it made me feel there was only the two of us in the whole world.

After chatting, and getting shit-faced with Emma the other night, she'd convinced me to be more open to him. To let my guard down and let him in. I'd done just that. While he was in London we'd spoken on the phone several times, and he was constantly sending me messages to check-in. He was so thoughtful.

He'd only been in London for four days, but it had honestly felt like four weeks. I could no longer deny the connection between us or my developing feelings.

I was trying not to get carried away, though. He was, after all, God's gift to women, and I wasn't sure of his feelings for me. I knew he was enjoying our time together, but beyond that I couldn't read him.

We arrived at the bar and were taken to the best seats in the place; I expected nothing less, since that was just the way things were in his world. The best of everything. Was I the best though? Did he really think that out of all the women here tonight, who were all clearly fawning over him, that I was the best?

I tried to push the thought to the back of my head. *They aren't with him, Tess, you are,* I chastised myself.

We drank, laughed, joked—oh and made out in the bar. I was having a great night until I began to feel unsettled. Like we were being watched.

I scanned the room, searching for anything that could be to blame for the uneasy feeling that had made base camp in my stomach.

Then I saw her. A stunningly beautiful woman who sat at the bar. She was early fifties, with long, flowing brown hair and a figure to die for. She wore a short black dress that didn't really leave much to the imagination, though I think that was the point. The word cougar sprang to mind.

As I moved my eyes to take her in, I realised she wasn't watching me at all. Well, not at that moment anyway. Her full attention was on Luke; her eyes looked hungry.

The uneasy feeling was gone, replaced by another sensation, jealousy. She was looking at Luke like I wasn't even there, like I was invisible to her. He was everything, and I was nothing.

I'd had the same feeling when I'd first seen Bee in his kitchen. It was a new sensation, one I'd not really experienced before.

I turned my attention back to him; I smiled as he continued to talk. I'd zoned out though—I was no longer sure what he was talking about. My focus was broken, now singled in on the woman.

Turning again to see if she was still eye fucking my date, I was surprised to see her staring directly at me. Our eyes locked. I'm pretty sure that hers narrowed, I think with disgust. Definitely disgust, if the rest or her face was any indication. She wasn't attempting to hide her dislike for me.

"Red, is everything alright?" Luke asked, startling me for a second before he followed my gaze to the woman at the bar.

"Sorry, I'm fine. What were you saying?" I tried to say calmly, though my cracking voice was failing me.

"I need to make a business call. It's quieter outside. Would you be okay if I step out for a second?" His smooth voice soothed me.

"Of course, I'll be here. Take as long as you need." I tried to be cool; I didn't want him to go, though. The woman might follow him, seduce him while he was on the phone. Jesus, I needed to get a grip.

He leaned in and kissed me gently before making his way to the door that led outside. My eyes immediately returned to the bar where the cougar in black had been sitting.

The seat she had occupied was empty. *Shit*, I thought. She hadn't wasted any time. I continued to scan my surroundings, watching the door to see if I could see her follow Luke outside, but she'd gone, and I couldn't find her.

I wanted to sprint to his side to check, to make sure she couldn't get to him. I tried to calm my overactive mind. *Try and be normal, Tess, please.* I reached into my clutch and pulled out my compact, then set about reapplying my bright red lipstick.

Not too shabby, considering Luke had smudged it all across our faces back in my condo. My lip curled into a smile as I thought back a couple of hours. My dirty memories were, however, interrupted by a cough.

I lowered the compact and was taken back by the sight before me. The cougar stood at the end of our table, arms folded across her chest and a stern look on her face.

Neither of us said anything; we were both still eyeing each other, attempting to suss the other out.

"Can I help—"

"You need to leave this bar and him. You are not worthy to even be in his presence, never mind being on his arm," she spat with such disdain and hatred.

"Excuse me?" I said defiantly. "Who the hell do you think you're talking to?"

"I know people like you, and you're not deserving of someone like him," she said matter of factly, like the words that she was speaking weren't vile or cruel. It was almost like she was asking about the fucking weather.

"I think you need to leave me the fuck alone, lady, before we have more of a problem than we already do."

I was done talking to this rude, crazy bitch. I closed my compact and began to slide it back into my clutch. She began to move closer, but stopped dead in her tracks at the sound of Luke's voice.

"Do we have a problem here? What do you want?" he said, addressing the woman, indifference in both his voice and face.

The cougar's whole demeanour changed in an instant—I'd never seen anything like it. Before she was confident and dominant, now she was meek and timid.

"Sir, forgive me, I was just speaking with this young lady," she replied quietly. I had to strain to be able to hear her above the sound of the music.

"What about?" Luke asked casually. He took a seat next to me and placed his hand on my thigh.

I saw the cougar's eyes widen at his actions. She was *definitely* not pleased with the situation. "Sir, I was telling the lady that she is not worthy of you. That she should leave and never see you again." She was a bitch, but she never once looked him in the eye. She was clearly in awe of him, and somehow he held power over her.

"Excuse me?" Luke replied, clearly becoming more pissed with every word that came from her mouth. "You need to leave. Now," he commanded.

The cougar was having none of it, however. She stood her ground, although still not making eye contact with him. How did she know him? Did she work for him and that was why she was calling him sir? And what the hell made her so sure I wasn't "worthy" of him?

"Sir, please," she begged. "She is no one, an insignificant, you must see that?" Her whole demeanour had creeped me out.

"Stop!" Luke bellowed at the woman, causing her to take a step back. She seemed to dip into a sort of bow. I have to admit that the outburst scared the shit out of me; I hadn't expected that response from him.

"Who in the fuck are *you* to tell *me* who I can spend time with?" He waved a hand in my direction but without looking at me and continued, "She is mine, do you hear that? Mine. Now get the fuck out of my sight. If you aren't gone from this bar in ten seconds, I might end up doing something that I regret. Now go!"

People in the bar were looking at the scene in front of them, and I shrank back away from their stares, from the cougar, and more importantly, from Luke.

He'd frightened me. His outburst had come from nowhere, and it took me by surprise. I'd never seen this side of him, and in all honesty, I hated it. It reminded me of Daniel and the many scenes he caused throughout our relationship.

I realised the woman was gone, nowhere to be seen. I hadn't seen her leave, but she was no longer in the bar.

"Was that necessary?" I asked. I tried to keep my voice as calm as I could, attempting to stop it from cracking.

"It's not up to anyone else what I do with my life, Tess. You're mine, end of discussion," he said dismissively. He wasn't even looking at me when he said it; instead he scanned the bar, likely making sure she had left.

"Excuse me," I said as I stood up.

"Where are you going?" he said sharply.

"To the bathroom, if that's allowed?" I replied with a frostiness in my voice. I didn't wait for a reply before I moved away from the table.

I made my way to the entrance of the bar where the toilets were. As soon as I knew he could no longer see me, I darted over to the doors. Stepping outside, I took a deep breath and tried to stop my heart from hammering in my chest and my body from shaking.

I managed to hail a cab straight away, then jumped in it quickly so he wouldn't follow me. The cab moved away from the bar and headed through the busy traffic.

Fuck this. I couldn't go through that again; I didn't need another fucked-up, possessive man in my life.

31

LUCIFER

I HATED WITCHES.

Well, that might be an oversimplification of the issue. In general, most witches were loyal to a fault. They were incredibly useful, but in all honesty, I tried to avoid them as much as I could.

They always thought they had something to offer me, something new that I'd never seen before. They all thought they were worthy of me, and many had promised they could provide me with an heir. In all honesty, I'd never thought of having a child, so I'm not sure what they thought telling me that would accomplish.

I'd been with witches over the years, but they always got more attached and read into things that clearly weren't there. I was in it for sex, and that was my only motivation. They, however, thought that because I'd slept with them that they were now my soulmate.

A couple had become obsessed, to the point that I'd had to reveal my true form to them. That, unfortunately, did not have the desired effect; they'd instead believed I was baring my soul and that by revealing myself I was declaring my affections. Fucking crazy witches.

I'd never seen the one that had approached Tess before, though that wasn't uncommon. I didn't know every single unholy creature personally. They knew me, though.

I was livid with the gall of the woman. Who the fuck did she think she was to presume to tell me who I could and couldn't spend my time with? She was lucky I hadn't torn her head from her neck where she stood. Instead, I'd let her leave, couldn't really allow Tess to see my darker side.

To be fair to Tess, she'd held her own against the woman —gave as good as she'd got. But I knew it would play on her mind. She'd already mentioned the amount of attention I got, and it was clear that the interaction would affect her. I'd have to handle the whole thing carefully.

I sat, waiting and waiting. I checked my watch and realised it had been about fifteen minutes since she'd gone to use the facilities. An uneasy feeling hit me, so I decided to give her a call.

No answer.

The uneasy feeling in my gut grew, and I made my way through the crowded bar, ignoring the multiple looks I got on the way. I had to find Tess, get to her and make sure the witch hadn't caused too much damage.

I pushed through the door and made my way into the ladies' bathroom to find her; she had to be in there. The bathroom wasn't massive, and there were a few women at the vanity, applying more lipstick and running their fingers through their hair.

"Why hello there, handsome. I think you're in the wrong place—unless you were looking for me?" said a woman in her early twenties. For someone so young, she was very sure of herself.

"Have you seen a tall, auburn-haired woman come in here?" I asked the women.

"Sugar, I'm the only woman you'll need tonight," she purred as she began to walk towards me.

I scanned the stalls and saw that they were all empty; she wasn't here. Had she left? Of course, she had—the witch must have rattled her more than I thought. *Fuck.*

I turned to head back out of the bathroom when I felt someone grab my wrist. I spun around to see the cocky kid holding on to me. I didn't say anything; I just looked at where she held me.

"Don't leave so soon. We could have a lot of fun together," she said while winking at me.

"Take your hand off me now," I said in a low growl.

She must have been too drunk to sense my tone and instead chose to shove herself up against me. I could feel her fake breasts firmly pushed against my chest. Her drunken breath hit my face as she purred, "I'll do anything you want, sugar."

I pulled my wrist free from her grasp and moved my hands to hold either side of her upper arms, then pushed her away from me. I let a little of my darkness show, thought I'd frighten her just a little. "Look, you dumb fuck, leave me alone."

She cowered away, moving back to her friend who hugged her. That seemed to have done the trick. *Now to find Tess.*

As I walked from the bathroom, I pulled out my phone and called her again, though there was no answer. I linked Conrath next. He'd been tasked to watch over her and continue with the surveillance. He confirmed to me that she'd left the bar around twenty minutes ago and jumped into a cab.

Fuck.

What game is she playing?

I tried her number again—it rang and rang until finally, she answered. I was about to ask if she was okay, tell her I was worried, but she cut me off before I even got a chance.

"Luke, please leave me alone. I need some time. What I just saw at the bar… I need to process it," she said quietly.

What was she talking about? I had no control over the woman; I'd tried to protect her, save her from the abuse. "Tess, that woman didn't know what she was talking about, please just ignore her." I did my best to stay calm.

"I'm not talking about her. I'm talking about you, Luke." She was deadly serious. What was she talking about? What had I done?

All I could muster was, "Me?"

"Yes, Luke, you," she replied. "You don't own me. I'm not yours to possess. The way you threatened that woman was out of line."

"You're overreacting, Red," I replied.

"No, Luke, I'm not. I've seen enough possessiveness and male aggression to last a lifetime, and I'm not prepared to go through it again. Now please, leave me alone." I attempted to reply, but before I could say anything she'd already hung up.

Shit.

I'd been an idiot. I had to see her in person. Explain everything and try and do damage control.

I knew it would take her at least half an hour to get to her place, so without thinking, I portaled directly to her building. I hadn't even considered the right way to explain how I'd gotten there before her. I just had to see her.

I waited outside of her building for her to return. While I did, I tried to process everything that had happened. How could I have been so stupid? Of *course,* my display had triggered memories for her. The years of abuse at Daniel's hands had clearly affected her.

My outburst had reminded her of him. I tried to shake the feeling of disappointment away. She had been frightened of me. Many people feared me, as they should, but I never wanted Tess to. I never wanted her to look at me like so many others did.

I had been trying to protect her and show her that she was worthy. That I wouldn't tolerate people talking ill of her. That I would stand up to people, for her. Instead, my actions had had the opposite effect, and now she didn't think I could protect her at all. She thought the opposite, that I could hurt her.

A car backfiring shook me from my thoughts, and I realised Tess still hadn't returned. I checked my watch and realised I'd been standing outside of her building for over an hour.

She wasn't coming home. I needed to know she was safe. I once again linked Conrath, who informed me she'd gone to Emma's. Of course, she had. She wouldn't want to be alone when she was like this. I found a door and portaled to Emma's building.

I found Conrath and got him to fill me in on what had happened. He told me she'd arrived around forty minutes ago and that Emma had met her at the front of the building to pay for the taxi.

My heart sank when he told me that she was crying when she'd gotten out the cab. Emma had wrapped her in a big hug before pulling her into the building. He said that the two remained inside and hadn't come out. Conrath told me he didn't expect to see either of them till morning, but I had to see her, just to check that she was okay.

I made my way up the fire escape of the building, careful not to be seen by anyone, hiding in the shadows and using the darkness to my advantage. I made my way to Emma's floor and found what I was looking for.

Tess was curled up on Emma's sofa, her head resting on Emma's lap. The rest of her long body was curled up into a tiny ball. I could see the tears streaming down her beautiful face, and all I wanted to do was hold her. I knew I couldn't, though, so instead I watched. I watched for hours until she finally cried herself to sleep.

Emma managed to slip from under Tess without waking her up; she covered her friend with a blanket before clearing up the tissues that littered the floor, and then made her way to bed.

I continued to watch Tess from the shadows. I couldn't bring myself to leave her alone, not even while she slept.

Shit, why did I feel like this?

What was happening?

32

DANIEL

IT HAD BEEN a couple of weeks since I'd woken in the strange London apartment with an unquenchable thirst. I'd finally found my way to the kitchen and drank water straight from the tap, gulping as much as I could get. Still, I'd felt a thirst, and my throat burned, the water quenching absolutely nothing.

I had stood over the sink, breathing heavily, trying to figure out what was going on. I heard a pounding, a thumping, and I turned to see where it was coming from. A woman stood in the door. In that exact second, I couldn't tell you what she looked like. The first thing that I noticed, the very first thing that drew my attention was the artery pulsing in her neck, just below her skin.

The noise was coming from her; it was the sound of her blood pumping through her body and her heart beating and forcing the blood to every last part of her.

In an instant, I felt fangs puncture my bottom lip. They were my fangs. I could taste my own blood in my mouth, but I wanted her blood. The woman before me, I wanted to taste her blood.

I knew then that Lilith had kept her word. She had turned me; I was now a vampire. This woman before me, though, she was human. I instinctively knew.

At the thought of Lilith, she appeared behind the woman in the doorway and pushed the scared thing into my arms. I grabbed the woman by the throat and tilted her head to one side so I could fully expose her neck.

She screamed. I knew at that point it was only going to get worse for her. I leaned in and whispered in her ear, "That's right, bitch, scream for me."

With that, I sank my fangs into her neck. The rush of blood that filled my mouth immediately calmed the burn. I began drawing out her essence with long pulls. The more I took, the more my thirst was quenched. I drew, and drew, and drew until finally there was nothing left to savour. I had drained her dry.

I pulled my mouth away from her neck and released my grip on her throat. As I did, she crumpled to the floor. Her dead eyes stared up at me, and I felt nothing. No remorse, no guilt. Nothing.

"We'll teach you to control yourself," Lilith said from the doorway.

I looked at her, studying every part of her face. She had looked young, but now I could tell she was older—not from her appearance, but from something else I didn't understand. "I don't need to control myself. She wasn't anyone, so she didn't deserve to live. I'll take what I want," I calmly replied.

"That is your choice, Daniel, but we have rules that you must live by. Otherwise, I'll kill you myself." She was unmoved by my outburst, disinterested even. I'd love to see her fucking try. "On your first feeding, it's usual to completely drain someone, but from now on the thirst should get easier to control."

I didn't reply; I simply chose to watch and listen to whatever she was trying to sell me. Then silence, it had engulfed the room, and made me uneasy. It was almost painful—I couldn't bear it. "Now what?"

"Now, Daniel, I prepare you for the task at hand. That means I train you, teach you, and tell you everything you need to know. You practice, learn, and listen to everything I have to say," she said as she walked towards me.

This bitch couldn't tell me what to do. She may have turned me, but I was stronger now; I wouldn't take orders from a woman. She had her back to me, and I moved to grab her from behind—but I never even got that far. I was frozen to the spot, unable to move. My eyes flicked around the room and met the back of her head.

She was shaking it, turning to face me. I blinked, and she was in front of me. Her hands had painfully grabbed my cheeks and she looked into my eyes. Then I felt it. A connection, one that I hadn't noticed before. It wasn't just a connection though—it was an allegiance, fealty. *What the hell?*

"Please, Daniel, do you really think you are the first to try and end me? I see you feel it now. It takes a short while for the connection to establish, but now that it has I'm sure you understand," she said, searching my face and releasing me from whatever she'd done.

"I do," was all I could muster. I now felt ashamed of myself, all I wanted to do was please her. I wanted to matter to her, to prove myself to her. "How did this happen?" I asked meekly.

"Well, my dear, I fed on you. Drained you near enough to the point of death. When you were balanced on the edge of life and death, I fed you," she said seductively.

"Fed me what?" I asked. I couldn't remember anything from that night. It was a complete blur.

"My blood, Daniel. I fed you my blood." Like it was nothing, the most common occurrence in the world. "The blood that flows through your body is mine and has given you this most precious gift. That is why you're connected to me, and why you now feel the way you do." She smiled smugly.

That was why I felt differently, why I wanted to please her and do anything she asked of me. I had to excel, *for her*. Was this what all vampires felt like with their sires?

My attention snapped to a man who stepped into the room. Lilith, though, did not take her focus off me. I could sense that this man wasn't human; he was a vampire, like us. Without looking at him, she began to speak, "Please dispose of the body, Matthew," she asked cooly—like she hadn't just asked him to get rid of a woman I'd just murdered.

"Yes, ma'am," the man replied with a bow. *Who the fuck was this prick?* He left without the body, and I didn't understand why. I also thought the bow was pointless, since she wasn't even looking at him. *Is she his sire? This prick? Should I bow to her? Shit, I have so many questions.*

I felt the burn in my throat again. *Is this a sign that I need to feed? Was that what my new body was trying to tell me?* I didn't understand all these new feelings and sensations. I had to learn to control them.

"I'm keen to start your education, Daniel. We have much to cover before we go to New York," she said, turning her back on me and making her way to the door. She gestured to someone outside, but I didn't see who it was.

"When will we be leaving?" I asked. I was keen to see Tess and do what needed to be done. For me, and now, because Lilith wanted it too.

She returned and stood in front of me. "Soon," she said, gently stroking my face with her finger. "First, though, you need to learn about all of your new abilities and exactly what you are capable of. I'll teach you to get a handle on your thirst so that it doesn't control or consume you. Then we'll go."

The burn in my throat continued. It felt like my gullet was melting from the inside out, now becoming painful. Was that what she was talking about? Being able to control this thirst, this feeling? I tried to push it to the back of my mind.

"So all you want from me is to take out Tess?" I questioned, trying to do anything to ignore the fire in my throat.

"She is insignificant to me, but I need her gone. For good. All I want is for her to be away from Louis. Permanently." Her tone was now murderous. She hated Tess; it was evident in every word she spoke.

"Louis?" I said without thinking.

"You know him as Lucifer. To me he will always be Louis." Her voice was now laced with adoration. She loved him like I loved Tess.

The door to the room opened again, and Matthew returned. *Prick.* He was followed by two women: one vampire and one human. Never once taking her eyes off of the dead body on the floor, the human moved to stand next to Lilith. At the same time, Matthew and the female vampire made their way to the lifeless body on the floor.

"Your Majesty, there are matters which require your attention," the female vampire said as they began to lift the corpse.

Hold on, your Majesty?

Before I could stop myself, the words blurted out of my mouth, "Who exactly are you?"

Lilith smiled slyly as she grabbed the woman by her side, took one of the woman's wrists, and handed the other to me. I watched as Lilith's fangs protruded from her mouth; in response, mine did the same. It was like they were answering to her, and I had no control over them. She pricked her fangs against the woman's wrist, and blood began to pool and then drop to the floor. The burn in my throat erupted, and I watched her, waiting.

"I am Louis's partner, and Queen of the Vampires," she said before sinking her fangs into the woman's wrist. My body followed her lead as my own fangs punctured the woman's wrist, the blood squirting into my mouth and cooling the burn.

We drew and drew and drew until there was nothing left. We pulled away, and the woman dropped. She was dead, yet I couldn't tear my eyes away from Lilith. She was majestic; she was my Queen.

Now I was in New York. I had been for a few days and it was one hell of a city. London was something, but this place was unbelievable. No wonder Tess had decided to come here.

I'd become familiar with my surroundings and found my bearings quickly due to my new skillset.

The first thing I did was locate Tess's building. I'd been given all of the details I needed by Lilith and her people. As soon as I stepped foot on American soil, it was my first instinct to find her, to see her.

It hadn't been long before I saw her, running back to her building. Her long auburn hair was tied in a bun on the top of her head. She had running leggings on and a tank top. Her tits bounced when she moved, and it took everything in me not to run over and bury my face in them, biting and sucking them till she screamed. I wanted her to scream. Not from pleasure, though.

Her face and chest were covered with a sheen of sweat. This was new; I'd never seen her exercise before, and she looked good for it. Like she could put up a fight.

She always had struggled against me. Despite her being tall, she was no match for me. I could cage her body with my big frame and she had no choice but to surrender. Despite her new level of fitness, it still wouldn't be enough. Not now.

She stopped outside of her building and removed her

headphones before pushing the door open and disappearing from view.

It took a lot of restraint to not rip her throat out where she stood, but that wasn't the plan. I had to make her suffer; I couldn't climax too early. It wouldn't do.

I knew she hadn't seen me since I lurked out of sight. I was a creature of the darkness now, moving in and out of the shadows.

TESS

AFTER I HAD LEFT Luke in the bar, I hadn't gone home; I'd gone straight to Emma's and cried myself to sleep. I'd done it again, fallen for a guy that was no good. *What's wrong with me? Why can't I find a nice guy?*

The following day when I'd woken up looking like a puffy-eyed panda with a jackhammer in my head, I trudged into Emma's bedroom and flopped face-down next to her on the bed.

She'd told me I needed to give Luke the chance to explain and that I might have blown things out of proportion. She might be right; I'd done it in the past. But this, this I didn't think I'd blown up. She'd had a point, though: he did deserve a chance to explain.

I spent the next week dodging phone calls from Luke. He phoned me at least twice a day, and sent text messages begging to see me, saying he'd take everything at my pace. He would come to me, I could go to him, or we could meet somewhere neutral. He said he didn't care as long as he could see me, explain what had happened.

I'd told him that I needed time to gather my thoughts,

figure things out in my head and that I'd let him know what I decided. He still rang and texted. I wasn't sure if it was sweet or overkill.

The whole situation was affecting me more and more. I'd felt really uneasy for a couple of days. It was like my nerves were on edge, and I was unable to shake the feeling I was being watched.

It was like the last two years of my life had vanished. Like I was back in London, looking over my shoulder being skittish. I hated it. Was this just the fallout from my fight with Luke, or was it something more?

I'd been cooped up in my condo for twenty-four hours without any fresh air. *Enough is enough, Tess*, I scolded myself. That wasn't who I was anymore; I wasn't some scared little girl who would hide away and let things get her down. No, I was stronger now.

After my pep talk, I decided I'd go for a run, blow off some steam and release a bit of my nervous energy. I often ran around Central Park when I needed to clear my head, and this felt like one of those times.

After making my way to my closet, I found some leggings and a hoody, grabbing my trainers too. With my hair pulled into a high ponytail so it wouldn't bother me, I made sure to grab my phone and headphones; I always listened to music when I ran, since it helped motivate me.

I locked my door and headed down to the lobby of my building. I greeted a couple of my neighbours on the way. I set my phone to play my running mix. Putting my headphones in, I began to run down the street to the park.

There was a chill in the air today, and I was glad I'd worn my hoody as I began jogging my usual route around the park. I passed the place where I'd bumped into Luke, and my thoughts drifted back to the time we'd spent together.

It had been amazing—until it wasn't. I pushed on,

running away from the spot, trying to put it to the back of my mind.

His face drifted back into my thoughts. Had I been wrong about him in the first place? I'd had the feeling that something was off, something that I couldn't quite put my finger on. I'd dismissed it as my own insecurities, but maybe I had been right all along. Maybe something *was* off.

The feeling was back, like I was being watched. I carried on running, scanning my surroundings as I went. There was no one, just other runners and families. I thought I'd stick to the more well-travelled routes today, just to be on the safe side.

I carried on running, thinking about Luke and what I'd do. Regardless of my initial hesitancy, I had grown close to him. I'd developed feelings for him, strong ones. Being honest with myself, I thought I was falling in love with him. I shook my head, trying to dislodge an answer, trying to find anything that could point me in the right direction.

Until the encounter with the cougar, he'd always been so open with me, calm and collected. I'd had so much fun with him, and he had made me feel alive for the first time in far too long. I never held anything back from him. I told him everything and was completely myself. There were no pretences; I was truthful about everything. I did that because I wanted to be. I wanted him to know everything that had happened to me. Not so he'd feel sorry for me—no, so he could see how far I'd come.

Maybe I'd just have to see him, hear him out before I made a decision. I couldn't do anything without hearing what he had to say. I would make sure, though, that I wouldn't be blinded by his charm and unbelievably sexy face. I wanted answers, and he'd need really good ones to repair the damage that had been done.

I continued running, my feet pounding on the ground

and my heart thudding in my chest. My music blared through my headphones, and I realised it was one of my favourite tracks.

The path ahead seemed a little too quiet for me, so I decided to turn down another, one I knew would be busy. I was about halfway down the track when I realised I was alone. The usually busy route was deserted, and my heart began to thunder as a sick feeling took over.

I was being watched; I knew it. It was like there was a darkness drinking me in, studying my every move. I hated the feeling and picked up speed, trying to find more people. It moved with me, yet I was alone—not another soul was on the path.

Fuck, fuck.

I stopped and spun around on my feet, ready to confront whoever was following me. "What do you want?" I screamed. But there was still nothing; no one was there. The feeling hadn't gone away, though. I scanned around, looking in the bushes trying to see someone, anyone.

It was just me, alone on the path. *Am I going crazy?*

Suddenly I heard movement to my left and once again took off running, thankfully reaching a busier track with more runners and walkers. People sat on benches, laughing and joking, and I felt the relief wash over me.

I slowed to a walk, trying to take deep breaths and calm down.

My phone rang and buzzed in my pocket, once again sending my heart-rate skyrocketing. I literally jumped with fright. I pulled out my phone and saw that it was Luke ringing.

I was spooked and really wanted to hear his calming voice. I decided to answer, since I wanted to sort this whole thing out one way or another. I couldn't go on like this, and I was ready to hear him out.

LUCIFER

Tess had finally agreed to meet up with me. It had taken some persuasion, but here we were.

She didn't want to meet at either of our places, which I understood, and she'd instead suggested we meet at O'Malley's. I knew it was because she felt comfortable there; it was like a second home to her. She wouldn't be alone, and she'd have her support system nearby. It was also very public.

I hoped it wouldn't come to that though.

I walked through the door and searched for a booth, preferably in the quietest part of the bar. If we were having a heart-to-heart, it would be good if we could hear each other.

I managed to find one and slid into one side, the side facing the door, so I could see when she came in. Not that I'd need to see her arrive; I'd instinctively know she was there. I couldn't explain why, though.

I saw Emma at the bar; she'd clearly already spotted me. I didn't think it was a coincidence that she was working tonight. She was now making her way over to me and stopped in front of me.

"What can I get you, Luke?" she said. She was still warm,

but not as much as she had been before. It also took me by surprise when she used my name; we'd never actually been properly introduced.

"Two Johnnie Walker Blue's please, Emma," I replied, trying to give my voice as much emotion as I could.

"I hope you two can work this out," she said to me. "I've never seen her this happy, well before..." she trailed off, then turned without waiting for my reply and headed to the bar to get the drinks. I stopped and thought about her words; Tess had never been happier, and in all honesty, neither had I.

I knew it sounded clichéd, but she'd changed me, awoken a part of me that I thought had died, actually one I didn't think existed.

Then I felt her, felt her presence before I even saw her. I lifted my head and watched her walk in. She looked phenomenal; my mouth fell open slightly before I quickly gathered myself. She wore black jeans, a green t-shirt, her black leather jacket, and a pair of biker boots. Her hair was straightened and flowing all around her. She wasn't particularly made up, but she was radiant.

Maybe it was because I hadn't seen her for a week, but to me it had felt like an eternity. Time had seemed to move slowly without her in it. She was here now, though, and hopefully, I could fix things.

I could tell she was trying to look confident, waving over at the bar staff and attempting to push her nerves away. Her heartbeat gave her away, though. It raced in her chest. She searched the bar until our eyes locked. She dropped her gaze and began to make her way towards me. She slid into the booth opposite me.

Before either of us could say anything, Emma returned with our drinks and set them down on the table. She turned her back to me and squeezed Tess's shoulder. "I'm right at the bar if you need anything," she said quietly to Tess, her voice full of reassurance. With that, she moved away in the direction of the bar.

"Tess, before we start I just want to apologise for my behaviour. I'm so sorry if I scared you. The thought of you being frightened of me…" I shook my head, unable to finish my sentence.

She was still, eyeing me for a moment. "Luke, I've been down this road before. Daniel was possessive, and his actions led me to move halfway across the world to get away from him. I won't put myself in that position again."

"I'd never hurt you or lay my hands on you as he did. That's not who I am. I need you to believe that."

She held up a hand to stop me from continuing. "It's not just that. You told that woman I was "yours," but I'm not an object to be owned. That's how Daniel saw me, as a commodity." She looked down at the table, picking at her nails. She didn't want to be having this conversation—I wished she didn't have to. I was going to find that fucking witch and make her pay.

"Please let me explain, Tess." I'd do and say whatever I needed to in order for me to keep her. I searched her face; she stopped picking her fingers and looked up at me. She didn't say anything. She just nodded, which I took as my opportunity to explain.

"You know I've been with… a few women, I've never made any attempt to hide that. But recently I haven't been involved with anyone seriously. This was my choice after some issues I've had with women in the past." She watched me, listening to everything I had to say.

"It's been like that because women have gotten attached to me. Possibly because of who I am, but it has always ended badly. The easiest way to describe them is stalkers." She remained silent, watching intently. "There was one woman in particular who took things too far, and the repercussions for both her and me were long-reaching," I said, remembering the incident. "People think they know me, know who I am and what I'm about. For that reason, they seek me out, thinking they are the one for me. That's always so far from the actual truth," I said, shaking my head. It was true: most people who approached me, wanted to tame the Prince of Darkness or to rule by my side. It was endless, and I wasn't interested. Sure, I'd fucked them, but that was it.

"When we were approached by the woman in the bar, she was one of so many similar women I've known my entire life. They think they know me, that they are the one for me, someone who can be my equal." She started to say something, but I stopped her. "Let me get through this, Tess." She nodded for me to carry on.

"You are no one's possession, Tess and I'm sorry if that's how my actions made you feel. You are so much more than a thing to be claimed. What I was trying to get across, very inarticulately, was that I *chose* you. I chose you to be my equal. *You* are *my* choice, Tess, and I don't care what anyone else thinks of that. I especially do not care for the opinions of people that I don't know or those who don't know how extraordinary you are."

She was watching me. I leaned across the table, taking her hand in my own. She didn't flinch or snatch it back. "I've enjoyed our time together, and I really hope that you'll give me the opportunity to continue getting to know you and prove that I'm not like him."

None of what I'd told her was a lie; I hadn't been completely forthcoming either. Couldn't really tell about my crazy exes—after all, I wanted to keep seeing her.

My bat-shit crazy exes could still cause problems for me; they had been for centuries. Some had ended up paying for it with their lives, and some were still out there. After this long, they had to have finally gotten the message that I didn't give a fuck about them—who knew though?

I studied her face; she still hadn't said anything. She remained mute. She was mulling everything over in her mind. We sat in silence for a while until I could no longer take it.

"We can take everything completely at your pace, Tess. If you want to stop things here then I completely understand that. I just want you to know—and believe me when I tell you that—I have never felt like this before, cared about anyone as I do for you. I'd really like to see where this could go." It was a last-ditch attempt, one last bid to salvage something from the shit that had happened.

She picked up her drink, and I expected her to sip it slowly. Instead, she downed it in one gulp. It was apparent to me that she needed the Dutch courage. She was building to something. I watched and waited; I'd said everything I needed to say, and it was now her turn. I had to sit and wait until she was ready, until she had decided what she would do.

It felt like an eternity, sitting there in silence.

"Okay," she said softly, "I believe you."

Relief flooded through my body; I was awash with it. A huge smile broke out across my face, and I squeezed her hand in thanks.

"But, if you do anything to make me feel like that again, it's over."

"Agreed," I replied quickly.

I pulled her hand up to my lips and brushed her knuckles with them before placing a gentle kiss on the back of her hand. I looked up at her, and I saw she was smiling at me.

I needed to find out more about the hold that she had on me; she wasn't just another human. There was something different about her, and I had to find out what it was. She had a hold over me I'd never experienced before and I had to figure it out.

I wasn't certain about who I thought could be helping Daniel. Now, though, as I'd told Tess about my past, I realised I'd need to check in on a couple of exes. It was possible they'd been helping him. If any of my exes were, then they would die.

That could wait until tomorrow though; tonight, I was going to enjoy the time with Tess and try and make things up to her in the only way I knew how.

I was going to ensure the make-up sex was going to blow her mind.

TESS

I HADN'T EXPECTED the story Luke told me about his past relationships, if you could call them that. It was the furthest thing away from what I thought was going to come out of his mouth. It wasn't just a story, though. I could tell it was the truth, and I believed him.

I'd asked him to be honest with me, tell me why the hell I should stick around, and he had done just that. I was shocked at his revelation about his stalker exes. Guess he knew a little of what I'd gone through after all.

It didn't excuse the way he'd acted, but now I understood his reaction.

I had to admit, telling me that he'd never had feelings like the ones he had for me shocked me a little, though I felt exactly the same. There was something between us, something I couldn't explain.

So we agreed to put it behind us and move on. He ended up coming back to my place. I hadn't planned on it happening, but I just couldn't help myself around him. By the time we got back there it was around 11:30 PM, and we eventually fell asleep around 4 AM. Apparently, he'd missed me and wanted to show me just how much.

I can't say that I minded—that man did things to my body that I didn't even know were possible. He had a direct link to my orgasms and just tapped straight into them. He could make me come as easily as snapping his fingers.

He was extremely talented, though I didn't like to stroke his over-inflated ego any more than I had to. I also tried to play it down, but I'm sure he was aware of how much he affected me.

My mind wandered to his experience. Everyone had a past, but the way Luke was with everything made me think that he'd been with a lot more people than I originally thought. My stomach churned at the thought of him with other women. It made me feel sick—which was ridiculous, and I had no right to feel like that. Whatever happened before me was out of my control, but it still bothered me.

I contemplated asking him about it, asking what his number was, but I thought better of it. I really wanted to know, but honestly I wasn't sure if I could handle the response. It was a double-edged sword. I wanted to ask him about the women who'd affected him, as Daniel had with me, but the thought of it tore me up inside. I'd have to decide if I could handle all of the details before asking him.

I pushed the thought to the back of my mind as I made my way to work. It was now 8 AM, and I was beyond tired. I had back-to-back shoots all day. Never one to turn down work, I knew today was going to be a killer.

I'd left Luke outside my building with a long, tender kiss and told him I'd have to catch up with him tomorrow. I knew I was going to be slammed today. He seemed a little put-out, but he didn't argue.

I'd stopped at my favourite coffee shop for a latte and muffin and was on the subway heading to the first shoot. As I sat tearing chunks off my muffin, the uneasy feeling settled once again in my stomach. It was busy, but I searched the train car for anything odd.

I mean, it wasn't unusual to see something strange on the subway—I'd once seen a man carrying a goldfish bowl with a turtle in it. Oh, and that time I tried to get onto a car only for it to be filled entirely with clowns. That one freaked me out; I'd slowly backed out and caught the next one.

As I continued to scan the other commuters, the uneasy feeling grew, and I jumped when my phone buzzed in my pocket. I fumbled while trying to grab it from my bag, and it had gone to voicemail by the time I pulled it out. I'd see who it was later.

I reached my stop and hustled to get to the location before everyone else. Thankfully, I was the first there, so I managed to set up in peace. I was booked here till midday, then had to move quickly to get over town for my next job an hour and a half later. That was due to go on until about 10 PM, depending on how things went.

The first job of the day was another ad campaign, this time for some up-and-coming designer. He'd wanted some high-end shots of his products so he could circulate them on social media and boost his brand. He'd picked everything: the models, the set-up, and the theme. He was a little bit of a control freak and wanted everything just so. I understood; it was his livelihood after all. It just made things a little more difficult for me.

I knew he was going to micromanage everything, but he was paying, so I'd try and be as accommodating as I could.

Sure enough, the morning seemed to drag. He had such high expectations for things that were just not possible. In my best calming voice I'd managed to rein the crazy bastard in, telling him it wasn't possible to get the models to balance on the ledge of one of the tallest New York buildings without any safety equipment. I'm pretty sure he wouldn't have cared if they'd fallen, just so long as he got the shot.

I was pleased with the work we'd done, though, and I think he'd eventually come around too. I made my way over to pack up all of my equipment and noticed I was running a little late. I'd have to get an Uber if I was to make it to my next call in time—I couldn't chance the subway.

Pulling my phone out of my camera bag, I noticed I had eleven missed calls. I clicked onto the number but didn't recognise it. Potential job perhaps? I checked the voicemail, but there were no messages. That wasn't unusual, since people hated leaving messages and would prefer to talk in person.

I'd deal with it tomorrow; I didn't have time to worry about it now. I booked a car, and then packed my cameras and lenses away. A couple of minutes later, my phone buzzed to tell me Uber was here.

As I made my way across town, I felt my phone buzz again. This time it was a message from Luke.

TOMORROW NIGHT I NEED YOU, DON'T MAKE ANY PLANS. I'M GOING TO SHOW YOU JUST HOW CRAZY YOU DRIVE ME AND HOW MUCH MORE THERE IS TO COME! HERE'S SOMETHING TO KEEP YOU GOING!

My phone buzzed again; an image of Luke filled the screen, shirtless wearing only his black joggers. His taut muscles glistened and the V of his hips were just visible. *Holy fucking Christ*, he was hot. I might have to frame it and hang it in my bedroom somewhere; he was an actual work of art.

THAT'S NOT FAIR, ESPECIALLY SINCE I HAVE TO WORK. THANKS FOR THE PHOTO, THOUGH. I'LL BE SURE TO POST IT TO MY INSTAGRAM! ;)

My phone immediately buzzed.

Go for it. I have nothing to hide.

I decided to reply with the angel emoji saying,

I'm a good girl, I'd never do that to you!

He texted back straight away.

Red, we both know you are no angel!

Another photo pinged through. This time it was a photo of his back, red scratches etched across the surface of his skin. Shit, had I done that last night?

I had absolutely no clue what this demi-god of a man wanted with me. My insecurities rose their ugly head again. He was amazing, and I just wasn't. I'd always thought of myself as fairly plain, nothing compared to someone like Emma. I wondered what his exes had looked like, were they pretty? Did they have more experience than me? How serious had they been before it all went to shit?

My thoughts were interrupted by the driver telling me we'd arrived. I lugged my equipment out of the car and made my way into the event. This was a charity gala, and I'd been hired to take various shots throughout the afternoon and early evening. I'd been booked until 10 PM, but I knew it was more likely that I wouldn't get home before midnight.

Sure enough, it was 11 PM before I managed to escape the event; they'd provided a car to take me back to my place, which I was thankful for. I was dead on my feet and looked forward to grabbing a shower and then crawling into bed to pass out.

I pulled out my phone, again realising I'd not checked it

since the Uber ride earlier. There were another thirteen missed calls, all from the same number. Again, no voicemails.

What the fuck?

That was weird. Someone really wanted to get in touch with me.

Knowing Luke, if he needed to see me about something urgent he'd just show up wherever I was. Plus, after everything we'd spoken about recently he wouldn't act like that. We'd agreed to take things slowly and see what happened.

I definitely still had my guard up with him, but he'd broken down so many of the walls I'd built up, I knew it wouldn't be long before that came down too. He was intoxicating to me, and I really wanted to see where things went. Plus, the awesome sex was a bonus.

The calls weren't Luke though; they were excessive.

I made my way into my condo, ensuring I secured all of the locks on the door just like I did every night. I showered quickly and made my way to bed. Checking my phone again, I noticed a further call that I'd missed while I'd been in the bathroom. Who was phoning this late?

I decided I'd call the number in the morning; I was too tired to deal with anything now. Right when I was about to plug the phone in to charge, it buzzed again. It was the same number. I contemplated letting it go to voicemail, but decided I should answer it—it might be important.

"Hey, baby, you missed me?" A smooth voice spoke from the other end of the line.

I knew that voice. It took me a second to register it, but I knew it… Daniel. My body stiffened, and I could feel the life drain from me. A wave of nausea overtook me, and I silently gasped. It felt like the air had been sucked from my lungs, and I could feel myself struggling to breathe.

"I've missed you, Tess, more than you'll ever know." He spoke calmly, but I knew he was far from calm. "So, New

York. Big city, Tess. You knew deep down, though, that I'd find you, didn't you? I think secretly you wanted me to find you." He was arrogant and cocky; nothing had changed. If anything, he seemed worse now.

I was still, listening to everything he was saying. Mute and unable to speak. The words caught in my throat, so I stayed silent. I continued trying to force air into my lungs so I could stop myself from hyperventilating.

"I know you're there, baby. Tell me, are you looking forward to me fucking you again? It's all I've thought about for so long, Tess. Having you again, being together again. Don't get me wrong, there have been others, but no one takes it like you do, Tess. No one." His voice had turned, and it was now cold and calculating.

I couldn't do this anymore. I'd run away from him, backed down too many times. I was stronger than this, than him. He'd made me feel small the entire time we were together, and I wasn't that person anymore. I was sick of him and his bullshit.

It was time this ended.

LUCIFER

I'D MANAGED to convince Tess to carry on with whatever it was we were doing. I'd never really been in a relationship before, so I wasn't sure if that's where this was headed.

I had slightly mislead her. I couldn't really explain that the people I'd been talking about were witches, demons, and vampires who all thought they could claim me. They were never anything more than sex, and that was all it took for them to convince themselves it was more.

There were a couple of women, though, who weren't just about the sex. There weren't any feelings involved; they were just different.

Again, I couldn't really explain that to her, so I thought my story about crazy "ex partners" seemed the most plausible answer. It was based on truth, so it wasn't a lie, I'd never lied to her. Omitted things, yes, but never lied.

I hadn't seen her yesterday after I'd left her place. She'd been at work all day. Thankfully the make-up sex the night before kept me going, although I still had an insatiable need for her.

I honestly think she was like a drug to me; I was

becoming addicted to her. The softness of her skin, the smell of her hair, the curves of her body, and how she squeezed around my cock like she was made to take it.

We were getting back on track, but I knew I had to be careful. Not just for her sake, but for the sake of Hell and its inhabitants. My actions had caused quite the stir within Hell: that I'd reneged on an agreement because of my selfish desires. No one had dared say anything directly to me, but the rumours had gotten back to me.

If only they knew the half of what was going on with Tess and me. I'd also heard some rumblings about how out counterparts in Heaven were taking the news. I thought they'd be pissed that I wasn't fulfilling my duties, and I was sure he'd have something to say about it. Not that I gave a fuck what he thought—that's how I landed the job in the first place.

I'd never backed out of an agreement in all of my years ruling, although at this point the deal didn't matter. We'd still been unable to find Daniel, so, as it stood, there was no deal.

On the one hand, him staying lost would solve some of my problems; on the other, I'd never be truly at ease if I didn't know what happened to the arrogant prick.

Everyone I had was on the lookout for him. My people searched everywhere and left no stone unturned. Favours had been called in, and nothing was out of bounds.

But he continued to evade us.

Bee and Levi sat in my inner circle with me, catching up and discussing the events that had led us here. They were as baffled as I was.

"He has to be getting help from someone. No doubt about it. He couldn't stay hidden from us for this long without help. A spell maybe?" Levi thought aloud.

He was right; everyone had drawn a blank. Daniel had disappeared, which told me that whoever was helping him was powerful and had contacts.

"Bee, it might be worthwhile looking into my previous female conquests. If they thought I was getting close to someone new, it might have pushed them over the edge," I said knowingly.

As I mentioned it, she shook her head. She was annoyed with herself for not thinking of it sooner. I saw her link someone—I presume whoever she had leading the search. She looked furious with herself. This wasn't on her though as I hadn't thought of it straight away either.

I had been too wrapped up in Tess.

"We've crossed paths with this person before. They know how we operate and how things down here work," she said. "There is no way he could do this alone; Levi is right."

"Wait a second, did you just agree with me?" Levi said with a grin.

He was right—the two of them got on well, but it was rare they agreed on things. Most of the time I think Bee just disagreed with him to get a rise. Piss him off.

"Don't get used to it," she said, shooting him a glare.

He laughed and held his hands up in surrender.

"What I don't understand is what someone would have to gain by helping Mr. Turner? Who thinks that going against you is a wise decision?"

"Who do we know that has nothing to lose?" questioned Levi.

She shook her head. "Everyone has something to lose, Levi."

She was right; if it was someone from my past, they'd know I'd kill them for their disobedience. Unless... that was what they wanted? Me to annihilate them? That's what would happen when I found them. Surely no one was that stupid.

"Bee, there are a couple of things I need to speak to you about." She looked at me intrigued. "I need to find a loyal witch to undertake some tasks for me. Someone who can be trusted."

She knew how I felt about witches. They were useful, but I was, for the most part, not a fan. "I can do that. What's this about?" she queried, leaning forward in her chair and picking up her wine glass.

I proceeded to tell them about the witch who'd approached Tess at the bar and let her know she was unworthy to be with me. Levi whistled, wide-eyed. He knew that there was a whole world of pain waiting for the witch.

Bee nodded her head in acknowledgement. "What's the other task?"

"I want to find out as much as I can about Tess's father."

"We couldn't find any trace of him at all when he completed the dossier on her. It was like Mary all over again, an immaculate conception," she said with a smirk.

Levi burst out laughing.

I must admit the thought of it brought a grin to my own face. If that was the case, I was sure God would be really pleased about that. It was impossible though; he'd have already put a stop to it. He'd never have let things get this far. In his infinite wisdom, he'd have killed her before he let me have her.

"Leave it with me, I'll find someone loyal," she declared.

"Oh, and Bee... someone discreet. I don't want anyone else to know my suspicions about Tess's father."

At that moment, Conrath linked me and asked permission to enter my circle. He had an update for us. "Come in, Conrath," I said. With permission granted, the wards and other protections fell away and he walked in.

I studied his face before he said anything. He did indeed have news, and I knew immediately that I wouldn't like it. By the look on both Bee and Levi's face, they'd realised the same thing.

Conrath approached us, dipping his head low.

"What is it? What do you have?" I asked impatiently.

He stopped in front of me, unable to look me in the eye. That definitely wasn't good.

"We've managed to track Daniel's whereabouts," he said. His voice faltered.

"Where?" Was my only reply.

"He's not in London anymore." He paused before he continued on, like he didn't want to speak the words. "He's in New York."

TESS

I NEEDED to end this for good.

I could no longer let him hold any power over me.

The only way to do that was for me to confront him and tackle it head-on. I was done running and hiding like a scared little girl.

As soon as I'd heard his voice on the phone, I was taken back, back to a place I wanted to forget, that I'd fought so hard to escape. I'd accomplished so much since I'd left Daniel, but he still had the ability to make me cower.

He made me feel insignificant, like I wasn't worthy of anyone's love or affection. I knew that wasn't true—I was worthy—but hearing him made me question everything.

I'd arranged to meet him, to finish what had started so many years ago and tell him he no longer had any power over me. I would rid myself of him and everything about him.

It was no surprise to me that he was keen to meet. He'd see it as an opportunity to get me back, to persuade me to leave my life and go with him. He'd controlled me for nearly four years, which was four years too long.

The place I'd arranged to meet him at was always busy—a coffee shop far, far away from my place. I didn't want him anywhere near where I actually lived. I'd make sure that I took a long and varied route home. I knew he'd try to follow me.

The coffee shop was a deliberate play on my part. It was a tourist spot, so there were always tons of people. I wanted somewhere public, since I didn't want to be on my own with him and needed as many people as humanly possible to be there. That way he couldn't start anything, and if he did, at least there'd be witnesses.

We'd arranged to meet around 6 PM. It was open much later, but I didn't want to do this in the dark.

It was now 4 PM, and I knew it would take about an hour and a half to get across town. I already had a car booked for the journey over there. My return trip had been planned too, and it would allow me to zig-zag across the city.

I'd been preparing myself mentally all day. Psyching myself up to finally stand up to him.

I was currently in the shower, letting the water wash over me while I tried to ease my stressed and tense body. It wouldn't help; nothing would calm my nerves. I stood thinking about Luke. Maybe I should have told him what was going on, but he'd have offered to help, and I didn't want to drag him into my mess.

He was due to come over tonight, and I was really looking forward to seeing him, with the knowledge that Daniel would once and for all be out of my life. I'd tell him about the meeting then—he might not be too pleased, but I'm sure he'd understand.

After all, if anyone could understand messed-up exes, it was him. I'd been surprised when he told me that he'd had stalkers. Not just one, but multiple stalkers. Guess it went with the territory of being both successful and sexy as hell.

Stepping out of the shower, I focused again on the task at hand and pushed Luke to the back of my mind. I grabbed my towel, wrapping it around me and cocooning myself in its fluffiness. I picked up another for my hair and wrapped it up.

I made my way to my closet, figuring out what to wear. It had to be plain, not even remotely sexy. There had to be no hint of anything that he could misinterpret. I finally decided on a pair of black jeans, a white t-shirt, a chunky green cardigan, and a pair of Vans. It most definitely was not sexy. I would have worn a sack if I owned one. Nothing sexy about a fucking sack.

I dropped my towels in the hamper and pulled on my clothes. I gathered up my jacket and shoes and made my way to my bedroom.

I'd tie my hair up in a bun; no make-up either. I'd need to be as plain as I could. This was going to be difficult enough, and in all honesty, despite being the happiest I'd ever been, I didn't want him to see that.

My heart immediately started hammering in my chest as I stepped back into my bedroom. I stopped dead in my tracks, unable to take another step. Nausea took over, and I fought my body hard to stop from passing out.

My eyes fixed on the opposite side of my bedroom.

How did he get in here?

How did he know where I live?

Why is he here?

I didn't need to ask myself the last question; he was here for me.

"Hey, baby, you miss me?" Daniel spoke from across the other side of my bedroom, standing between my bed and the window. He was smiling. It wasn't his usual smile, though. It had an eerie quality—there was something off about it.

He was different. Something unknown that I couldn't put

my finger on. Whatever it was, I already knew that I didn't like it.

I remained still and silent, unable to move or speak. I had to pull myself together, or I was in for a whole world of pain. I could run for the door. I could make it; he was on the other side of the bed.

If I was going to do it, I'd have to do it quickly and right now. I turned on my heels and ran towards my bedroom door. Before I even got there, he'd blocked me in. His massive frame consumed the doorway. I was stuck in my bedroom, unable to leave.

How the hell did he do that? I couldn't understand how he'd moved so quickly. It was like I'd blinked and he was in front of me.

He grinned at me and I realised in that moment that he was going to show me just how much he'd missed me. I wasn't sure I'd survive it.

I backed away from him, weighing up the options in my head; I could try for the fire escape. But before I could finish formulating anything, he spoke and it sent shivers down my spine.

"Tess, Tess, Tess. There isn't anywhere to go. No one is coming to save you. You're mine now, just like you always have been." The words were calm, but his voice dripped with venom.

"You should have known I'd find you. It took longer than I'd hoped, but here we are. You look good," he said, moving towards me.

I instinctively backed away from him. He smirked at my response, and I instantly regretted it. I should have stood my ground, but I knew where this was going, and the feelings of helplessness had begun flooding back through me.

I hated the way he made me feel.

Before I knew what had happened, he had his hand

around my throat, gently squeezing. Enough to make me struggle for breath, but not enough to choke me. He looked down at me, studying my features. He looked intensely at my face, a face he hadn't seen for years.

I wanted to look away, turn my head, but I was powerless. Then I remembered my self-defence—he already had me by the throat, but I had a clean shot to his balls. That would take the fucker down.

With a swift motion, I kneed him forcefully to the crotch, causing him to release his grip. I quickly made a move for the front door and ran as fast as I could, but just as I reached it, I felt his arm around my waist. He pulled me back against his body, my feet dangling off the floor.

"You'll regret that," he spat.

He threw me across the room, and I crashed into my coffee table. I instantly felt the pain in my side. I'd experienced it before. I was pretty sure he'd just broken a rib or two.

I was a heap on the floor, holding my side while I tried to catch my breath. He once more made his way to me, and I backed away from him with no success. He grabbed a fistful of my hair, lifting me from the floor. Once I was upright, he forced my head back.

"Look at me," he bellowed.

I did as he said, my eyes finding his. Long gone were the eyes I knew—these were bright red. What the hell? What was going on?

"I have a few new tricks up my sleeve, baby. Shall I show you?" It wasn't really a question; he was going to show me no matter what I said. I nodded my head. It was probably best to play along.

He smiled. "That's my girl." It was then that I noticed the fangs that protruded from his mouth, hanging over his bottom lip. He licked them, as if trying to draw my attention to them.

I remained still, not really sure what I was looking at.

He gripped my hair harder, tipping my head to one side and exposing my neck. He moved closer, trailing those pointed teeth against my neck. I tried to move, but he was just too strong. Stronger than I remembered.

Everything I'd learned couldn't help me; nothing was working against him. Maybe I could reason with him? Fat fucking chance of that. It hadn't worked the entire time we were together, so why would it now?

"What do you want?" I finally managed to squeak out.

"You," he replied menacingly.

"What do you want from me, Daniel?" I said, more forcefully.

"I want you to die, Tess, but first we're going to have some fun. You see, I'm different now. I've changed since you last saw me."

"You're still a small-dicked scumbag. That hasn't changed," I quipped.

Hey, if I'm going to die here, I'm not going to make it easy.

He punched me in the stomach, knocking the wind out of me. I tried to double over, but he wouldn't let me; his hand still gripped my hair. He dragged me to the bedroom and threw me into it. I crashed against one of my bedside tables, breaking it and smashing the legs.

"Don't fucking test me, you little bitch," he snarled. "I could kill you with the flick of my wrist." I didn't doubt it for a second. I'd die here, but I'd fight until my last breath, making him work for it. I wouldn't give him the satisfaction of surrendering.

I composed myself and shakily rose to my feet. "Come on then, Daniel. What have you got?" I taunted.

He didn't reply; he just remained still. He smiled, and I

once again saw his pointed teeth. This time, though, I saw them elongate, change to actual fangs. Like an animal. What the fuck? He saw me looking at them, and now he was grinning.

"Neat trick, huh?" he purred, "wait till you see the rest."

"The rest?" I questioned. Maybe not the smartest idea, but at least if he was talking to me he wasn't killing me.

"Becoming a vampire comes with lots of neat tricks, baby," he said calmly, like he hadn't just told me he was a blood-sucking leech.

He'd finally lost his mind. All the drugs and booze over the years had taken their toll. *What is he talking about? Vampire?*

"It's true, and you're about to learn just how much pain I can inflict. Are you ready?" he asked. Like I had a choice in the matter; he was going to do what the hell he wanted. He always did.

I'd play along with his little delusion for a while. "Come on then, Vlad. Show me."

38

LUCIFER

I WAS MAKING my way to Tess's place. We'd arranged to go for drinks, and I'd said I'd pick her up around 9 PM. I was running a little late with everything that had been going on.

I pulled up outside of her place around ten minutes after 9 PM. I'd sent her a few messages earlier on but hadn't received any replies. It worried me a little, but the demons on surveillance duty had said she was alone in her condo and that no one else had entered. I wondered if she needed to charge her phone, or perhaps it had broken.

I decided that despite not hearing from her, I'd still go on as planned. Selfishly, I wanted to see her. I'd ask her about her phone later.

I slowly made my way up through her building to the elevator. I'd decided I was going to tell her that I'd had people looking into Daniel. Obviously not *everything*—I wasn't fucking crazy. Just that I wanted to look out for her and ensure she was safe.

After stepping into the elevator, I pressed the button for her floor. It started to move, and I once again focused on what I'd tell Tess. I wasn't sure how she'd react to the news that I had people looking into her ex. She might be pissed, but I wanted to be as honest as I could.

The doors opened onto Tess's floor, and I was met by darkness. I sensed it—something wasn't right. I made my way through the corridor to her door. I tried using my powers to discern what was going on inside but nothing. There was definitely some sort of magical block.

She was in trouble.

I felt it in the pit of my stomach.

Knocking calmly on the door, I strained to hear any noises coming from inside. There was nothing, absolute silence.

She didn't answer. I knocked again, this time calling out to her and trying the handle—still nothing and the door was locked. I needed to get in there, check she was okay.

I thought it best to portal in, since that would be less of a shock than me breaking down the door. I found the closest unlocked door and portaled through it, finding myself in Tess's living room.

I didn't need to look far to see that things clearly weren't okay. There were signs of a struggle, and the coffee table was smashed. Where the hell was she?

An unknown feeling struck me. I wanted to know if she was alright; I *needed* to know. Was this fear? Not for myself, since I knew there was little that could be done to me. I felt fear for Tess, fear that she wasn't okay. I'd never experienced this before; it was a feeling I didn't care for.

I decided to announce I was there, so I called out her name. I didn't expect a reply. Sure enough, there was none. But I could feel her—so I began to search her place.

I made my way to the last room, the bedroom.

I stopped dead in my tracks.

Motherfucker, I thought to myself.

Here he was. We'd searched for him, and he was in her

fucking condo like nothing had happened. He stood behind her, using her as a shield, hiding himself from me.

Ignoring his presence, I spoke to her. "Tess, are you okay?"

"Don't you dare talk to her," he spat from behind her.

I saw he had his hand wrapped around her throat and was applying a little pressure. Just enough to control her.

"Tess, it's going to be okay," I said, trying to be reassuring. Trying my best to calm her.

"Don't lie to her, this is going to be anything but fine," Daniel said with a laugh.

I studied her face, hardly paying any attention to the scumbag behind her. She was injured, I could tell. More broken items of furniture in her room told me he'd thrown her around. The busted lip and the way she held herself confirmed it to me.

"Luke, please just leave," she said. She was worried about my safety. With her words, I saw him squeeze her throat a little more. He was pissed at both of us. It was nothing compared to the way I felt at that moment. I wanted to rip his head off and mount it on a spike at the entrance to Hell, as a warning to those who even dared think about crossing me.

I didn't move, just stood still and looked at her, trying to be as cool as I could given the circumstances. I was livid, my blood boiled in my veins, and I knew it wouldn't take much for my true self to be revealed. I had to keep calm, not for him, but for Tess.

"Thank you for coming to check on Tess, but as you can see, she's fine. You can leave now," he said coldly. He eyed me from behind her, willing me to push his buttons. He was goading me; he wanted me to release Hellfire because then she'd know.

I tried to be as calm as I could, but it was tough. "No, Daniel, I think it's you who should leave before things get to the point of no return," I said threateningly. *Does he really think he can win this? Against me?*

He couldn't be that stupid; he knew who I was and what I was capable of. I knew he had power now, I could sense it, but he was still no match for me.

"Please, Luke. Leave," Tess begged. She was crying. Tears silently slipped from her eyes and down her face, along with the blood that was also dripping down her chin and onto her neck.

"No, Tess, I won't leave you," I said. My tone was no longer gentle; it was harsh. It wasn't for her, though. It was for him. I wanted him to know that this would only end one way. No matter what he did now, he would die at my hands. His soul was mine.

He shifted slightly from behind her, and I could see his face more clearly.

Fuck.

Red eyes, pointed teeth—pale, waxy skin.

Who the hell turned this prick into a vampire?

TESS

I WAS TIRED AND ACHING.

Until Luke had shown up at my place, I hadn't been scared. I knew what was coming. It was only a matter of how long I had left. Daniel was going to kill me, and I'd come to terms with it. It wasn't a question of if, it was a question of when.

Daniel was taking his time, stringing the process out as long as he could. He'd make me suffer, the way he told me he'd been suffering since I'd left him.

I hardly thought it was the same.

I would no longer beg or plead. It only gave him more strength and power over me. I would go silently, without giving him the satisfaction of my screams. I wouldn't die terrified.

But things changed when I saw Luke in my bedroom. Now I was frightened, horrified that he might get hurt because of me. Scared that Daniel might hurt him, maybe even kill him. Daniel seemed to know a lot about Luke, including that we were together.

Daniel had clearly been in New York longer than I thought. He'd been watching both me and Luke. That uneasy feeling I'd been having finally made sense. The presence I'd felt was him, him and his vampire blood.

I couldn't quite believe it—I still wasn't sure I did—but I was out of plausible explanations for the change in him.

He tightened his grip on my throat again, and I winced. It was instinctive. He'd hurt me pretty bad. It wasn't the worst he'd ever inflicted, but not far off. Least I'd managed to knee him in the balls. That made me feel a little better.

"So help me, Daniel, let her go, or I will kill you in front of her," Luke said through gritted teeth. I admired his efforts, but it was pointless against Daniel. He'd never stop. Not until I was dead.

I felt my body sag—I was struggling to stay on my feet— the pain was intense. Daniel felt my body drop, and he held me up. In no way was it for my benefit though. This was all about the performance he was giving Luke.

"Come now, Luke, this is what I wanted all along. You couldn't give it to me, so I got help from elsewhere." I could hear the smirk in his voice. He was enjoying himself.

Wait, what was he talking about? Did they know each other? I shook the thought from my head; it was Daniel's mind games. He was just trying to get Luke to leave, grasping at straws.

I looked up to meet Luke's eyes. Watching him, I saw the worry on his face. More tears slipped silently from my eyes, but I mouthed *leave*.

I felt my lip split again with the movement. It released a new trickle of blood, which ran down my chin and my neck. I felt Daniel change his position. He slid his hand to the side of my throat; his face moved over my shoulder. I felt his tongue lick up my neck, cleaning the blood that had dripped down. His tongue made its way up my neck and chin until it landed on my mouth. He licked my bloody lip, never once taking his eyes off Luke, who was struggling to stay still.

I felt Daniel grin, and at that moment, he roughly kissed me, biting my lips with his fangs and releasing more blood. It hurt; his fangs were so sharp, but I remained strong. I didn't scream.

Luke's jaw clenched, and I could see the anger flare inside of him. He took a step forward just as Daniel moved back behind me. "I don't think so, Luke," he said. I could hear the triumph in his voice. Luke was his new target. His new victim to torture. He wanted to hurt me to get to him.

I couldn't do this anymore.

I needed him to leave.

I pleaded, begged in my head, willing him to get the messages. I couldn't say it aloud, it would play right into Daniel's hands. I thought he might be able to tell from my eyes if I repeated it enough times.

Luke, please leave, please. I can't let him hurt you. Please leave.

I repeated it again and again. I searched his face.

I could hear them talking, but I was too focused on getting Luke to see me, to hear me. I managed to pick up the odd snippet of their conversation. Something about deals, opportunities, souls. It made no sense.

Luke, please leave, please. I can't let him hurt you. Please leave.

I continued repeating it until something happened. I stopped, clearing my mind.

Tess, I can hear you. Are you okay? How is this happening? I heard him say. I looked up into his dark eyes. I studied his face.

You can hear me? I said in my head.

Yes, I don't know how this is happening, but we don't have much time. Tess, he's going to try and kill you. I was looking

Luke directly in the eyes. I'd heard him speak to me, but as I watched his face, his mouth remained shut. This was all happening in our heads.

What the fuck? How is this even possible.

I know it's crazy and we'll figure it out later, but now we need to get you away from him.

I begged with my eyes and spoke through the link. *Luke, you have to leave now. I can't drag you into this. I won't have you getting hurt because of me. Leave, please.*

I watched as his eyes softened on me. *Tess, I can't leave without you, I just can't.* His emotions were written all over his face.

We don't have any more options; he wants me. If you leave now, you can be safe. It was the truth, as awful as it sounded.

Tess, he's a vampire, so he's weakened by silver. Are you wearing your necklace?

Yes, but what am I supposed to do with that? It's only a necklace.

I'll distract him. You use the pendant, stab him with it. It'll weaken him long enough for you get to me. It's the only chance we've got, Tess. Please trust me. He stared at me, searching my face for anything.

"I'll kill her in front of you, Luke, I don't care *who* the fuck you are." Daniel's words hissed in my ear.

"I'll rip your throat out before you even get chance," Luke replied. His eyes had shifted from me to Daniel. The look that he gave him had me believing every word he said. He would kill Daniel. But I didn't want that; he couldn't be responsible for that. He couldn't ruin his entire life just for me.

Tess, please trust me. We need to do this to get you out safe. Once you've stabbed him, you need to run, fast. I'll deal with him after that.

Was this really happening? I didn't understand anything that was going on. I was lost.

I had to make a decision.

Now.

LUCIFER

I WATCHED HIM CLOSELY, his every move pissing me off.

I was going to enjoy watching him suffer, again, and again, and again. He was going to Hell as my own personal pet project.

His suffering would become my new favourite hobby. I'd enjoy thinking of new and inventive ways to torment him and prolong his agony for all time. I couldn't kill him; then he'd be gone for good. Vampires's souls disappeared when they died. No one knew what happened to them but they certainly didn't go to Hell. Once he was dead that was it, he'd be gone.

I'd have to be careful not to push too hard. It wouldn't be a complete travesty if he died, it would just mean I wouldn't get to enjoy the torture.

"You're a son of bitch, you know that don't you?" Daniel spat. He was talking to me like Tess wasn't even there. I thought for a second he'd forgotten she was.

"You found her, and you didn't fucking tell me. You kept her for yourself." His voice oozed with contempt.

I saw Tess look at me; likely she was wondering what he

was talking about. My eyes met hers, and I wasn't sure what to say.

Daniel laughed menacingly. "She doesn't know, does she?"

Tess's eyes once again met mine. Uncertainty swam in them. She spoke to me. *What's he talking about, Luke? Do you know each other?*

I was about to respond when he once again tightened the grip on her throat, leaning down so he could whisper in her ear. "Your new man isn't quite who he said he is, baby." He smiled at me knowingly.

I hated the way he called her baby; it made me feel sick. I was enraged at just the thought of them together. She was no longer his, she was mine, and the way he held her now made me want to literally raise Hell.

"What's he talking about, Luke?" Her voice was shaky and unsteady. His prolonged grip on her throat had made her sound hoarse. Laced with uncertainty, her tone concerned me.

She searched my face for any signs I could give her. I didn't want to tell her. I wasn't ready. I hadn't lied to her about anything. Every question she asked me, I'd answered truthfully—sort of. I had omitted certain aspects of my life, but I'd never lied.

I had eventually intended to tell her.

Or had I?

I wasn't sure.

Telling someone you were the Devil and ruler of Hell wasn't really something you just dropped into everyday conversation.

I heard Daniel speak again. "Oh, baby, you thought I was bad. You've just moved into the big leagues," he cackled.

"Fuck off, Daniel," I bellowed. I felt my eyes go black. The rage was surfacing, though I was trying my best to push it back. It was becoming more difficult, though, with each passing moment.

They both saw the change. Tess looked on wide-eyed, but Daniel grinned. "There he is."

I took a step towards them, and Daniel took a step back, dragging her with him. "I don't think so Luke," he said from behind Tess.

"Tess, ignore him. He's trying to drive a wedge between us, please don't let him," I said, disregarding Daniel and focusing on her.

I could sense she was torn. She wanted to believe me, but she'd seen things tonight. She'd met a fucking vampire, and everything she knew had changed. If I told her, everything would be different. She'd never accept me for who I was. How could she?

"I've been honest with her, and she knows *exactly* what I am. Can you say the same?" Daniel said gleefully. He was enjoying every second of this.

"Tell me about that, Daniel. You're a vampire. Who made you?" I wanted to shift the focus back onto him, and I wanted an answer. After all this was done, I'd be paying them a visit.

"Well, if we're telling that story I think we should go back to the beginning, don't you, Luke?" The fucker was enjoying this. I shot him a look. Fine, if he wanted to go down this road, I'd end him. The look on his face told he no longer cared what happened to him.

"See, baby, I approached Mr. Albright here to help find you." Tess's eyes shot to my own, pleading for me to tell her it wasn't true. "But once he'd found you, turns out he wasn't willing to give you up. So I was approached by an interested third party. She said I could have you *and* piss off Luke at the same time. Seemed perfect."

"Cut the bullshit, Daniel. Who turned you?" I demanded.

"Let's not skip ahead. I was offered a choice, become a

vampire and get what I wanted, or stick with you and lose everything: Tess and my eternal soul. Wasn't really much of a choice."

Seriously pissed off, I bellowed at him, "Who fucking turned you?" I was aware my eyes had now gone completely black; my true self was showing. The mask had truly begun to slip and Tess had noticed. She watched me carefully.

Daniel stood tall behind her, allowing me to see more of him. He was enjoying every second of this, and there was a glint in his eye. "My mistress is someone very well known to you, Luke."

I wracked my brains. Which vampire could it be? I'd known a few in my time. But I hadn't pissed anyone off that much. Then it hit me; realisation struck and I looked up at his grinning, smug face.

No, it couldn't be her.

Before I could say anything, he cut in.

"It was my Queen that turned me. She was the one to give me this opportunity. She wants what is hers. You." His voice dripped with victory.

"Lilith wouldn't do this, she's not suicidal," I spat back.

He stared me down, pure rage on his face. My response had struck a nerve. I'd not only just insulted his queen but his maker too. "Don't you dare speak about her like that. She is everything. You don't fucking deserve her."

I'd clearly pissed him off. This just took an unexpected and unwelcome turn. I didn't need the extra drama that Lilith brought to the table. I'd push his buttons now though, since I knew his weakness, and it wasn't Tess.

"Lilith is no queen; she's just some crazy bitch who can't take a hint. I've been trying to rid myself of her for years, but she just won't get the message. That tells me she's fucking stupid." I made sure my voice dripped with contempt.

He was livid, and I saw him slightly loosen his grip on

Tess. I was getting to him; no newly turned vampire could resist the loyalty pull to their master. I knew they'd still be linked.

"Enough!" he screamed. I saw Tess flinch, and I knew we had to move quickly.

Tess, we need to move soon, are you ready? I asked. There was no response; she just stared at me blankly.

"Tess, are you okay?" I asked aloud this time.

She didn't say anything.

Daniel grinned from behind her; I wasn't sure what was happening.

"That's right, baby, he's not what he says he is and you know it." He stroked her cheek gently with his thumb when he spoke softly into her ear.

"Get your hands off her now, or I'll kill you where you stand." My voice boomed throughout the condo.

"Nice of you to finally show up. Now come on, I've shown her mine. I think it's about time you showed her yours… Lucifer."

TESS

LUCIFER?

What the hell? That's not his name.

His name is Luke. Isn't it?

I stared at him and remained silent, trying to process why Daniel had just addressed him with another name. Not just any name either, the name of the Devil? What was going on?

"Come on, Lucifer, I'm sure she's got questions for you. Probably be easier if you just show her." Daniel was goading him for a response, and it seemed like it was working. I watched as Luke's eyes continued to change, going darker and darker, now black. They were so different from the eyes I'd become so fond of.

His fists were clenched into balls by his sides, and his knuckles went white with the pressure he was exerting on them. His jaw was clamped shut, and I could see the tick of his muscles as he clenched his teeth.

He was livid.

Why was he so angry? Daniel was just being Daniel. Luke's reaction, though, told me he'd struck a nerve.

Then, their earlier conversation flashed back across my mind. Daniel's words, *"You couldn't give it to me, so I got help from elsewhere."* How did they know one another? What linked the two of them?

I chose to ignore Daniel. "Luke, how do you know each other?" Daniel laughed from behind me, but before Luke spoke, Daniel answered for him.

"Baby, Lucifer was supposed to find you. Find you and bring you to me. That was our deal. It turns out he changed his mind." He was calm, which unnerved me even more.

I looked at Luke, studied his face while waiting for him to tell me they were lies. That it was all just bullshit. Then, I remember what he told me about his job. Acquisitions. His business was acquiring things for people. Could that stretch to acquiring people?

"Tess, please—" Luke tried to respond, but I cut him off before he could spill more lies.

"How much am I worth, Luke? What was the price?" I said coldly. "Five thousand? Ten thousand? What's the going rate for an ex-girlfriend these days?"

I felt Daniel shift behind me; he laughed. "It's not money, baby. Lucifer here takes payment of a different sort. Don't you?" He turned his attention now to Luke. "Are you going to explain all of this to her? I think we're past the point of keeping her in the dark, don't you?"

Luke stared Daniel down. As I studied him, I felt a shift. The rage rolled off him, and I suddenly felt darkness. An intense darkness, one that far outweighed Daniel's. What was happening?

"You are going to pay for this, over and over and over again. You and Lilith." Luke spoke directly to Daniel. Ignoring that I was still completely in the dark about what was going on. I'd had enough of this crap.

"Luke, tell me now!" I screamed. I was sick of being the only one in the room who didn't know what going on with my own life.

He seemed shocked by my outburst. His eyes met mine, and they softened. "I'm sorry, Tess, it was never supposed to be like this. I wanted it to go differently. Please remember that." He was pleading with me, yet he still hadn't answered my question.

"For fuck's sake, *I'll* do it. Baby, Lucifer here is the Devil. I sold him my soul, in exchange for you. In exchange for your life. He was supposed to find you and deliver you to me so that I could kill you. He didn't follow through on his end of the bargain, though, so I sought help from elsewhere."

This couldn't be true. How could this be true? Luke wasn't the Devil. The Devil didn't exist. It was a story, a myth. Then I realised that I'd also thought vampires were a myth, but one stood behind me with his fangs pushed to my throat, so I wasn't sure of anything anymore.

"Luke?" I questioned. I wanted him to tell me it was all lies, that it wasn't true. That Daniel was crazy. But he said nothing. He didn't move. He just stood, staring at me.

His silence was deafening, and in that moment I realised the truth.

"I—I don't believe you, either of you," I cried, my voice cracking with emotion.

Daniel spoke first. "It's true, baby, I want to kill you, and Lucifer here was supposed to help. He's the Devil, trust me on that."

"Tess—" Luke began.

"I'm sick of lies. I want the truth now." I needed the truth from him, no matter what it was.

He stared at me for a while before he said, "It's true. Daniel and I had an agreement, I would hand you to him once I'd found you, but I couldn't. Once I met you, spent time with you, I couldn't give you to him. He doesn't deserve you; no one does..." he said softly.

"Fuck you, Lucifer," Daniel spat. "She's mine, and that will never change."

"No, she's not. You will never have her," Luke said with certainty.

"What about the rest of it? About who you are, is that true?" I questioned. He didn't reply; his words had failed him. Instead, he just nodded his head. One little action shattered all that I thought was true. "Show me," I said. "I need you to show me."

"You don't want to see this, Tess, not really," he pleaded. His eyes met mine, and I could sense his reluctance.

"I do I need to," I answered, staring him down.

He shifted his weight from side to side; he was stalling. "Tess—"

"Show me!" I screamed, interrupting whatever line he was going to spin. "Now."

It seemed to happen in slow motion. I watched on in disbelief as the scene played out in front of me.

I heard the tear first—I wasn't sure what it was. It was like material ripping, and it wasn't until I saw huge wings appear from behind him that I realised it was Luke's clothes. They had ripped at the back to allow his wings to be free.

Yes, fucking wings.

Once they were completely unfurled, he spread them out, and I had a chance to study them. Stretched out, they spanned at least ten feet across. They were black—not totally black though. They reminded me of the feathers of a raven. But they had a red lustre to them, making them seemingly shimmer. If it wasn't for the absolute craziness of what I was witnessing, I'd have thought they were beautiful.

As my gaze moved from wing to wing, I caught sight of his eyes. Just blackness, they were eyes I didn't recognise.

I continued to study the rest of him. His skin was red, but not like you'd imagine. It glowed, changing constantly. It reminded me of the embers of a fire. I suddenly felt warm, like there was a heat in the room; I wasn't sure whether it was all in my head or whether his ember skin was actually radiating heat.

"Tess," he said, in a voice I didn't recognise. It was much lower than his usual voice, harsh and gravelly. Him speaking my name made me flinch against Daniel's body, something that was not missed on Luke.

We stood there for what seemed an age. The three of us weighed each other up, staying completely silent, getting the measure of the situation. I was shocked; I couldn't move or speak. I just stood frozen, stuck in Daniel's grip, no longer fighting.

Then I heard him in my head, though it wasn't the new voice. It was his voice, the one I'd gotten to know, the one that melted me.

Tess, please. It's still me, he pleaded.

Are you fucking serious right now? I don't know who the fuck you are, Luke. Shit, that's not even your name.

He looked at me across the room, and I heard him speak to me again. *Please, focus on what you need to do. You need to get away from him; if you don't, he will kill you.*

I looked deeply into his inky eyes, trying to read him, to get anything from him. But there was nothing beyond black pools of emptiness. *I can't trust you anymore, Luke, I just can't.* I focused hard to block him out, to shut my mind back off to him. His pleading slowly grew quieter until there was only silence.

A wave of realisation hit me. I couldn't trust *either* of

these men, if I could call them that anymore. I couldn't put my faith in either of the two beings that stood with me in my bedroom.

I was alone. Completely.

I had to do this myself.

From what I could ascertain, Daniel had to be my main focus; he wanted me dead. I had no clue what the Devil wanted with me; I would have to figure that out later—if I survived.

I scanned the room for anything I could use to help me take Daniel down. I was careful not to meet Luke's penetrating eyes. Silence still encompassed the room. It was eerie.

Finally, my eyes landed on my broken bedside table that Daniel had thrown me against earlier causing it to smash. There was a splintered wooden leg close enough for me to grab. I'd seen plenty of vampire films to know a stake in the heart should do it—at least I hoped.

Steadying myself, I took deep breaths, closing my eyes and preparing. Could I do this? Could I kill Daniel? Was I capable of it?

I had loved him once; he'd been a good man when we met. He was my everything for so long.

Contemplating my options, I knew I had no choice.

I was still making excuses for him. Yes, I'd loved him once, but he wasn't a good man. He never had been. He was an evil, lying, manipulative, abusive bastard. I knew him as a human, and he was fucking crazy. He'd never stop now that he was a vampire.

I had to do this. I had to end him before he killed me. He'd told me that that was why he was here; he got some sick twisted pleasure from telling me he was going to kill me, and that he'd enjoy doing it.

I was ready to be free of him for good.

Keeping my eyes tightly shut, I filled my lungs with deep

breaths and prepared myself. I reached up finding my necklace; I clutched it with my hand. Opening my eyes, I saw Luke. He was watching me. It was like he wanted to help, but this was my fight.

"Daniel," I said seductively. "Let me see you; let me see your face. If you're going to kill me, I want to see you do it."

"That's kinky, baby," he purred. Still holding my throat, he turned me to face him. Now face to face with the man who had tormented me for so long, I looked into his eyes. I knew Luke was watching; I could feel his eyes on both of us. I leaned into Daniel and kissed him, hard. I felt his fangs puncture my bottom lip; I felt the teeth elongate more when my blood spilled into his mouth.

His hand moved from my throat to my hair, and he grabbed a handful of it, pulling me towards him. His other hand snaked around to firmly grab my arse; it was a deliberate "fuck you" to Luke, who could see everything. Daniel was enjoying the torture he was inflicting.

My own hand moved to his cheek, and I gently left it there.

I was doing my utmost not to be sick. I didn't want to kiss Daniel—I'd rather eat shit—but I had no choice.

With my free hand, I gently pulled the necklace and pendant from my neck. It stung as the silver chain dug into my flesh before snapping. With it now in my hand, I managed to manoeuvre it so I could use it as a weapon.

Daniel continued the kiss, still licking at the blood that spilled from my lip. This was it, my only shot and I was about to take it.

I pulled away from the kiss, and he grinned at me. He had no idea what I was about to do. He still thought of me as broken and timid; he was about to find out how wrong he was.

I glared at him and then shoved the pendant into his eye.

He stumbled back, releasing me from his grasp and swearing loudly. He clutched at his face, though the silver pendant was still lodged in his eye, which was now bleeding. I moved to grab the splinted leg, clutching it in my hand as I stepped back towards him.

"No, Tess. Don't!" I heard Luke shout from behind me.

Before he had the chance to stop me, or before Daniel had the opportunity to recover, I plunged the splintered wood through Daniel's chest, causing him to stagger back.

He looked from me to the wood protruding from his chest, back and forth between the two. He desperately grabbed at the wood, and when he pulled the stake out, he hissed.

He took a slow, pained step towards me, reaching desperately for my arm. "Baby, help me," he croaked as his skin began to pale. It was turning grey, and seemed to be losing its elasticity. His muscles disappeared before my eyes as he became more emaciated. He took another step towards me, but I couldn't move. I was horrified by the sight unfolding. He was withering before my eyes. I knew this wasn't going to be quick; it would be prolonged and painful for him.

"Baby, please," he begged when he made a move to grab my arm. When he finally made contact, there was no strength to his grip. In fact, as soon as his fingers laced around my wrist, they crumbled to dust. I recoiled in horror and he let out a shocked gasp.

I stepped farther back when he took another tentative step towards me. When his foot made contact with the floor, it shattered, and he fell to his knees.

His face was gaunt, skeletal; his skin was disintegrating slowly. He looked at me, questioning what I'd done.

I'd ended it, ended him.

I continued watching while his skin flaked from his body

and his bones decayed. His eyes stayed on me, never once leaving my gaze until there was nothing left. Nothing of him remained. Not even ash. No trace of Daniel Turner.

Just the wooden shard on the floor.

Now I just had to deal with the Devil.

42

LUCIFER

I WATCHED ON, helpless.

She'd done it. She'd killed Daniel. Rid herself of the monster that had followed her for so long.

She thought she was free; she thought this was the end.

She had no idea.

I watched as she backed away from Daniel's body. She watched while his body withered and decayed, until there was nothing left. There was no trace of the vampire that had come to kill her. The man she'd once shared her life with was gone.

Just a shattered piece of wood on the floor.

We stood in silence. I was waiting for her to make a move. This was her show now.

"Why are you still here?" she questioned. She continued to stare at the floor, unable to turn around and face me.

"Because you are. Tess, are you okay?" I asked gently.

She spun around to stare me down. "Are you fucking kidding me? Of course, I'm not okay."

In hindsight, it was a stupid question, not my finest hour, but in all honesty I didn't know what to say to her. I saw her looking me up and down, and I realised I hadn't returned back to my human form.

I concentrated, and my eyes and skin shifted back, though my wings were more reluctant to retract. They appeared to be enjoying their freedom. Hell, they might as well stay out— she knew everything now anyway. I tucked them behind me, and I attempted to take a step towards her.

She immediately backed up. "What are you doing?" she asked.

"I want to check you're okay. I think you should go to the hospital." I was genuinely concerned; I cared for her. Dare I say I think I was falling in love with her. I couldn't tell her that now, though, it wasn't really the right time to declare my love.

Her words shook me from my thoughts. "I just said I wasn't okay. Who the *fuck* would be, after everything that has just happened?" Tears began to slip down her cheeks, but she made no sound. I desperately wanted to comfort her, pull her into my arms and assure her that everything was going to be fine. Tell her I'd protect her, that I'd make things right.

I knew I couldn't, though.

Not now.

Not after what she'd just done.

"I need you to leave. Now," she whispered.

It wasn't happening; I couldn't leave until I knew she was okay. I had to get her checked by someone. "Not until I know you're not hurt." I moved again, but she backed away. "Tess, please, I won't hurt you," I said calmly.

"You already have. You lied to me. And you're the fucking Devil, Luke—Lucifer." Her words seeped deep into me; the feeling was intense. I'd never experienced it before. I was losing her. She was about to walk out of my life, and I'd never be with her again.

"Please," I begged. "Let me take you to the hospital, and I'll leave once I know you don't have any life-threatening injuries. Please, Tess." I was actually begging her, something I'd never done in all my years.

"No. I can take care of myself. Just leave." She wasn't budging, but neither was I.

"Why did you do that to Daniel? I told you I would do it," I asked, trying to change the subject for a second before I made my move.

"I finished it; it was for me to do. Not you. I had to be free of him, and the only way to be sure of it was to do it myself." She looked me in the eyes. Her tears had begun to stain her face.

A realisation dawned on her as she looked at my face. I wondered if she could see the utter despair that I knew was clearly visible in my eyes. "What? What is it?" she asked worriedly.

"Tess, you've taken a life," I said, my voice cracking.

"I did what had to be done." The words fell out of her mouth like she was trying to convince herself.

She didn't comprehend what that meant. "You don't understand. You've ended a life. Snuffed it out. Murder is a sin that can never be forgiven." I swallowed hard, trying to get rid of the lump that had lodged itself in my throat.

"What are you saying? What does that mean?" I rubbed my face with my hand, fidgeting from side to side. I didn't want to tell her. I was trying to find the words when she said, "Tell me."

I looked at her beautiful face and spoke the words I desperately wished weren't true.

"It means that your soul belongs to me, Tess. You're mine."

43

TESS

WHAT?

What is he talking about? My soul belongs to him; what does that even mean?

I watched him as he stood, silently staring at me for some sort of reaction. His wings disappeared behind him, and he took a tentative step towards me. I didn't move. I was still trying to digest what he'd just said.

I was his? How? In what way?

He moved closer still. He looked like himself, like the Luke I'd met that night in the bar. The Luke that had worked his way into my life, and my heart. The only Luke I'd thought there was. He seemed sad; it was written across his face.

Why was he sad? Surely he'd just gotten exactly what he wanted.

"Tess, did you hear me? Do you understand what I've just told you?" he asked gently. He looked at me for some sort of acknowledgement.

He was closer now; he stood directly in front of me. One more step and his body would be pressed against mine. I wanted him to do it. I wanted him to hold me and make everything go back to how it was, but I knew that was impossible.

I looked up into his dark, beautiful eyes. "I heard you, and yes, I understand." My reply was quiet, more so than I'd thought it would be. I knew what happened to sinners, those who didn't repent. I wasn't religious, but I think everyone knew what would happen if you were bad. That's if you believed in all of that stuff. I hadn't until today, but now it looked like that was all shot to shit.

"I need you to tell me who you are, Luke. I need to hear you say it." I needed to hear the words spill from his mouth. I wasn't sure if hearing him say it would change something, make things different.

He remained silent, his eyes pleading with me. "You already know who I am," he softly uttered.

I remained silent, watching him, willing him to admit the truth to me. He sensed I wasn't backing down and that I needed this from him.

"My name is Lucifer, the first fallen and ruler of Hell. I'm also the man who loves you, and wants to protect you from the evil in this world. If you'll let me, that is."

Is he fucking serious?

This had to be some sort of sick, twisted joke.

"Are you kidding? You don't love me; I was a business deal, Luke, a fucking acquisition." He tried to interrupt, but I wasn't finished. "I meant nothing to you; I was the means to a soul, nothing more."

My heart broke as I spoke the last words, and I crumpled to the floor. I was sobbing, desperate for this not to be happening. He fell to his knees in front of me. I could tell he wanted to comfort me but thought better of it.

I wanted him to hold me.

I was so pathetic.

"It's not like that, Tess. Yes, that was the original agreement, but it changed the second I met you. Everything that happened between us was real. I never lied to you, never." There was an adamance to his voice, like he truly believed he'd never lied to me.

"You may not have lied, but you certainly didn't tell me the whole truth. I can no longer believe a single word that comes out of your mouth; it's all dishonest. You're just like Daniel." I sobbed.

"I'm nothing like that scumbag. I'd never ever hurt you, Tess, please believe me when I tell you that." There was anguish to his voice, from me comparing him to Daniel. I didn't feel bad, though, since it was how I felt.

"The damage is done, you've already hurt me. I'm broken again, and you did it. I opened up to you, I trusted you, I was falling for you, and yet I have absolutely *no* idea who you really are." My voice cracked with emotion. I was overcome and had to struggle to catch my breath.

He reached for my hands, but I pulled away. "You need to breathe, Tess, or you're going to pass out," he spoke urgently.

It was no good—I couldn't force air into my lungs. I was starting to see spots; my sobs became more laboured, and I was struggling more.

I looked up at him panicked, and the concern was visible on his face. "Tess, breathe. Breathe for me." He tried to stay calm, but the urgency in his voice betrayed him.

I gasped as I looked at him, staring at the man who had broken down my walls. A man whom I'd let in, who I had thought was good. In fact, I'd just repeated my cycle again, falling for another bad guy—and there was no one badder than the fucking Devil.

With that thought swimming in my head, I stopped struggling and allowed the blackness to fill my vision.

EPILOGUE

LILITH

HE WAS DEAD. I sensed he was no longer connected to me. As he'd failed to complete his training, our link was still active. I could sense his energy, yet it had just been snuffed out. I wasn't upset by it. He had been a means to an end.

Daniel's life had little consequence to me, as long as he had succeeded—as long as she was gone.

"Is it done?" I spoke into my phone.

"We are waiting for confirmation, your Majesty," the voice responded.

"I want to know immediately," I said before I hung up.

If Daniel had succeeded, there was no doubt in my mind that Louis had killed him. I was very aware of that when I'd sent him in there. His death had been unavoidable.

I wanted Louis. I cared about nothing else.

I waited, and it felt like hours, but it was mere minutes until my phone rang again. "Speak," I commanded.

"Your Majesty, Daniel is dead." I knew that already. There was hesitation down the line—the person didn't want to say any more.

"Tell me, child," I spat.

"The girl lives. She was the one to kill Daniel, not Lucifer as we first believed. She is aware of Lucifer's true identity now, though, your Majesty." The voice was small, and I could hear the apprehension through the line.

I didn't answer. I simply hung up the phone.

Then, I screamed, louder than I'd ever screamed before. It wasn't fear that ripped through me; it was unadulterated rage. The windows in the old warehouse shattered all around me as I continued to scream from the bottom of my soul.

The man who was tied to the chair next to me tried to cower. He was unable, though, as he was bound tightly. He was no one, just a plaything.

I stopped screaming. I'd genuinely forgotten he was there while I'd been lost in my rage. I turned to face him. He was panting with pain; blood trickled from his ears, and I assumed his eardrums had burst. Tears streamed down his face, soaking into the gag forced into his mouth.

"Shhh, it'll be over soon," I said soothingly while stroking his face. I yanked him out of the chair, breaking his bindings and holding him in front of me. In an instant, I savagely bit into his neck and felt his warm blood dripping from my mouth and down my chin. I drew and drew relentlessly before I finally ripped out his throat and dropped his limp body to the floor. The rest of his blood flooded from his torn-out throat, pooling beneath him. The crimson of his blood glistened in the moonlight, and I felt strangely soothed by the sight of it. There had been no reason to kill him other than me being pissed off.

I looked into his glassy eyes as he bled out in front of me; it wasn't a pleasant way to go, but I was not in a *pleasant* mood. He would have felt it—he would have suffered. I wanted him to be in pain. I wanted someone else to feel anguish like I was—it wasn't fair I was going through it alone.

I licked the blood from my lips, tidying up as I looked down at the man's corpse at my feet. It was a waste, really.

I gave it little further thought.

She *knew*. All was not lost. The little tramp knew that he was the Devil.

Luke, that's what Tess had thought his name was. He'd had many names over the years, but he would always be my Louis. He was special to me, and I to him, despite what he might say. We shared things no one would understand; we had been there at the beginning.

He said he was through with me, that it was a mistake, but I knew those were lies. He loved me as much as I loved him. We needed each other; that was why he'd done what he did all those years ago.

Louis was mine—he had been for all eternity, and no one else could have him. Especially not some little human whore. I would destroy her, and then he and I would be reunited and remain together for the rest of time.

Just because she knew who he was, though, didn't mean this was over. Louis had a way of being persuasive; he could twist and manipulate everything. It was his skill. He could sway her. Sway her straight back into his strong arms, arms that didn't belong to that little bitch.

She was human, so he had to know it couldn't last. She was so fragile and finite. Her life would end, since she was not immortal like us. What could he possibly want from her?

I wasn't prepared to take any chances this time. Whatever he wanted from her, he wouldn't get it. I wasn't going to let anyone else handle this. She couldn't return to him—I wouldn't allow it.

If I wanted her gone, I'd have to do it myself.

He'd know I was involved by now. I hadn't wanted to get my hands dirty. Now, I had no choice. I could snap her neck like a twig—it wouldn't be a hardship for me, and now I *really* wanted to.

I'd have to kill Tess myself.

HELL HATH NO FURY

DARK DESIRES BOOK 2

Tess now knows the truth: Luke Albright is the Devil. He lied to her and kept that side of himself hidden. Now she's in over her head, but she needs to know what else he's been keeping from her.

Lucifer wants Tess. She's buried herself deep into his soul and he can't see a future without her. But now it seems like she'll never trust him again. He tries to prove he is worthy of her, but he's already decided if she doesn't want him then he'll protect her anyway.

And Tess needs protection now more than ever. An old threat lurks in the shadows, desperate to rip the two apart and claim Lucifer as her own. Tess is collateral damage, and the queen of the vampires wants her dead.

Can the pair conquer the growing threat, or will it drive them apart forever?

Buy Hell Hath No Fury now…

HELL'S ANGEL

DARK DESIRES BOOK 3

Tess has answers about the power she holds—an ancient power, one thought lost forever. However, that power comes with even more questions. Tess must learn to control and harness her new abilities, as well as discover the truth about her father.

Lucifer is painfully aware that everything is far from resolved. Tess is in more danger than ever before and he needs answers in order to keep her safe.

Tess is a threat to everything. Her existence threatens a balance that has been in place since the beginning of time. A powerful entity has decided he can't risk her existence being known and will do anything to keep her a secret... even if that means he has to kill his only daughter.

Buy Hell's Angel now...

MAILING LIST

To keep up with all the latest news and releases from author M.L Mountford, be sure to sign up to her mailing list.

You will receive regular updates on new projects, as well as information on deals and exclusive offers.

Your email address will never be used for spam and you are free to unsubscribe at any time.

Sign Up Now.

ABOUT THE AUTHOR

M. L. Mountford loves to read and write paranormal romance. She tries to make her characters interesting, sassy, and quirky, as well as creating whole other worlds hidden within our own.

She is from the North-East of England, where she lives with her husband and two young daughters.

Her busy life means she's fuelled entirely by coffee and sugar. When she's not writing she can be found eating everything in sight, binge watching whatever new documentary Netflix has to offer, swearing far too much, or with her nose buried in her Kindle.

For more information
www.mlmountford.com

ACKNOWLEDGMENTS

The first, and most important, thank you goes to my amazing husband Lee Mountford. Without you paving the way and sharing your knowledge and expertise, I would not have had the confidence to complete this book. I couldn't have done any of this without your support, thank you. Also, to my two wonderful girls. I am very lucky to have such an amazing family.

I'd like to take this opportunity to thank my editor, Josiah Davis https://www.jdbookservices.com for all of his help with this project.

Thanks also go to Dianne McCarty for being an additional proof editor on this project.

The amazing covers were designed by the talented, Raven Nordmann https://www.facebook.com/groups/ravenbookcovers Her work is beautiful, and she helped turn my ideas into an amazing set of covers.

A huge thank you goes to my wonderful Beta readers: Laura Holland, Amanda Lynn-Domanowski Mashburn, and Cheryl Gray. Thank you all for your keen eyes.

My final thank you, is to you for taking the time to read this book. I hope you had as much fun reading it as I did writing it!

Copyright © 2021 by M.L. Mountford

All rights reserved.

No part of this book may be reproduced in any form or by any electronic or mechanical means, including information storage and retrieval systems, without written permission from the author, except for the use of brief quotations in a book review.

❀ Created with Vellum

Printed in Great Britain
by Amazon

78690327R10181